THE ACTOR'S GUIDE TO
ADULTERY

Books by Rick Copp

THE ACTOR'S GUIDE TO MURDER

THE ACTOR'S GUIDE TO ADULTERY

Published by Kensington Publishing Corporation

THE ACTOR'S GUIDE TO
ADULTERY

Rick Copp

KENSINGTON BOOKS
www.kensingtonbooks.com

KENSINGTON BOOKS are published by

Kensington Publishing Corp.
850 Third Avenue
New York, NY 10022

Library of Congress Card Catalogue Number: 2004105346
ISBN 0-7582-0497-3

First Printing: November 2004
10   9   8   7   6   5   4   3   2   1

Printed in the United States of America

For Holly:
Thank you for a lifetime of love and laughter.

Acknowledgments

Once again, without the unflagging support of my editor and friend John Scognamiglio, the adventures of Jarrod Jarvis would be stuffed in a drawer somewhere.

I'd also like to thank my Writers' Group for their keen eye to detail during the writing of this book: Dana Baratta, Melissa Rosenberg, Dan Greenberger, Rob Wright, Allison Gibson, Alexandra Cunningham, and of course Greg Stancl, who is a major fan of the genre.

Thanks to Rob Simmons, Laurice and Chris Molinari, Joel Fields, Liz Friedman, Robert Waldron, Bennett Yellin, Marilyn Webber, Mark Greenhalgh, Lori Alley, Woody and Tuesdi Woodworth, Joe Dietl, Ben Zook, David A. Goodman, Patricia Hyland, Craig Thornton, Sharon Killoran, Laura Simandl, Susan Lally, Dara Boland, Liz Newman, Brian O'Keefe, Michael Byrne and Vincent Barra. I am blessed to have you all in my life.

Thank you Yvette Abatte for your wonderful friendship and for your bang up job on the website. And thank you Todd Ransom for your tireless efforts to get the word out.

My deepest gratitude to my parents Fred and Joan Clement and to Jessica, Megan, and Justin Simason for showing me how lucky I am each and every day. Also thank you to fellow mystery lover Nancy Schroeder for challenging me to come up with a better ending.

ACKNOWLEDGMENTS

Also to my crack team of William Morris agents—Jonathan Pecarsky, Ken Freimann, Lanny Noveck, Cori Wellins and Jim Engelhardt—to whom I am forever grateful.

To Milan Rakic, thank you for bringing such joy to my life.

And finally, Linda Steiner, you are a constant inspiration and I would be lost without you.

Chapter 1

"I believe this man poses a serious threat to me and society in general, and I strongly urge you to keep him locked up behind bars where he belongs." I paused for dramatic effect. There was a chill in the air. I was nailing this. Why couldn't I have been this persuasive last week when I auditioned for the role of a powerhouse prosecuting attorney on *Law & Order: Special Victims Unit*? Maybe it was because today the stakes were much higher. The guest-starring gig was fifteen grand and another year of guaranteed SAG insurance, but this performance would decide whether or not I would spend the rest of my life living in fear, looking over my shoulder, expecting to find a knife-wielding madman bearing down on me. Today I was delivering testimony at the parole hearing of Wendell Butterworth, a forty-four-year-old mentally unstable career criminal, who when he was in his early twenties, tried kidnapping me three times.

When Wendell saw me make my acting debut on an Oscar Mayer bologna commercial just shy of my fifth birthday, he became convinced that I was his long-lost soul mate from another lifetime. He kept watching TV, hoping to see me, and he did on a slew of commercials for Juicy Fruit gum, GI Joe action figures, and Kentucky Fried Chicken. When I landed my hit series a few years later and became a big star, Wendell decided it was time for a long-overdue reunion in this lifetime.

My first encounter with him was during our first season of *Go to Your Room!* He had conned his way past the security gate at the studio posing as a messenger, and found me hiding from my tutor, who was on the warpath because she found out I'd lied when I told her I had a photo shoot for *TV Guide*. It was just a ruse to get out of one of her annoying little pop math quizzes. Wendell pretended to be a production assistant sent to retrieve me for a network run-through rehearsal. We were halfway to Barstow before a quick-thinking cashier at a Mobil Station recognized me from the special "Missing Child Star" news bulletins on TV and dialed 911. I never even knew what was happening. The whole time I thought I was on my way to a promotional appearance at the network's Las Vegas affiliate station.

The second time, Wendell bought one of those "Maps to the Stars' Homes," and drove out to our Pacific Palisades house, where he locked our maid Gilda in the pantry and jumped out to grab me while I was pouring a bowl of Lucky Charms cereal. Believe me, I didn't feel so lucky that day. But fortunately, my parents arrived home just as Wendell was hustling me into his Dodge pickup. My father wrestled him to the pavement while my mother called the police from the car phone.

Finally, with his frustration growing to dangerous levels, Wendell got his hands on a Smith & Wesson and decided that if the Devil's Disciples (namely my parents) were going to keep us apart in this world, then he had no choice but to escape with me into the other world. His plan was to shoot me dead, and then take his own life. We could finally be together for eternity.

This was still a few years before the haunting and brutal murder of another sitcom child star, Rebecca Schaffer, in 1989. That's when people finally started taking celebrity stalkers seriously. Rebecca was dressing for an audition for *The Godfather 3* when a whacked-out fan rang her bell, and fired a gun at her as she stood right in her own doorway. She died at the scene. And Hollywood was finally jolted awake.

But my nightmare ended on a sweltering hot summer day in August. And as fate would have it, Wendell Butterworth would not succeed with his insidious plot. As my mother and I pulled out of the studio gate and stopped for a red light at the intersection of Melrose and Gower next to Paramount Pictures, Wendell ran up to the passenger's side window, which was open, and pressed his newly registered gun to my temple. Before either my mother or I could even react, Wendell pulled the trigger. There was a loud click. And then silence. Wendell had forgotten to load his gun. As he fumbled in his pockets for the bullets, my mother grabbed my shirt collar and dragged me out of the car, both of us screaming and running into the street, bringing traffic to a screeching halt. A quick-thinking motorist saw Wendell stuffing bullets into the chamber of his gun, and slammed on his accelerator, plowing into Wendell and knocking him to the ground unconscious.

For weeks reporters and TV journalists besieged us with requests for interviews. I almost had an exclusive sit-down with Barbara Walters until she found out I made fun of the way she talked. Hell, I was only twelve. How did I know she was so sensitive?

More disturbing details bubbled to the surface about Wendell as the press dug deeper into his past. He was initially portrayed as a wayward orphan whose parents were brutally murdered by intruders in the summer of 1971 while he slept peacefully upstairs in his room. The killers were never caught. Well, a *20/20* investigation after his attack on me revealed that there was no home invasion by unknown intruders at all. It turned out his parents had refused to allow eleven-year-old Wendell to watch the series premiere of *The Sonny and Cher Comedy Hour*, so he took matters into his own hands by butchering both of them with a meat cleaver, watching the show, then going upstairs and turning in. After all, it was past his bedtime.

After a battery of psychological tests following his arrest, Wendell was found to be deeply disturbed (let me put on my big surprise face), and once convicted (his lawyer's "innocent by reason of insanity" ploy failed), he was committed to a special psychiatric ward at Angola State Prison, where he managed to escape once and tried to find me again during our show's second season. Luckily he was quickly recaptured and transferred to an even more secure facility at Vacaville State Prison in Northern California, where he has remained ever since.

It was tough making the six-hour drive up to Vacaville to speak at Wendell's parole hearing. I hadn't seen him since that terrifying day at the traffic light outside Paramount. When I entered the sparse, stuffy room where he was seated at a table, flanked by two beefy prison guards, I almost didn't recognize him. Almost. Eighteen years had passed, and he was much older. In his twenties, he had only just started losing his fine blond hair, and he was muscled and compact. Now he was much paunchier, with only a few wisps of dull yellow hair combed over his forehead. His complexion was ruddy and pale from years of incarceration, and more than a few wrinkles creased his face. But one thing was the same as I remembered. His eyes. They were still a dull gray and they still had the wild look of a sociopath. He stared at me, and appeared to be fighting back a smile. I half expected him to jump up and grab me in a bear hug, as if he still believed we were separated soul mates. And that's why I'd made the long trip up north. Because in my heart I knew Wendell Butterworth wasn't cured. He wasn't ready to reenter society a well-adjusted, law-abiding citizen. And I wasn't ready for him to get out either.

Wendell sat quietly watching me as I delivered my speech. My hands were shaking and the paper made a loud rustling sound in my grip.

"I do not believe that Wendell Butterworth has made enough progress, and I fear that if you release him, he will continue his campaign of terror against me, as well as others."

The sound of the paper was so thunderous, I was sure the parole board couldn't hear a word I was saying. I glanced up at them to gauge some kind of reaction to my presentation. There were three of them. A corpulent man in his fifties who was bursting out of a cheap brown suit. A prim-and-proper frail gray-haired woman with a stern gaze over a pair of horn-rimmed glasses. And a handsome doctor with curly, unkempt hair and soft, caring eyes. I made eye contact with him, because, after all, he was the cutest one on the panel. He smiled at me and I immediately lost my place. I had to consult my stack of pages again. More rustling. I kept reminding myself I was in a loving, fulfilling relationship with an LAPD detective named Charlie Peters. Damn, where was I?

"I'm sorry . . . Let's see . . . campaign of terror against me . . . Oh, right. Here we go. I simply don't believe Wendell Butterworth is a changed man. And I beg you . . . for my own peace of mind, and for my family's, please do not let this man out of prison because I know it will only be a matter of time before he strikes again."

There was a moment of silence as the parole board digested my words. Then the gray-haired lady spoke first.

"Mr. Jarvis, we all appreciate you coming here today to speak with us. You make a very convincing argument."

"Thank you."

"I'm curious though. Did you read the psychiatric evaluations we sent you in the mail?"

"Yes, ma'am. I did."

"Five reputable doctors believe Mr. Butterworth has made remarkable progress, and in order for him to continue in a positive direction, he should be able to reconnect with a life on the outside."

"I don't believe that to be the case."

The cute doctor leaned forward. "Why not?"

"Look at his eyes," I said. "They haven't changed one bit. They still scare the hell out of me."

Wendell averted his eyes from me, and fixed them on the

floor. He didn't want me blowing his chances of getting out of here. Not with something as inconsequential as the look in his eye.

The gray-haired lady broke out into a smile dripping with condescension. "Mr. Jarvis, are you disputing the findings of five doctors based on the mere fact you don't like Mr. Butterworth's eyes?"

"That's right," I said.

She stifled a chuckle, and then flashed her two colleagues a look that said, "How long are we going to indulge this idiot?"

The corpulent member of the board checked his notes before addressing me. "What about Cappy Whitaker?"

"What about him?" I said.

"He was a child actor just like you. He had a rather notable career in his own right, though admittedly not nearly as successful as yours, and he, too, was a target of Mr. Butterworth's obsessions."

"I'm very familiar with Cappy's ordeal. It was very similar to mine."

"And yet, we've received a notarized letter from Mr. Whitaker supporting a decision to release Mr. Butterworth at our discretion."

This floored me. It downright knocked the wind out of me. Cappy Whitaker was an adorable moppet who hit the audition scene right about the same time I did. He had this cherubic face dotted with freckles, big twinkling brown eyes, and bright orange hair, and he made a lasting impression on the American public in a Disney adaptation of *The Prince and the Pauper,* which led to a situation comedy as Debbie Reynolds's grandson. The show lasted six episodes, but Cappy's TV Q rating was high enough to win him a memorable series of Kraft commercials, where he stood next to a ten-foot box of macaroni and cheese and wailed, "Hey, *I'm* supposed to be the big cheese!" The catch phrase caught on for a bit, and made the front of a few million T-shirts. It was bigger than that cute old lady screaming, "Where's the Beef?!" for Wendy's Hamburgers, but didn't have the lasting impact of my very own "Baby, don't even go there!" It did, however, become an instant footnote in eighties pop culture, and further endeared Cappy to the viewing public as well as Wendell Butterworth. He decided that Cappy, like me, was also his soul mate, and it was grossly unfair that they be kept apart. He staked out the apartment complex where Cappy lived with his grandmother, who was raising him after his alcoholic mother died in a drunken traffic accident. He made one botched attempt to snatch Cappy when his grandmother took him to the beach in Santa Monica one gloriously sunny Sunday afternoon, but he failed miserably when a gaggle of buff lifeguards beat him to a pulp when Cappy screamed for help. It caused quite a stir, landing the wholesome heroic hunks on the cover of *People* in their tight red swim trunks and holding life preservers. Some believe this story was the inspiration for the popular waves and babes show *Baywatch*. Days later, Wendell was quietly released for lack of evidence. He convinced authorities he was simply asking Cappy for directions to the Santa Monica Pier. That's when Wendell turned his attention back toward me.

I cleared my throat, gathered my thoughts, and addressed the three members of the parole board. "I can understand why Cappy Whitaker no longer believes this man poses a serious threat to society. He wasn't attacked in his home while eating breakfast. Mr. Butterworth didn't press a gun to his head at a traffic light and pull the trigger. I don't mean to compare emotional scars here, but I believe my experience with Wendell Butterworth was far more harrowing and has haunted me a lot longer. I respect Mr. Whitaker's opinion, but where is he? Why isn't he here? Because he didn't care enough to make the trip. I did." I pointed a finger right at Wendell's face. "Because this man is with me in my nightmares every time I go to sleep!"

Finally I had gotten to them. The parole board members sat in stunned silence. The corpulent one started making notes. The gray-haired lady stared at the floor. And the cute one, well, he looked at me with sympathetic eyes, and gave me an understanding nod. He opened his mouth to speak when suddenly a chirping sound pierced the air. Everybody sat up and looked around. Where was it coming from?

I frowned, annoyed. It was obviously someone's cell phone, and I was offended it had interrupted the impact of my speech.

The gray-haired lady looked up at me. "Mr. Jarvis?"

"Yes?"

"I think it might be yours."

She was right. The aggravating chirping sound was coming from my back pants pocket. I had planned on leaving my cell phone in the car, but I was expecting a very important call from my manager/best friend Laurette Taylor. I had been cast in one of the lead roles in an NBC comedy pilot some months ago that insiders predicted would be sandwiched in between the network's two biggest hits on Must-See Thursday. I played a lascivious massage therapist with designs on all the girls in a hip twenty-something apartment house. As a proud gay man in his early thirties, I had to congratulate myself on my ability to stretch as an actor. And the suits loved me. The networks were in the process of selecting their new series for the fall TV season. Laurette had promised to call me the minute she heard something. I checked the small screen on my cell phone. Sure enough, it was Laurette. I had to take the call. This could be one of those life-altering moments that could shift the entire trajectory of my career as an actor.

I sheepishly looked up at the bemused parole board. Even the cute doctor wasn't smiling anymore. "I'm sorry. I really have to take this." There was an audible huff from the gray-haired lady as I hastily slipped out of the room.

Outside, the drab, sterile hallway was even more depressing than the room where the parole board was conducting their hearing. It was empty except for a two-man cleaning crew mopping the floor a few feet away from me. I pressed the talk button and took a deep breath.

"Laurette?"

"Hi, doll face. Where the hell have you been? Haven't you gotten any of my e-mails?"

"I haven't been online today. I'm in Vacaville."

"Where in God's name is that?"

"Up north. Between Sacramento and San Francisco. I drove up for my stalker's parole hearing."

"I really need to get you a job. You do the strangest things to keep busy."

"They want to release him, and I'm here to make sure that doesn't happen."

"Do you know how many actors would kill to have a stalker? You can't buy that kind of publicity."

Laurette was always thinking of my career.

"Listen, I have to get back inside. They're going to make a decision soon," I said. "But I didn't want to miss your call."

"Good. Because I have exciting news."

This was it. After years of struggling to shed the baggage that came with being a former child star, I was about to land my first significant series role as an adult. I had worked so hard for this moment. I sat down on a hard wooden bench to savor the news.

"I'm getting married," Laurette said.

That didn't sound like, "The network picked up your pilot."

"I'm sorry. What?"

"I'm getting married. Can you believe it? After a lifetime of horrible dates and misfired relationships, I've finally found him. The one. Just when I came to accept the fact that he'd never show up, he's here."

"What about the pilot?"

"Oh, God, that loser? He hasn't called in months. Last I heard he quit Delta after his divorce was final and moved back to Atlanta. Truth be told, he had this mole on his back I just couldn't get past."

"Not the airline pilot. The network pilot."

"What network pilot?"

"*My* network pilot. On NBC. The one I've been waiting weeks to hear about. Did it get picked up?"

There was nothing but dead air. I figured the news wasn't good.

"Oh, honey . . ." Laurette said, her voice filled with a motherly, comforting tone usually reserved for occasions like telling a kid his pet hamster died. "It's not going to happen. They passed on it."

Now I felt just like that kid with the dead hamster.

"Why? You said all the suits loved it."

"They did. And then they tested it. I think it set a new record for low audience scores. Didn't I call you? That was something like, four days ago."

"No, you didn't call me."

"Oh, I guess I've been so caught up in this new romance, I forgot. So, back to me. Isn't this wild? I'm finally going to walk down the aisle!"

This was a double blow. First, my best friend neglected to break potentially devastating news to me as early as possible, so I could grieve properly and move on to my next career disappointment. Second, this same best friend, who always insisted on relating every last detail of her life, was getting hitched to a man I had never even heard about.

"Who is this guy? And why haven't I met him?"

"We just met two weeks ago."

I opened my mouth to speak, but felt there was no way she would not detect a hint of judgment in anything I said.

"I know it's fast," she said, reading my mind. "But it was one of those moments when you just know. We ran into each other at a screening at the TV Academy. It was some CBS Sunday night movie based on a true story about a little girl in Tennessee who was trapped in a mineshaft for eight days. The movie was crap. The kid they got sucked. But he played one of the firefighters, and believe it or not, he was quite good. He's very talented. His name is Juan Carlos Barranco."

10

Juan Carlos Barranco. The name sounded vaguely familiar, but I couldn't place it.

Laurette had discovered a propensity for Spanish men on our nine-day trip to the coast of Spain last summer. But an actor? I love actors. I'm one myself. But I know that most of them are one big red flag for inevitable emotional distress.

"So he's an actor, huh?" I said, hoping she'd pick up the obvious concern in my voice.

"Yes," she said, choosing to ignore it. "They had a reception after the screening, and we both went for the last finger sandwich. It was chicken salad. Not bad actually."

Laurette and I also both have to fill in complete food descriptions during any story we tell the other.

"Anyway, he graciously let me have the sandwich," she said. "And I told him how impressed I was with his performance, and then we wound up back at my place. And he's been there ever since."

"He's living with you?"

"Don't tell my mother, but yes. That's why we're getting married right away. I don't want to compromise my Catholic upbringing."

"Sweetheart, you compromised your Catholic upbringing in 1986 on our road trip to Fort Lauderdale when—"

"Don't say it. Just tell me how happy you are for me!"

I sighed. There was no way to slow Laurette down once she made a decision. She was a freight train and you just had to go along for the ride and hope you didn't derail from the high speed.

"I'm really happy for you," I said.

"Now get your ass back down to LA so we can start making plans."

"I want to meet this guy, and make sure he's good enough for you."

"Wait until you see him! He's gorgeous! And so sweet. He brought home takeout from Red Lobster because he knows how much I love their garlic cheese rolls. He hid the ring in one of my popcorn shrimp! I almost choked to death."

Laurette was laughing at the memory. I was still hung up on the fact she was planning to marry an actor. If I could just get her to talk to my boyfriend Charlie, he'd certainly tell her to run screaming for the hills, having lived with me for three years.

I was momentarily distracted when the door to the parole hearing opened and the three members of the board filed out into the hallway. They were followed by the two prison guards, who escorted Wendell Butterworth down the hall toward the processing room.

"Laurette, I have to go," I said. "Something's happening."

"All right, but call me when you get home. I want you and Charlie to be the first ones to meet my new husband. Can you believe I just said that? Husband!"

"I'll call you from the car."

I hung up the phone and approached the curly-haired cutie from the parole board.

"Excuse me, are we taking a short break?" I said.

The handsome doctor turned and flashed me his winning smile. "No. We're finished."

"Well, what happened?"

"We unanimously voted to grant Mr. Butterworth his parole."

I felt as if someone had just slammed me in the gut with a fist. I staggered back, not sure at first if I heard him right.

"You're letting him out?"

Eavesdropping, the gray-haired lady stepped up behind me and sniffed, "We asked if anyone else had anything to add, but you were out here on the phone." With a satisfied smile, she marched off toward the exit.

My head was spinning. I didn't know what to do. I thought I might pass out. That's when the curly-haired doctor put a comforting hand on my arm. I thought he might offer some encouraging words, maybe a little advice on what steps I should take to protect myself now that Wendell Butterworth was free to start following me around again.

"I was wondering," he said. "Are you seeing anyone?"

Chapter 2

After extricating myself from the curly-haired doctor's advances, I didn't stick around to witness Wendell Butterworth's official release after two decades of imprisonment. My stomach was churning enough as it was. Laurette's bombshell had shaken me up pretty good, and I had to race back to LA to judge this new fiancé for myself.

I called Charlie from the car when I was still a good four hours away from home. I knew he was working on a gang-related assault case on a homeless man and wouldn't be in his office so I left a message on his voice mail.

"Hi, it's me. You're not going to believe this one. They're releasing Wendell Butterworth so you better check the alarm system at home. Oh, and by the way, we're hosting a dinner party tonight . . . for Laurette and the actor she's going to marry. Yes, you heard me right. I said 'marry' and 'actor' in the same sentence."

When I had left LA the day before to drive up to Vacaville for the parole hearing, Charlie told me he was looking forward to the two of us ordering Indian food and watching a DVD, just the two of us, upon my return. I had a habit of disrupting his plans so I had to tread delicately.

"I know you were looking forward to coconut chicken curry and Reese Witherspoon tonight, but we don't know anything about this guy. Who he is. Where he comes from. Zilch. So I think it's best we put that off and have them over to the house. I knew you'd agree with me."

I hung up quickly, knowing perfectly well his reaction when he heard the message. But Charlie loved Laurette almost as much as I did, and I knew he, too, would want the scoop on this rather sudden shocking turn of events, even at the expense of his favorite Friday night ritual.

The next order of business on the drive home was calling every actor I knew to see if any of them had ever heard of Juan Carlos Barranco. The first six fellow thespians couldn't even manage to repeat back the name, let alone reel off a list of credits or a bio. But I struck pay dirt with Annabelle Lipton, a former scene partner from my Master Acting Class a few years back with the late Tony Randall of TV's *Odd Couple*. Annabelle and I had teamed up for a scene from Clifford Odets's *Golden Boy* that had left Mr. Randall in tears. I recently caught Annabelle in a feminine hygiene ad on Lifetime, so it was good to know the class had paid off for her in some way.

"Juan Carlos Barranco? I dated him for a while about seven months ago," Annabelle said. I could almost hear the bile rising in her throat. I hadn't seen her in over two years, but from what I remembered, she was adorably cute with a pixie cut and huge hazel eyes.

"When did you two break up?" I said.

"We never officially did. He stayed over one night because my place was close to an early-morning audition. He kissed me good-bye and said he'd be back in an hour. I never saw him again."

Some people are reluctant to talk about painful moments from their past. Luckily actors can go on for hours, all day even, as long as the topic is related to them. And Annabelle, being a consummate actress, had plenty to say. "We met at the Viper

14

Room. He asked me to dance, bought me a few drinks, just showered me with attention. It was right about the time I had received a small inheritance from my great aunt who had died back in Grand Rapids. Got about fifteen grand. He was working as a massage therapist at the time. That was his side business when he wasn't working as an actor. Right about the time we finished blowing my aunt's money together was when he disappeared. Interesting timing, wouldn't you say?"

"Could be a coincidence," I said, not believing a word I was saying. Neither was Annabelle.

"Yeah, right. Then I started getting all these calls from his massage clients trying to find him. It seems he offered a package of ten massages for the price of five. Pretty good deal, right? Well, after everybody paid him in advance, he took off. When people called up to schedule an appointment, they found out his cell phone was no longer in service. And the only other contact number he gave out was mine."

"Sounds like a charming guy."

"You have no idea, Jarrod."

True, Annabelle had a flair for the dramatic. She once stubbed her toe on her bathroom door jam and tooled around in an electric wheelchair for two weeks. But I believed every word she was telling me about Laurette's new love.

"Next thing I know," she said, "I see him on *90210* kissing Tori Spelling."

Of course! That was how I knew him. He played a really hot Rugby player on *Beverly Hills 90210* during its last season (I was and still am an unapologetic fan). I knew a couple of actors on that show, who confirmed rumors that he had slept with the very much married executive producer in order to get the part. He must have been good. He was signed up for a six-episode story arc.

"So why are you asking me about Juan Carlos?" Annabelle said.

"He's about to marry a friend of mine."

Dead silence. For a minute I thought the cell phone had cut out. But then Annabelle spoke in a grave, measured tone. "Tell her to get out while she still can."

I roared up Beachwood Drive, heading straight for the world-famous Hollywood sign and the English Tudor home I shared with my boyfriend, Charlie, and our loyal Pekinese, Snickers. Charlie and I both would have preferred a bigger dog, maybe a shepherd or even a Lab (a pet that wouldn't scream *gay*), but when Charlie was called to the scene of a murder-suicide involving an elderly couple driven to despair by their useless HMO, he found their cute little dog sniffing around the bodies of his former owners, confused and whining, and just a few minutes away from a one-way trip to the Humane Society. Charlie just couldn't do it. He brought her home, we fed her some left over chicken tikka (yes, it was Indian food/DVD night), and she went to sleep at the foot of our bed. She's been a fixture there ever since.

I whipped up the windy roads of the canyon, turning the last corner to see Charlie's new Volvo parked outside the house. Right behind it was Laurette's gas-guzzling Ford SUV. I knew when I hit that unexpected traffic just north of the city, I would be cutting it close. I hit the garage door opener, and pulled my Beamer inside. As I jumped out, I could hear the excited jangling of Snickers's tags behind the door leading to the kitchen. I took a deep breath, and marched inside to meet the already infamous Juan Carlos Barranco.

Charlie was at the stove stirring a pot full of mashed potatoes and boiling water for corn on the cob. I knew instantly that the steaks were probably already on the grill outside in the backyard. Laurette sat at the kitchen table, which resembled a fifties diner booth (a by-product of my gay kitsch gene), downing what I presumed from the half-empty bottle was her third glass of wine. Charlie didn't drink.

There was no sign of Juan Carlos.

As Snickers ran in circles to celebrate my arrival, Laurette jumped up and grabbed me in a big welcoming hug. "We thought you'd never get here."

I muffled a reply into her ample bosom, as the bright colors from her stylish print top blinded me.

Charlie turned around and gave me a wink. "Hi, babe." He looked as sexy as always in an open-collar J.Crew shirt and a pair of ripped jeans. Even after mucking up his Friday night plans and making him prepare a whole dinner for four because I was late, he still looked genuinely happy to see me. God, how did I get so lucky?

"So, where is he?" I said.

"He had an audition for some low-budget horror thing in Silver Lake. He'll be here soon," Laurette said confidently, obviously unaware of his history of never returning from acting auditions.

Charlie turned back to the stove and started scooping the freshly whipped potatoes into empty skins that he had lined up on a cooking sheet. I saddled up behind him and wrapped my arms around his waist.

"Twice-baked potatoes," I said. "My favorite."

"Got filet mignon, corn on the cob, tossed salad, and rolls. Am I forgetting anything?"

Laurette piped up. "Juan Carlos is bringing dessert. He said it would be a surprise. Something sweet and Spanish, I'm assuming. Like him."

I turned and smiled at Charlie. "Looks like you took care of everything. I owe you."

"Yes, you do, and I intend to collect . . . later." Another wink.

As Charlie slipped the cooking sheet in the oven, I poured myself a glass of wine and sat down with Laurette at the kitchen table.

"So . . . an actor?" I said.

Laurette laughed. "I know, I know. Trouble with a capital T. But Juan Carlos is different from any man I've ever dated."

"Or married, I hope." I added. Five years ago Laurette had married an aspiring director who was trying to mount an independent production about a family horse-breeding business set in Lexington, Kentucky. Once Laurette had secured financing through her ample contacts, and he went off to shoot his epic, the whole thing fell apart. The marriage, not the film. The film went on to win an audience award at Sundance and a successful art house career for its director. The marriage was dissolved after Laurette's husband impregnated an extra on the set who was fresh out of high school.

"Yes. Joel was a prick. He used me. My therapist says I have to stop picking men who need me professionally so I feel I have a value in the relationship. That's why Juan Carlos is perfect for me. He doesn't need me."

"Um, Laurette, honey, I don't mean to be a wet blanket or anything, but Juan Carlos is an actor and you're a talent agent. A talent agent who knows a lot of studio executives and TV producers."

"Yes, but Juan Carlos is doing just fine without me. He hasn't asked me to do him one favor. Not one. Joel and I were on our second date when he handed me his script and asked if I could get it to Jennifer Love Hewitt."

It was just about dark outside. The flashing beam of a car's headlights passed by slowly out front, signaling the arrival of the man in question. He turned around in the driveway and parked behind Laurette's SUV. Snickers's ears perked up and she scurried to the door, barking all the way. As I followed Snickers, I glanced out the window and noted that Juan Carlos drove a Lexus convertible. Very nice for someone whose last film role was "Firefighter #3" in a CBS TV movie. I opened the door, and put on the warmest, most welcoming smile I could muster. Juan Carlos wasn't the only actor in Laurette's life.

"Hi, you must be Juan Carlos. I'm Jarrod." I wanted to add, "And Laurette's best friend who will hunt you down and gut you with a knife if you hurt her in any way," but it seemed too early in the evening.

"I've heard a lot about you, Jarrod." There wasn't a trace of a Spanish accent. Maybe he was second or third generation. Or maybe he had been working with a voice coach to pound it out of him.

Despite my suspicions based on Annabelle's stories, I couldn't help but be impressed upon first glance with Juan Carlos. He was, just as Laurette promised, gorgeous. About six feet, broad shoulders, jet-black hair, and smoldering brown Spanish eyes that glistened in the light from the lamp just outside the front door. He was wearing a Hugo Boss suit, but the tie had been undone and the shirt was open, giving me more than a hint of his toned muscular smooth chest. He looked even better in person than he did on *90210*.

"Sorry I'm late," he said as he shook my hand and entered before I had a chance to invite him inside.

Laurette ran into the entryway from the kitchen and threw her arms around him. She smothered him with kisses on his face, ears, and neck. Whatever was in reach of her lips. I noticed him tense slightly as she hugged him. It was just for a split second, and then he relaxed and allowed her to maul him. Finally, he gently pulled away and smiled. His teeth were fluoride white and perfect.

"I nailed it, honey. I'm pretty sure I got the part," he said.

"Oh, honey, that's wonderful. I'm so happy for you," Laurette said, before turning to me. "See, I told you he was good."

Charlie was the next to amble out of the kitchen, and stride over to Juan Carlos with an outstretched hand. "I'm Charlie. Nice to meet you, Juan Carlos."

Juan Carlos gripped Charlie's hand, and looked him up and down. It was subtle, barely detectable in fact, but I caught it. If I didn't know better, I'd swear he was checking Charlie out.

"I better head out to the backyard and check on the steaks. How do you like yours done, Juan Carlos?" Charlie said.

Juan Carlos smiled and slipped his hand behind Laurette, lowering it until his palm was firmly clamped on her butt. "Blood red."

Charlie nodded and walked away. I thought I saw Juan Carlos peek at Charlie's ass as he strolled off, but he instantly averted his eyes when he felt me watching him. I had to be imagining this. Laurette had excellent gaydar. She of all people would likely know if the man she was planning to marry was straight or not. But it did depend on how good an actor Juan Carlos was.

"So, sweetie, what did you bring us for dessert?"

Juan Carlos frowned, and then gave us both an apologetic look. "In all the excitement about the audition, I forgot to pick something up."

"That's all right, darling," Laurette said. "I have to lose twenty pounds in six days anyway if I want to fit into my wedding dress."

They embraced again, and Laurette mouthed the words, "Isn't he fabulous?" over his shoulder to me.

That's when it hit me what she had just said. "Did you say six days?"

"Yes. You don't already have plans or anything, do you? We just didn't have time to send out formal invitations."

"No, we don't have plans. But six days? I had no idea you were going to get married so soon."

Juan Carlos flashed me a self-satisfied smile. "We both know this is it, the real deal. What's the point in waiting?"

Laurette took his hand and gazed longingly at him. I had to snap her out of it somehow. I didn't have time to get the full story on Juan Carlos in only six days. "But there's so much to plan. You have to pick out a venue, a dress . . ."

"It's done," Laurette said. "You know I've always wanted to be married at the Hearst Castle. There was a last-minute cancellation next weekend. It cost me most of my savings, but I got it. My dress is being altered as we speak. I've booked a band. Invited everybody I want to be there. There's not a whole lot left to do."

My head was spinning. I knew Laurette was a freight train when she decided to do something, but I didn't expect her speed to rival a space shuttle.

"There is one problem, though," she said with a scowl.

Finally, something I could work with to stop this madness.

"I could only afford the Hearst Castle for three hours," she said. "With setup and cleanup, that leaves approximately one hour and seven minutes for the ceremony and reception. It's going to be tight."

I was speechless. There was a momentary silence before Juan Carlos picked up the slack in the conversation. He beamed at his blushing bride. "Oh well," he purred. "More time for the honeymoon."

And then the happy couple proceeded to suck face right in front of me, devouring each other like a pair of five-year-olds chowing down on their first hot fudge sundae.

I felt sick to my stomach.

La Cuesta Encantada, or the "Enchanted Hill," is located in San Simeon, midway between Los Angeles and San Francisco, and is situated sixteen hundred feet above sea level on a sprawling two hundred and fifty thousand acres. Housing one hundred and sixty-five rooms, two spectacular swimming pools, and an astonishing collection of art and antiques, the magnificent compound was built by publishing magnate William Randolph Hearst over a twenty-eight year-period. Since Hearst and his longtime mistress, the comedy actress Marion Davies, loved hosting Hollywood royalty, including Charlie Chaplin, Jimmy Stewart, Greta Garbo, and Cary Grant, the camp value alone made it the ideal spot for Laurette's nuptials. Ever since her parents carted their wide-eyed eight-year-old daughter on a bus up to the grounds for a tour, Laurette had been fascinated with the history and beauty of "the ranch," as Hearst liked to call it, and felt it was destiny that she be married among the ghosts of the Hollywood elite. Since her first wedding was a Vegas quickie so her husband could jet off to Prague for an obscure film festival, Laurette decided to arrange a more formal affair at the Hearst Castle upon his return. But when he did arrive home six weeks later, he kept putting her off until she finally gave up on both a San Simeon wedding and her ill-fated marriage.

Juan Carlos was an entirely different animal altogether. The thought of an expensive party at a sprawling hilltop retreat looking down on the blue sea and up at the blue sky was not only a good thing, but a God-given right. Despite having no financial resources of his own from what I could see, this charmer certainly had cultivated tastes. He was more excited about getting married at this exotic location than his blushing bride was.

Charlie didn't share my suspicions about Juan Carlos's character. He felt I was being overprotective of my best friend, and should just lay off and be happy for her. So naturally my persistent suggestions that he run an ID check on Juan Carlos using his police sources fell on deaf ears.

The drive up to the tiny seaside hamlet of San Simeon took about three and a half hours, not counting the hour-and-a-half stop at the Biltmore Hotel in Santa Barbara for their remarkable all-you-can-eat Sunday morning brunch. Charlie tried reminding me that there would be food at the reception, but since Laurette could only afford to rent the Castle for such a limited amount of time, I didn't want the pressure of having to scarf down enough shrimp cocktail before we got kicked out.

Since I insisted on going back for a third serving of pineapple sponge cake at the Biltmore, we fell behind schedule, so by the time we reached the Hearst Castle, there were only a handful of guests left at the bottom to be bussed up to the property for the ceremony.

Five of us boarded a blue bus driven by a portly African-American man with a pleasant smile, and began our ascent heavenward to the estate that was so high up it often sat above the coastal fog drifts.

Charlie and I sat in the back and I watched the other three passengers, none of whom seemed to know each other. Directly in front of us was a young woman in her early twenties, with long cascading brown hair that fell down below her shoulders. She was a petite thing, very thin and gaunt. If only I had brought a doggie bag from the Biltmore, then maybe I could feed the starving little bird. Her face was striking, with gorgeous green eyes and full Angelina Jolie lips. If she hadn't started going the way of Karen Carpenter, she would be a real beauty.

The other two passengers were both men. Across from the girl sat an obese man in his early thirties, who ran upwards of three hundred pounds. He was squeezed in his seat, and droplets of sweat trickled down his cheek. His washed-out orange hair, or what was left of it, was unruly and frizzy with a few stray wisps combed over his bald plate. He looked grossly uncomfortable, and he kept his eyes fixed out the window. He had zero interest in conversing with any of us. A few seats ahead of him was a short, compact fellow who made up for his height deficiencies with a killer physique. He, too, was balding, but unlike the heavy man, he kept the sides neat and trimmed. He wore a tight white T-shirt to showcase his muscles and crisp hip-hugging jeans. This guy was definitely not dressed for a wedding.

I decided to break the silence. "So, are you all friends of the bride or groom?" I knew full well they were all acquaintances of Juan Carlos, but it was an acceptable icebreaker. Charlie smiled. He loved watching me force people to socialize.

The girl spoke first. Her voice was as tiny as her body. "Groom."

More silence. I wasn't about to give up.

"So, did you have to travel far to attend?"

"Florida," she said flatly.

The short man's ears perked up and he flipped around in his seat. He and the girl made eye contact and there was both surprise and recognition in their eyes.

"What are you—?" she started to say to him, but thought better of it. He gave her a polite nod and they instantly turned away from each other.

"You two know each other?"

"No," they both said in unison.

I kept forging ahead. "Oh, is Florida where you met Juan Carlos?" I asked the girl.

"Yes."

She wasn't giving me anything. And the other two didn't seem very anxious to talk to me either. So I stuck out my hand. "I'm Jarrod."

She looked at my hand as if it were covered with abscesses, and then reluctantly took it for a moment. After a brief handshake, she quickly pulled away.

"Dominique."

"That's a pretty name," I said, trying desperately to win points somehow. I'm an actor. I have a need to be loved. It didn't work. She just grunted what I assumed was a "thank-you" and looked away.

"We're friends of Laurette's," I said, plowing on. "Have you met her yet? She's wonderful. You'll love her."

This got her undivided attention. She whipped around, her

eyes narrowing and her face tightening as she said evenly, "I don't have any interest in meeting *her*."

"Oh. Okay," I said. Charlie signaled me with his eyes to drop the subject. I smiled at him and then turned back to Dominique. "Why not?"

I heard an exasperated sigh come out of Charlie.

Dominique thought for a minute, probably debating whether or not she should say anything more. But her anger got the best of her, and eyes blazing, she said, "Because it should be me marrying Juan Carlos today."

"So you two were—?"

"Yes," she said.

"I'm surprised you got an invitation."

"I didn't." And with that, she turned back around, sending me the clear message that our conversation was over.

This was too juicy. But I was more than a little worried that an old flame of Juan Carlos's might ruin Laurette's big day. I wasn't sure how I should handle it, whether I should tell Laurette, or try to get Dominique to leave quietly, when Charlie, reading my mind, squeezed my arm and whispered, "It's none of your business." He was right. I decided to focus on someone else.

"You a friend of the groom's too?" I said to the short, muscular man upfront, but both men turned around.

The obese one nodded and then, with a miserable look on his face, gazed back out the window. I've never seen someone so unhappy going to a wedding. Except for maybe Dominique.

The other man was a bit chattier. "Yes, I've known Juan Carlos for some time now. Austin Teboe. We met in Florida as well. Working in a restaurant. I haven't seen him in a while. I'm hoping he'll be happy to see me."

This was too much. "So he doesn't know you're coming either?"

"Nope. Doesn't have a clue. It's going to be a big surprise."

The more he talked, the more nervous Dominique appeared. She started fidgeting in her seat, folding her arms, trying to stay calm.

"So are we the only two on the bus who have actually been invited?" I said to Charlie, as I kept one eye on the obese man to our left. But he never even bothered to acknowledge me.

The bus pulled in and deposited us at the Neptune Pool on the north side of the property, where the wedding ceremony was scheduled to take place. Made up of fragments of ancient Roman columns, bases, and capitals, and decorated with sculptured figures of Roman gods, the picturesque pool area was reminiscent of an Italian Renaissance villa. Laurette could not have selected a more visually exciting locale. With rain clouds hovering overhead, however, there was an unsettling foreshadowing of storms ahead.

Most of the guests were already seated, and I got the distinct feeling from the annoyed looks we were receiving that the ceremony was being held up due to our late arrival.

Charlie, the obese man, and I slipped quietly into a row of seats in the back so as not to draw any more attention to ourselves. Dominique and Austin, however, remained standing, making a concerted effort to be conspicuous.

The organist off to the side launched into those first notes that introduce the "Wedding March" processional, and Juan Carlos, his skin a perfect shade of bronze against his all-white tuxedo, strolled out to take his place in front of a makeshift altar set up near a breathtaking sculpture of the Birth of Venus. He broke out into a smile with enough wattage to light Dodger Stadium. He was in his element, enjoying everyone watching him and admiring him and envying him. Until his eyes fell on Austin. And then the smile faded. His face twitched a little. He was confused, almost disoriented. Austin was enjoying every minute of it. He sent back a slight wave and then folded his arms, satisfied he had made some kind of point. But Juan

Carlos's reaction to Austin's presence was nothing compared to his horrified reaction to Dominique's last-minute arrival. He stared at her, mouth agape, mind obviously racing. I could tell what he was thinking. What was she doing here? How did she find him?

For a minute I thought he was going to bolt. Get the hell out of Dodge. But then it was too late. The organist started banging out the familiar "Wedding March" melody, and Laurette Taylor, decked out in a bodacious satin off-white wedding dress complete with gauzy veil and an endless train carried proudly by four preteen first cousins, made her way down the aisle, ready for her moment in the sun.

That's when it started raining.

Chapter 3

God was undoubtedly sending Laurette a message when he opened up the skies and pounded her hastily planned wedding with an unrelenting torrent of rain. She chose to ignore it. Not budging from the altar, resolved to leave the Hearst Castle a newlywed, Laurette gripped Juan Carlos's hand tightly and strained to hear the sermon from the doddering old minister whose fogged-up glasses prevented him from sailing through his notes in a timely manner. And since she could afford the property for just over an hour, an unmistakable tension began creeping into Laurette's smile as the long-winded and soaked minister ate up a lot of time talking about love and commitment and the importance of trust. She pretended to listen, but I knew Laurette's mind was on the three-tier German chocolate wedding cake, and if the staff had thought to move it under the canopy to protect it from the rainstorm.

Several guests dashed for cover, but the majority of us stayed glued to our seats, resigned to the fact that we were going to leave this place drenched to the bone. Besides, we had to take our cue from the bride and groom and neither was acknowledging the fact that the wedding party and all their guests were practically drowning. None of us could hear a word the minister was saying, but when Laurette leaned forward and whispered something in his ear, I presumed she was advising the old man to wrap it up because he seemed to skip right to the "I do's."

The minister cleared his throat and tried talking above the now blustery winds. "Do you, Laurette Taylor—"

"Yes," she interrupted him. "Yes, I do. Thank you. And he does too, don't you, darling?"

"Yes," Juan Carlos screamed.

The minister was not good at improvisation. He desperately wanted to stick to the script, but Laurette was having none of it. He was at a loss.

"So by the power vested in you," she offered, trying to help him out a bit.

"Yes, yes, by the power vested in me . . ."

He took a pause for dramatic effect in a lame attempt to add some theatricality to the already drama-filled affair. But Laurette never gave him the chance. She turned and faced the crowd.

"He now pronounces us husband and wife. He gets to kiss me now." Laurette peeled the wet veil off her face and puckered up her lips. Juan Carlos grabbed her by the shoulders and devoured her face with his mouth in an obvious play of machismo that rivaled Al Gore's attempt to show his amorous side by sucking his wife's face at the 2000 Democratic Convention.

The crowd erupted in applause and I turned around in my seat to get a good look at Dominique. She watched the proceedings with a steely gaze, never flinching, just frozen in time, like one of the Roman statues behind her.

Laurette snatched a fistful of Juan Carlos's tuxedo jacket and pulled him down the aisle as the poor organist, sopping wet, began the standard "Wedding March" recessional.

Hurrying things along, Laurette bellowed, "Try to move it along, people! We have a lot to do, and we only have forty-six minutes!"

Mercifully, the reception was under a tent erected on the South Earring Terrace of the estate, built around an ancient Verona wellhead that the caterers almost used as a giant punch bowl before cooler heads prevailed. The nearly one hundred guests squeezed under the canvas cover, and there was very little room to move let alone browse the buffet and load up on chicken salad finger sandwiches and mini-éclairs.

In the interest of time, Laurette chose to forgo the usual wedding traditions of announcing the bride and groom, the first dance, the tossing of the garter, and a receiving line. But since she worshipped food, a devotion both she and I shared, the cutting of the cake was an absolute must. The head caterer did indeed have the foresight to protect the cake and move it under the tent before it began pouring, knowing the bride would blow her stack if one creamy frosted flower got hit with a single raindrop. She'd taken longer picking out the cake than she had picking out a husband.

Laurette pushed her way through the crowd, advising people to eat immediately because the staff had to commence with cleanup in a scant twenty-six minutes; otherwise she'd be charged an additional hour at a whopping cost of a cool five grand. A lot of guests felt so much pressure, they simply couldn't eat at all. I didn't have that problem. Charlie and I grabbed plates and dived right in, starting with the cheese and crackers. Before I had a chance to start sampling, Laurette was hovering behind me.

"Jarrod, my dumb ass sister got wasted and banged one of the groomsmen last night, big surprise, and now she's so hung over she doesn't want to make a toast. I know what she's doing. She's pretending to be sick so she can steal focus from my big day. So typical. Could you do it?"

"Do what?"

"Make a toast."

"But . . . but I haven't prepared anything."

"Oh, honey, please," she said confidently. "You're fabulous

with improv. You should have your own sketch show. And I know you'll be brief, unlike that loser of a minister. Could you believe him? I told him to keep his sermon down to three minutes. Doesn't anybody ever listen anymore?"

"What do you want me to say?"

"How much you care about me, how perfect you think Juan Carlos is for me, how happy we're going to be together. Blah, blah, blah . . ."

So she wanted me to lie.

"Laurette, I don't know . . ."

"He'd be happy to," Charlie interjected, squeezing my arm tightly, sending me a clear message to just shut up and do it so everyone could go home happy.

"All right, sweetie," I said. "Just tell me when."

"Be ready in seven minutes. If I can get that lame duck photographer who's always running out of film in place, we can cut the cake at the same time."

I was so happy Laurette was taking the time to enjoy her big day.

She hurriedly checked her watch. "I better grab a ladyfinger before the caterers start packing up." She lifted her dress to barrel her way to the dessert table when she stopped cold.

"Who's that?" she said.

I turned to see Juan Carlos engaged in a heated discussion with Dominique. Her eyes were bloodshot from crying and her hand shook as she pointed her finger in his face, on the verge of losing her composure completely. Juan Carlos stood fast, arms folded, a thin smile painted on his face, trying to downplay the seriousness of their conversation.

"Oh, that's an old friend of Juan Carlos's. We met on the bus up here," I said, also trying to downplay the seriousness. Laurette was too smart for that.

"I don't remember her on the guest list. Is she just an old friend or an old *girl*friend?"

"Um, girlfriend, I think."

"I see," Laurette said. "Excuse me."

She seized the hem of her wedding dress, and plowed through the crowd toward her new husband like a linebacker carrying the ball to an end goal. She was upon them in seconds, and stuck out her hand to introduce herself to Dominique.

"This is going to be good," Charlie said, smiling.

The blood drained from Juan Carlos's face as he offered up introductions. Dominique never cracked a smile. She was too upset, and quickly walked away after shaking Laurette's hand. There was nowhere for her to go. There were too many people packed into the tent. She found herself face to face with Austin. He grinned and gave her a hug, but she recoiled and hissed something at him. She was furious with him, and I half expected her to spit in his face. He seemed to be enjoying her fury, almost relishing her discomfort. Finally, she pushed past him and left the protection of the tent, racing toward the line of parked buses that waited to transport the guests back down the hill to their cars. Dominique and Austin were both from Florida, and obviously knew each other despite their quick denials on the bus. My curiosity was piqued. What was Austin Teboe's personal business with the groom all about? And what was his relationship with the groom's ex-girlfriend Dominique?

I was about to embark on a fishing expedition and strike up a conversation with him when angry shouts steered my attention toward the buffet table. Juan Carlos was yelling at the antisocial obese man from our bus trip up the hill. He slugged him in the stomach, but the man's massive bulk prevented Juan Carlos from doing any serious damage. Within seconds, several groomsmen appeared on the scene, and began manhandling the big guy. As the groom's posse physically hustled the man away from the party, Juan Carlos, flushed with anger, dusted himself off, took a brief moment to cool down, and then rejoined his bride. He was back to smiling and glad-handing within seconds.

Laurette waved us over, and Charlie and I wandered over to the happy couple.

"We're just about ready for the toast, Jarrod," she said.

"Is everything all right?" Charlie asked Juan Carlos pointedly.

"Yes, why?" Juan Carlos said as if the previous scene had been magically erased from his memory.

"I thought there was going to be a fight."

"Oh, you mean Rudy Pearson?" Juan Carlos said, his voice full of disdain. "He's just a little bug. Not even worth the effort to squash it."

To my surprise, Laurette jumped in with an explanation. "He's a writer for *Soap Opera Digest*. He's been following Juan Carlos around ever since he played that rapist/preacher on *The Hands of Time*. He's called my office every day for the past two weeks trying to get the exclusive of our wedding, but I told him no press. This was our private day, not to be shared with the public. Besides, Juan Carlos isn't doing soaps anymore. There's no reason he should be following Juan Carlos around. I think the guy just has a big crush on him."

"He's a sleaze ball. If he comes around again, I swear I'll rip his face off," Juan Carlos said, seething.

"Don't you just love that fiery Latin passion?" Laurette said.

I glanced at Charlie. Neither of us thought much of Laurette's new husband, but neither of us was willing to express that out loud. Yet, anyway.

It was the time for my toast. The rain had subsided and the winds had died down, so luckily I wasn't going to have to shout my sentiments. The clock was also ticking. The caterers had begun wrapping up the food and folding up the card tables. We were down to two minutes before we had to vacate the premises. The buses were already sputtering to life in anticipation of our journey back down the hill. The staff quickly poured plastic flute glasses of champagne and handed them out to all the guests.

Charlie gave me an encouraging pat on the butt and sent me up to the front of the tent, where I addressed the crowd.

"When Laurette asked me to say a few words, and believe me, few is the key word since we all have to be out of here in less than two minutes," I said as the guests laughed politely, "I wracked my brain trying to come up with something profound or moving or funny or—"

"One minute, Jarrod!" Laurette said, prodding me to edit myself and keep it moving.

"But in the interest of time, I will just say this. To Juan Carlos and Laurette, every day may you . . . light up each other's lives and give each other hope to carry on." Okay, so I plagiarized Debbie Boone. But it worked in a pinch. Charlie chuckled, instantly recognizing my source material. Laurette and Juan Carlos didn't get the reference at all. Laurette, teary-eyed, her mascara running, blew me a kiss then grabbed the man of her dreams and sucked on his face some more. The rest of the guests wisely chose to wash down my treacle with champagne.

Someone started coughing. I looked around and spotted Austin Teboe, having just downed his glass of champagne. He was gasping and choking and gripping his throat with his hand. Everyone stood, stunned for a moment, before one of the groomsmen, who had just returned from ousting Rudy Pearson, ran forward and grabbed Austin in an attempt to give him the Heimlich maneuver. But Austin wasn't choking on a chicken wing. This sounded different. A white fizzy liquid spilled out of his mouth as he broke away from the groomsman's hold and staggered through the throng of people. His eyes bulged, his face was ghostly white, and his wheezing and coughing came to an abrupt halt as he stopped in his tracks, the life swirling out of him. There was an absolute stillness as all eyes in the tent watched him. He then fell forward, belly flopping dead into Laurette's perfectly decorated three-tier German chocolate wedding cake.

Chapter 4

Laurette was wrong to worry about her drunken, trampy sister stealing focus from her big day. The dead body in front of the buffet table was going to do the job for her. By the time the local San Simeon police arrived on the scene, the guests had been herded into the Refectory, the hilltop's sole dining room located in the main house, usually cordoned off for tours but today reopened due to the unusual circumstances. Charlie and I huddled with several of Laurette's fellow talent agents, who were all buzzing about the identity of the deceased. No one seemed to have the slightest idea who he was.

"Austin Teboc," I offered, never one to refrain from a good dish session. "We rode up the hill with him today. He worked in a restaurant in Florida, but he never told us whether he was a waiter, or worked in the kitchen, or parked cars."

"So he was a friend of Juan Carlos's?" asked a tiny woman in a smart suit with frizzy hair so big I was surprised she could hold her head straight. I recognized her as another agent in Laurette's Sherman Oaks office.

"He said he met Juan Carlos at the restaurant. And that the two had personal business that he was here to take care of . . ."

Charlie interceded and gently took my elbow, steering me away from the enraptured group of gossipmongers. "I think the police are ready to talk to us now, Jarrod."

We walked over to the corner of the room where four police officers stood over Juan Carlos and a confused and dazed Laurette, who sat on an antique love seat from the nineteenth century, ignoring the clearly marked sign that said DO NOT SIT ON FURNITURE. The team of investigators were led by a grizzled, balding, pot-bellied detective, who might as well have walked right off the set of *Hunter,* the Fred Dryer action series from the eighties, where I once guest-starred as a convicted counterfeiter's wayward teenaged son in their memorable sixth season opener.

He shook Charlie's hand. "Lieutenant Cranston."

"Charlie Peters, LAPD. This is my partner, Jarrod Jarvis."

Cranston nodded, ready to welcome me into the brotherhood of peace officers. "You guys up here working on a case?"

"No," I said. "I'm his partner in life, not crime."

This took Cranston by surprise. But it was a new world so he simply grunted and declined further comment.

Charlie was right in his element. He compared notes with Cranston. "We met the victim earlier." Charlie recounted our bus ride up to the Hearst Mansion, and how Dominique and Rudy Pearson, who were both fiercely determined to attend today's nuptials, had left rather abruptly. One by choice. And one by force.

Cranston turned to Juan Carlos. "How did you know the victim?"

"I didn't," said Juan Carlos, as he sat comforting Laurette.

Either Austin Teboe was lying. Or Juan Carlos was. I'd put my money down on the slippery, opportunistic actor any day.

"Well, according to Mr. Peters here, Mr. Teboe claimed to have known you, and that the two of you had some personal business he was here to talk to you about," said Cranston in a slightly confrontational tone.

"I said I never met him," said Juan Carlos.

Laurette took her husband by the chin and gently turned his face toward hers. "What I want to know is, who is this Dominique person?"

Juan Carlos glanced in my direction, trying to judge whether or not I had any knowledge about his past with her. I decided to make it easy on him. "An ex-girlfriend."

"How come you never mentioned her?" Laurette said.

"We only dated a few weeks. She meant nothing to me."

"Then what was she doing here?"

"She's had a little troubling letting go. I think she may be a little obsessed with me."

"A *little* obsessed? Honey, she crashed our wedding."

"I didn't want to worry you."

"Why? Has she tried contacting you before?" Laurette said.

"Yes," he said. "For some time now."

"Why didn't you tell me?"

Cranston stepped forward, interrupting the newlyweds. "Look, the ex-girlfriend is not why we're here. As far as we know, she's alive and well. Our focus is on Mr. Teboe, who sadly is not."

"I'm sorry," said Juan Carlos. "I can't help you. I already told you I've never met the man in my life. And if he's saying I did, he's got me mixed up with somebody else."

Charlie and I exchanged looks, both silently agreeing that Juan Carlos wasn't a very good actor after all.

"That's an awfully big mix-up if he traveled all the way from Florida to track you down at the Hearst Castle, which is up here in the middle of nowhere," I quietly offered.

Laurette stood up, and glared at Charlie and me. Then she pushed forward in my direction. "Jarrod, may I speak to you privately, please?"

I nodded and followed Laurette into the adjoining Assembly Room, where William Randolph Hearst had once smoked stogies with Clark Gable and Jimmy Stewart. I didn't dare take a seat on the historic antique furniture that gave the elongated space its Renaissance flair. Laurette was just too angry to sit.

"Why are you and Charlie attacking my husband?" she said.

"We're not attacking him. But there are a lot of unanswered questions involving his relationship with the deceased."

"What relationship? He's already told the police he didn't know him."

I gave Laurette my best "let's not fool ourselves" gaze. "I just think we should look a little deeper into this and see who might have had reason to off the murder victim."

"How do we even know he was murdered? Maybe it was a heart attack or a stroke or something?"

Laurette had seen the white fizzy liquid come pouring out of Teboe's mouth herself. You didn't have to be William Peterson or Marg Helgenberger to assume it could have been some kind of poison. It was only a matter of time before the coroner would be able to confirm it.

"I can see what you're doing," Laurette said.

"What?"

"You're going to get your kicks again playing Nancy Boy Drew. Just like you did last year when Willard Ray Hornsby died."

"Yes, but if you recall, somebody did indeed murder Willard, and I got to the bottom of it."

"You're not a detective, Jarrod. You shouldn't be sticking your nose into things that don't concern you."

"Why not? Because I might stumble across some dirty laundry belonging to your husband?"

"How dare you? You barely even know him."

"And how well do *you* know him? For God's sake, Laurette, how could you marry a guy you only met a few weeks ago?"

"Because I love him!"

We both stopped before we said things neither of us would be able to take back. Our relationship had always been strong and solid, but I was reluctant to go traipsing into uncharted territory that could do serious damage to our decades-old friendship. And sometimes Laurette was more manageable when she was hearing things she wanted to hear.

"Honey, I'm sure he's everything you think he is." A little white lie never hurt anyone. But a big one like this could bring the roof down on us. "But a man has died, and I think we owe it to him to find out what really happened."

Laurette sighed. "I hate when you get like this."

"Like what?"

"Like a pit bull that's gotten a hold on an old shoe. I can see it in your eyes, Jarrod. You see Juan Carlos as that shoe, and you're not going to let go no matter what."

She was right, of course. I was certain Juan Carlos was lying about not knowing the murder victim, and I wasn't going to rest now until I unearthed the truth. Unfortunately, this time it meant straining my bond with Laurette. But in the end, I knew whatever I found would be beneficial to her. Either it would put her mind at ease about the commitment she had just made, or more realistically, it would give her enough information to extricate herself from a catastrophic mistake.

Laurette whipped around, gathered up her bulky dress, and headed for the door leading back to the Refectory.

"Fine," she said. "Sniff around all you want. Once the police are done questioning us, we're off for a fabulous honeymoon in Maui anyway."

Still stung by my suspicions, Laurette marched off back inside the dining room to join her husband and her other guests. I could tell there was a sinking feeling deep inside her gut that was gnawing at her, reminding her that she didn't know Juan Carlos as well as she thought. And perhaps maybe there were dark secrets swimming their way to the surface that might wash away the rosy hue on her rose-colored glasses.

To my surprise, the police released the newlyweds and most

of the wedding guests within an hour after writing down all of our contact information. The Hearst staff was anxious to clear us out so they could resume their meticulously scheduled tours of the expansive property.

Laurette declined to toss the bouquet. We weren't allowed to throw rice or anything, given the time it would take for the staff to clean it up, so the process of sending off the bride and groom lacked the traditional fanfare and was decidedly anticlimactic, especially given the dramatic events at the reception. Laurette simply waved to all her friends and family, then climbed into the back of a white stretch limousine. It quickly began its descent down the long, winding paved road. Within moments, the giant limo was the size of a matchbox car and it suddenly vanished behind a lush green hill. All the guests then quietly formed a single-file line to board the blue tour buses for the fifteen-minute ride back down the mountain to our cars.

As our bus dropped a group of us off in the parking lot at the bottom of the hill, my stomach rumbled, which caused Charlie to raise an eyebrow.

"Hungry?"

"Yeah, so?" I said, rather abruptly. The fact was I was always hungry.

In my defense, during all the excitement, I never even took a bite from my hors d'oeuvre plate. And hours had passed since the all-you-can-eat brunch at the Biltmore Hotel in Santa Barbara. So Charlie knew to find the nearest roadside diner pronto or my mood would inevitably darken during the long drive home, and he would be the one to pay the price. After turning left for the Pacific Coast Highway scenic route south toward Los Angeles, Charlie spotted the San Simeon Beach Bar and Grill just across the road from sweeping views of the glistening, hazy blue ocean. He instinctively jerked the wheel and pulled in and parked right in front of the entrance in order to cut down on the length of time it would take to get some food into me, and thereby make his journey back home more pleasant.

"This look good to you?"

I nodded, choosing not to reply with a verbal response that could be laced with sarcasm or a slicing edge. When I was ugly from hunger, just staying quiet was my preferred method of dealing with my mood. This foresight was one of the chief reasons Charlie and I were still together.

The sea-blue paint on the one-level, dilapidated structure was fading from the sun's intense daily beating. The restaurant probably did a good business owing to the fact that it was so close to the Hearst property and all that traffic, not to mention there didn't seem to be another dining establishment within ten miles. And it was probably safe to say that this bar and grill in the tiny seaside hamlet of San Simeon, California, wasn't going to make any top ten lists in *Bon Appetite* magazine.

Charlie and I strolled inside, and took a table next to the window so we could gaze out at the impressive view. A hefty waitress in her late fifties, with a seen-it-all scowl, ambled up with her pad of paper and asked if we were ready to order before either of us had even opened the menu. I was fine with that. I didn't need to peruse. I was ready to eat now. One quick two-second glance at the lunch offerings, and I was raring to go.

"Club sandwich, no mayo, extra cheese, with chips and a small salad, peppercorn ranch dressing on the side, a Diet Coke, and a glass of ice water."

The waitress stared at me. I could tell she was impressed. I knew what I wanted with no annoying questions or irritating special requirements. Her day just got a little bit easier. Charlie, however, was another matter. He hemmed and hawed as his eyes scanned up and down the menu. The waitress, who was almost ready to give us a smile after my precise ordering, went back to scowling as Charlie considered his options.

43

"Let's see . . . what do I feel like? The omelets look really good, but I might be in the mood for some French toast. Of course, that sandwich you're getting sounds pretty good too."

Since Charlie was willing to put up with my hunger-related mood swings, it was only fair I dealt maturely with his incessant waffling when ordering in a restaurant. The waitress didn't share a bed with him like I did, so she didn't have to be patient.

"Should I just come back?"

"Yes," he said with a weak smile. "Two minutes."

As she started to walk off, I gently grabbed her arm. "But go ahead and put my order in, okay?"

She nodded with understanding, closed her pad, and huffed off into the kitchen. I stared out at the crashing waves across the road and we sat in silence for over a minute as Charlie glanced at the menu, but then he put it down on the table and said, "So what do you think? Do you believe Juan Carlos somehow poisoned Teboe?"

I took a moment to consider, but it was pointless. I knew my answer before he even asked the question. "Yes," I said emphatically.

"Me too." His tone was even more certain than mine. And as he launched into his intention to stay on top of the case, get a copy of the autopsy report, and stay in contact with the San Simeon investigation, my attention was drawn to a man who had just walked in the door. He looked vaguely familiar from the back as he approached the waitress, who had just come out of the kitchen with my Diet Coke and ice water. She pointed to a table across the room perpendicular to ours, and he sauntered over to it. Just as he slid in his seat, the waitress blocked my view as she stopped to deliver my drinks.

She gave Charlie a wary look. "Got any decisions for me yet?"

Charlie gave her an embarrassed shrug. He had been so busy discussing the Austin Teboe murder, he hadn't yet had the chance to make any.

"One more minute," he said as he cracked open the menu. "No, wait. I'll have . . ." But the poor guy just couldn't commit. Luckily, unlike a lot of gay men, he was much better committing to relationships. "No, forget it. Just give me . . . another minute."

The waitress shook her head slightly and tossed me a look, knowing I shared her contempt of indecisiveness when it came to food. And then she disappeared back into the kitchen again, clearing my obstructed view of the new diner.

My heart almost stopped. I could feel the blood draining from my face. Charlie glanced up from his menu, and instantly knew something was wrong.

"What's the matter?"

"It's him. He's here," I said.

Charlie looked across the room, and his face froze at the sight of Wendell Butterworth, my insane childhood stalker, sitting across the room from us, calmly skimming the lunch specials at the San Simeon Beach Bar and Grill.

Chapter 5

Charlie was up out of his seat like a shot, and charged over to where Wendell Butterworth sat with a satisfied smile on his face. He barely acknowledged Charlie looming over him. His dead gray eyes were fixed on me.

"What the hell are you doing here?" Charlie said with controlled anger.

Wendell glanced up at him and, with an innocent shrug, replied, "Just having some lunch." And then he looked back at me, and gave me a flirtatious wink.

Charlie's imposing six-foot-two frame towered over Wendell as he reached down, grabbed him by his shirt collar, and hauled him out of his chair, which tipped over in the scuffle.

Charlie pulled him forward in his grip until their faces were mere inches apart. "I want you out of here . . . now!"

"I'm just here to get something to eat," Wendell said calmly, going limp in Charlie's grasp. He wasn't going to give Charlie the satisfaction of fighting back.

The seen-it-all waitress, who'd just come out of the kitchen carrying my club sandwich on a rectangular plastic tray, apparently hadn't seen anything like this. Charlie let go of Wendell's collar and hooked an arm around the back of his neck, securing him in a headlock. Then, he yanked him toward the front door. Wendell let his feet drag across the floor, making it even more difficult for Charlie to maneuver him out of the restaurant.

The waitress dropped her tray in surprise, and let out a squeak before she turned back to the kitchen and screamed, "Joey, Lanny, you guys better get out here now!"

Charlie kicked the door open with his right foot, planted the palms of his hands squarely in the middle of Wendell's back, and shoved him hard outside. He then was instantly back at our table, where I sat trying hard not to show him how scared I was. He put a comforting hand on my shoulder.

"You okay, babe?"

"Yeah, it just kind of freaked me out, that's all."

I lovingly placed my hand over Charlie's and we were both still for a moment, contemplating the surreal nature of what had just happened.

Joey and Lanny, the cook and busboy, and prime contenders for a tag team WWE Smackdown title, came bursting through the revolving kitchen doors. They charged up behind the five-foot-two waitress, their bulky size dwarfing her.

Without taking her eyes off us, she said, "The tall one just accosted one of my customers. Kicked his poor ass out the door."

Charlie reached into his back pocket to retrieve his badge, but I stood up and took his hand under the judgmental stares of the obviously straight brutes.

"Let's just go," I said, noticing the remnants of my club sandwich littering the scuffed, dirty floor. "We'll stop somewhere else to eat."

I tossed a ten-dollar bill down on the table. Lanny, hairy everywhere except on the top of his head, waddled over to the front door and pushed it open. He glared at us as we passed by in a vain attempt to intimidate us as we were leaving.

With Charlie's martial arts background and advanced weapons training, it would take a lot more than a three-hundred-pound goateed gorilla in a stained white cook's uniform to intimidate me. On the other hand, if Charlie hadn't been by my side, I probably would have peed in my pants.

Out in the parking lot, we both cautiously looked around for any sign of Wendell Butterworth. He had obviously been released from prison for over a week now. Plenty of time to drum up a handgun. But Wendell had disappeared as quickly as he first appeared, like a ghost. I never once deluded myself into thinking he wouldn't pop up again to haunt me.

Charlie and I climbed into his Volvo, Charlie behind the wheel, and we pulled back onto the highway, riding south toward home in silence. I stole a brief glimpse of Charlie as he drove. He was lost in his private thoughts, and there were worry lines creasing his forehead. He hadn't been there for the hell and pain that Wendell's wrath had brought upon my childhood. But he was acutely aware of the scars and nightmares it had left on me. And it troubled him. He noticed me watching him, so I offered him a reassuring smile. I didn't want him to think I was going to let this guy get to me again. After all, I was older now, stronger, and wiser. I could handle one loony tune. But the reality was, all the fear and anxiety that had paralyzed me as a child was starting to come back. And the idea of this monster kicking off a new campaign of terror made me shudder.

"Monkshood. Very lethal. They call it that because the plant it comes from resembles a monk's cowl."

Charlie and I listened with rapt attention to Susie Chan as she talked while devouring her blackened swordfish at The Little Door on Third Street in West Hollywood. This quaint French bistro, aptly named for its small wooden front door, was one of the top dining spots in LA, and, with even the Diet Coke imported from Europe, very expensive. But the splurge was worth it tonight because in exchange for a forty-dollar piece of fish and a couple of hundred-dollar bottles of wine, Charlie and I were gathering invaluable bits of information.

"It was used in ancient Europe and Asia to poison enemy water supplies during times of war. Hunters also used its sap to poison spears, arrowheads, trap baits, you name it," Susie said between bites of her swordfish.

After returning from Laurette's wedding, Charlie had called his ex-wife, who was the best medical examiner the county of Los Angeles had to offer. She was a five-foot dynamo, appearing on television as a coroner to the stars. She had made quite a name for herself. But despite her enormous career success, she never quite got over her husband coming out of the closet. And she blamed me for breaking up her marriage even though Charlie and I met years after they'd divorced and he'd declared himself gay.

Relations between Susie and myself had always been strained, but lately they had been particularly dicey thanks to a blowup we had when Susie intimated on television that I was directly connected to the murder of my friend Willard Ray Hornsby last year. Of course I didn't do it, and I subsequently unmasked the real killer. But an apology never came from Susie, and we had barely spoken since. Charlie, in the interest of diplomacy, had maintained a cordial relationship with his ex-wife, and they still met for dinner once a month to catch up on each other's lives. I rarely attended these evenings, but tonight was an exception. Susie had agreed to conduct an independent autopsy on Austin Teboe to clarify the cause of death. And owing to her celebrity status, the San Simeon police were more than willing to accommodate her. Some of the officers probably even secretly hoped they'd make the pages of her next book.

Nobody seriously believed Austin Teboe had died of a heart attack. He was still in his early forties and in reasonably good shape. No, there was something else at work here, and Susie was more than willing to help out because, well, let's be frank, she was still in love with her ex-husband.

Susie gulped down a mouthful of a pricey Chardonnay. We were almost down two bottles, and Susie, the lush she was, would undoubtedly order another knowing full well it was my acting residuals picking up the tab.

"Interesting fact. In ancient Greece, legend had it that the plant originated from the slobber dripping from the fangs of Cerberus, the three-headed dog Hercules supposedly brought back with him from the underworld." I didn't give a rat's ass about the Greek myth of a poisonous plant. But I nodded as if I were caught up in a riveting Discovery Channel documentary.

Susie poured herself another glass of wine and then batted her big brown eyes at me. "Should we order another bottle?"

"Sure," I said, clenching my teeth.

Charlie flagged down the waiter.

"So, you're sure this is the poison that was mixed into Austin's champagne?" I said evenly, trying to get as much out of Susie as I could before she got too drunk to speak coherently.

"Yes. It's very bad. Causes burning and tingling, numbness in the tongue, throat, and face, followed by nausea, blurred vision, and paralysis of the respiratory system. Mr. Teboe probably felt as if there was ice water in his veins. And with the amount we found in his glass, it's fatal within ten minutes."

"Was there anything we could have done had we known what it was?" Charlie asked.

"Nope. There's no antidote, at least not that we know about." She pushed her plate away with a third of her swordfish still left. "I don't want to get too full. I hear their dessert menu is fabulous."

"So he was definitely murdered," I said just to confirm it out loud.

"Absolutely. Even the ME in San Simeon, who does maybe one autopsy every two years, knew there was foul play involved before he even cut Mr. Teboe open."

"Where do you think the killer got the stuff?"

"In Nova Scotia, monkshood survives as a garden plant. It's not impossible to come by. So I don't think it's going to help narrow down your lists of suspects."

"You've been a big help, Susie, thanks," Charlie said with a smile.

I felt it was in my best interest to agree. "Yes, Susie, thank you. You never cease to amaze me with your crime scene investigation talents."

Susie knew she was the best, and was always open to fawning accolades. She simply sat back and enjoyed letting them wash over her.

The waiter returned with our third hundred-dollar bottle of wine, and Susie nearly clapped with glee as he twisted the corkscrew into the top of the bottle and popped it open. He poured a small amount into one glass, which Charlie tasted and approved, and we commenced with another full round. Susie signaled another waiter, who was carrying a tray with the evening's dessert selections, and he hustled over to her side so she could ponder over which sweet appealed the most to her. She just couldn't decide, and the poor guy, who had about seven other tables to attend to, was left standing next to her, holding a silver tray lined with seven different dessert selections. At least Susie and Charlie had had one thing in common when they were married: culinary indecisiveness.

As Susie debated between the crème brûlée and the chocolate mousse cake, my mind wandered to Laurette's wedding. The killer had to be somebody in attendance. Austin Teboe had apparently known only two people at the ceremony. There was a definite history between him and Dominique, though it was still a mystery what exactly it was. But she left early, long before the wedding toast, so it would have been impossible for her to mix the monkshood poison into his champagne. That only left one other person: Juan Carlos Barranco. Charlie had made a few calls to Miami Beach, and found out Teboe had worked at a trendy Lincoln Road eatery called the Nexxt Café, which was one of the more popular spots in South Beach. He'd served as a chef, having resigned just two weeks prior to the wedding. Still, we weren't sure that was the restaurant where he had met Juan Carlos; Charlie couldn't verify whether Juan Carlos had ever worked there, or even dined there.

But although I wasn't yet sure about the details, I was convinced Laurette's new husband was behind the murder. And with the happy couple returning from their Maui honeymoon the following morning, I knew this already precarious situation was about to get a hell of a lot more complicated.

Chapter 6

Brave soul that she was, Laurette rang me the morning she got home from her four-day honeymoon at a resort world-renowned for their sumptuous all-you-can-eat buffets, and suggested we rendezvous at a Weight Watchers meeting so we could both weigh in. She decided that if either of us had dropped even a fraction of a pound, we could immediately drive to Hugo's, a West Hollywood brunch spot, and split a plate of their delectable pasta alla mama, to celebrate. From what I could speculate from our brief conversation, the honeymoon did not go well. Her voice was hushed and strained, and when I asked her if everything was all right, she deflected the question by asking how many Weight Watchers points a McDonald's breakfast burrito would cost her.

I hopped into the car and drove to the nearest Weight Watchers location, which was on Beverly Boulevard, in the heart of Los Angeles's teeming Russian immigrant community. There was no reason for Weight Watchers to be in this particular location as far as I could tell. The Russians in the neighborhood didn't look any heavier than the Americans.

I parked on a side street, walked to the two-level glass building, and made my way to the back where a line formed out the door with nervous-looking dieters awaiting their weekly weigh-in on a sturdy, top-of-the-line scale you just can't buy at Sears. There was no getting around the numbers that would pop up on the digital display screen. These industrial, professional machines were designed for accuracy. Which was good or bad, depending on what kind of week you'd had. Today was bad since I had overindulged at The Little Door with Charlie and Susie the night before.

Laurette and I had tried every kind of diet there was, but Weight Watchers was the one that seemed to do the trick since it was very easy for both of us to get caught up in counting points. It became a game we could play together as we spent hours trying to figure out how it would be possible to eat a filet mignon and half a pepperoni pizza in the same day. Unfortunately, with only twenty-seven points to spend a day, and one slice of French toast with a dollop of maple syrup totaling a whopping eight points, I was done eating for the day after breakfast.

I had been standing in line for just a few minutes when I heard a commotion up at the front counter. It was Laurette. She had arrived just before me and was determined to stock up on the three-point chocolate bars you could gorge on between meals during the week. But there was only one box left on the shelf and a formidable three-hundred-pound newcomer was certain her hand had reached the box first. I loved watching Laurette in action. She was a force to be reckoned with, and most rue the day they foolishly choose to get on her bad side. I had come close on her wedding day. It scared me to think about life without Laurette. She was just too bright a light in my world. And despite my misgivings regarding her new husband, I didn't want to jeopardize our friendship.

To my utter shock, Laurette let go of the box and muttered to the obese woman, "Fine. You take it."

The obese woman grunted, a victorious smile on her face, and took her seat in one of the hard, gray folding chairs that had been set up for today's lecture.

Laurette was clearly upset. Otherwise, she would have chewed up this woman and spit her out, in spite of her enormous size. Whatever was bothering her had to be big. It was extremely unusual for her to give up without a fight. And the stakes involved chocolate. Suddenly I was worried.

She spotted me in line, and ambled over to give me a hug. Her eyes were red, as if she had been crying, and she wore no makeup. Laurette never left the house without makeup. She prided herself on always looking dazzling. The more I studied her, the more concerned I became.

"How was the honeymoon?" I said.

"I think Juan Carlos is cheating on me."

Well, at least I didn't have to pull what was wrong out of her. That was what made Laurette such a good talent manager. No bullshit. She always just cut right to the chase.

"What makes you think that?" I said.

"While we were in Maui, someone kept calling our room at the hotel and hanging up. Juan Carlos said it was probably just kids playing a prank. But I know it was her."

"Who?"

"Dominique, his ex-girlfriend."

"Maybe he was right. Maybe it was just kids," I offered weakly.

Laurette shook her head. "No. Juan Carlos kept leaving me on the beach, said he was going to take a nap in the room. Finally, I called the room and there was no answer. He wasn't there. I think he was meeting her."

"She was in Maui? Are you sure?"

"No. Not a hundred percent sure. But one morning we got up early and did one of those sunrise bike tours down the side of a volcano. Halfway down, our group stopped for breakfast at a small restaurant, and I thought I spotted her outside, just standing there, staring at us. Juan Carlos told me I was being ridiculous. He refused to take me seriously, which just made me all the more suspicious. I know it was her, Jarrod. I saw her."

By this time, Laurette and I were at the front of the line, and it was my turn to bite the bullet and step up on the scale. I tore off my belt and shoes, and dropped my keys and loose change on one of the folding chairs. I was a seasoned pro at this. I didn't need any random coins or metal weighing me down.

I turned and let out a sigh. Operating the scale was Richard, this rail-thin former fatty whom I affectionately referred to as the "Diet Nazi." Richard had lost a hundred and forty pounds on Weight Watchers, and so was a self-proclaimed expert on what was good for the rest of us. When I lost ten percent of my body weight after four grueling months in the program, Richard called me up in front of the class and hailed me as a hero. Until he discovered I had celebrated my monumental weight loss with a huge Thai dinner. He berated me in front of the class, and told me I was not an example to follow, and that earning a few activity points by walking Snickers around the block did not give me license to splurge on pad Thai noodle with peanut sauce. Tension had brewed between us ever since.

Richard gave me a cursory glance, and waved me up onto the scale. I closed my eyes and did as I was told. There was an agonizing moment as Richard waited for the digital numbers to settle down, and then a sly smile broke out on his face.

"It seems we've put on a couple pounds, Jarrod."

I opened my eyes to see the digital readout: 172 pounds. Not good. Not good at all. It was more than a couple of pounds. It was five. The Diet Nazi could barely contain his euphoria.

"And it's not even the holidays. Looks like someone needs to work a little harder. Better luck next week."

I wanted to punch him in the face. Normally I would have found solace in Laurette taking her turn. One smart mouth remark from Richard, and she would have done what I fantasized about doing. She would have socked him square in the mouth.

But instead, after witnessing my public embarrassment, Laurette was too distraught to even attempt a weigh-in.

"I'm not up for this," she said and we hauled ass out the door.

As I walked Laurette to her car, she began to cry. I stopped and took her into my arms. "I'm sorry, sweetheart, I really am."

She pulled away, placing a hand on her chest in a vain attempt to regain her composure. "I love him so much."

"I know you do. Is there anything I can do? Anything at all?"

"Yes."

When I said it, I thought it was one of those rhetorical questions that would have triggered an automated response such as, "No, just being my friend is enough." But I should've known with Laurette, I was being lured into a plan.

"What?" I said, unable to hide my hesitancy.

"Follow him."

"What do you mean?"

She wiped away the last tear from her cheek, and looked at me with fierce resolve. "I want you to follow him and prove that he's a no-good philandering son of a bitch."

Now every little voice in my head was screaming at me to say no. Just tell her I don't feel comfortable staking out my best friend's husband to catch him in the act of adultery. But to be honest, my own curiosity was peaked. I wanted to know his story, and by tailing him, I just might come up with some answers to the questions surrounding Austin Teboe's murder.

Although Charlie would undoubtedly need to be kept in the dark about what I was doing, it proved to be too enticing to pass up. "All right. I'll do it, honey. But remember, this stays between us. If Charlie found out . . ."

"I won't breathe a word."

I nodded and our pact was sealed.

"I can't start on an empty stomach," I said. "Hugo's? My treat."

"Meet you there."

Laurette opened her car door as I walked up the street toward mine, but before she climbed in, she called out to me. "Jarrod?"

I turned around.

"If you do find out he's cheating on me, then will you help me do one more thing?"

"What's that?" I said.

"Kill him."

She was joking. I think. There wasn't a trace of a smile on her face. Or a humorous lilt in her voice. We would just have to cross that bridge if we came to it.

Luckily Charlie was in the shower when Laurette called at five-thirty the following morning to alert me to the fact that Juan Carlos was on the move. He was on his way to Gold's Gym in Hollywood, and had an audition for a national Home Depot commercial at ten-thirty. He was particularly vague about his afternoon schedule, so Laurette was convinced that if he was going to meet Dominique, it would be sometime after lunch. I arrived at Gold's in a rather drab, nondescript neighborhood just south of the multimillion-dollar renovation projects in downtown Hollywood, including the upscale Cineplex, the Arclight, built around the historic Cinerama Dome; and Hollywood & Highland, a trendy mall full of shops, theaters, restaurants, and the spacious Kodak Theatre, the new home for the Academy Awards. But even with all the opulent new developments a few blocks north, the street where I parked outside of Gold's was washed out and depressing. I was stuck there a solid two hours. I should have known Juan Carlos was a gym rat, completely obsessed with his physique. He was obviously in there pumping every kind of iron there was, not to mention chatting up a few pretty faces too.

Finally, around eight, he strolled out the front door, conversing with a couple of other well-built actors showing off their sculptured pecs in form-fitting T-shirts. Juan Carlos waved good-bye to his buddies, hopped in Laurette's white SUV, and drove west. I pulled out behind him, but tried staying a few cars behind him so as not to arouse suspicion.

He pulled into a Starbucks just outside the Farmers' Market, and I watched as he had coffee with a man and a woman, both in sharp Italian business suits. Agents or managers. Definitely. I watched them through the window from outside, and Juan Carlos never stopped talking. He was probably talking about his career goals and himself in general. For over an hour. The agents looked relieved when Juan Carlos checked his watch, and jumped up to leave.

Then, it was off to his audition on the west side in Culver City. It was in a brick building, home to several casting agencies. He primped in the SUV a good ten minutes before donning his Armani sunglasses, adjusting one stray hair on his head, and then finally marching confidently inside. He was in there an hour.

When he finally came out, he looked excited as he spoke feverishly into his cell phone. My guess was he got the part. Or at least a callback. There was almost a skip in his step as he headed for the SUV.

After lunch with another out-of-work actor I recognized from an MCI commercial, I was beginning to think Juan Carlos was exactly as he came across. A self-absorbed player who used his looks to get ahead, but in the end, a faithful husband. That was before he headed over the hill to the San Fernando Valley. I thought he might be driving to a last-minute audition, but when he drove north to a middle-class neighborhood near the Burbank Airport, and parked on a quiet street called Screenland Drive, I perked up. Something was happening.

Juan Carlos got out of his car, and walked up to a one-story pea green house that would never see the pages of *Architectural Digest*. He rapped on the door, and a stunning young blonde, spilling out of a bright pink tank top, welcomed him inside. As she closed the door, I saw Juan Carlos lean in and kiss her. On the mouth. Jackpot.

I leaped out of the car, and ran up the walk to the house. The blinds were drawn so I couldn't see inside, but after maneuvering around some shrubbery, I came across an open window leading into the kitchen. I could hear them in the living room. Their voices were faint, but distinguishable.

"It's got to be tonight," the blonde said. There was an urgency in her voice.

"So soon? We can't make any mistakes. I could lose everything," Juan Carlos said.

"Don't worry. We'll make it look like an accident. Something quick and easy."

"What kind of an accident?"

"Oh, keep your voice down," the blonde said. "Do you remember that woman who tried to kill herself on Fire Island?"

"So?"

"I took it away from her, remember?"

"Took what?"

"What she tried to kill herself with."

"What good does that do us?"

"I got it. I saved it. I'll show you. See? Poison. And it works fast."

This couldn't be happening. It was all so surreal. Juan Carlos and this blond woman were plotting some kind of murder. And I was ready to bet my house on two things. The poison was monkshead. And the intended victim was my best friend, Laurette.

I whipped out my cell phone to call Laurette and warn her when I heard a low, steady growling. I looked down to see a pit bull, ears back and teeth bared, ready to lunge for my throat. I dropped the phone. My only weapon. Perfect. I slowly raised my arms to protect my face (an actor's first thought), when the shades in the open window rolled up.

"Badger, what are you growling at?"

The blond woman stared at me. And then she let out a scream. A long, piercing scream. Juan Carlos was at her side in a second.

"Jarrod?"

"Hi, Juan Carlos," I said.

"You know him?" the blond woman said, shaking.

"Yes. He's a friend of my wife's. What are you doing here?" He didn't look angry. Just confused. He had no idea I was on to him.

"Does that really matter? I heard everything," I said with an accusatory look on my face.

"Heard what?" he said.

"The accident. Tonight. Laurette."

It took a minute for him to process what I was talking about. And then it dawned on him, and his eyes went wide. I probably should have dived for my phone and dialed 911, but I stood my ground. Juan Carlos looked at the blonde, and then, they both laughed. Big, hearty, guffawing laughs. I didn't see the humor in the situation, so I remained stone-faced.

Juan Carlos disappeared back inside and then returned with a DVD. He tossed it out the window and I grabbed it. It was a classic fifties melodrama, *Sudden Fear*, starring Joan Crawford, Jack Palance, and Gloria Grahame. What this had to do with anything was lost on me.

"You ever see it?" Juan Carlos said.

"Yes," I said. It was actually quite a potboiler. Playwright Crawford rejects actor Palance for her play, he returns later to romance her and plot her murder with his ex-girlfriend Grahame . . . Oh no.

I slowly raised my eyes to Juan Carlos, who had a big grin on his face. I didn't dare ask. I didn't have to.

"We're doing a scene for our acting class."

The blonde piped in. "Our teacher's a Crawford fanatic. Everyone's doing scenes from her films. It's so funny that you thought . . ."

I shrugged. The joke was on me.

Once Juan Carlos and his scene partner stopped laughing, and Badger finally stopped growling, there was a deadening silence. I knew what was coming.

"So what *are* you doing here, Jarrod?" Juan Carlos folded his arms and his eyes narrowed. There was no getting out of this one.

Chapter 7

As I stood in the hedges, caught, embarrassed, and totally screwed, my mind raced with a number of scenarios I could attempt to use to explain my way out of this botched stakeout. But I decided the truth was probably the best way to go. Well, almost the truth. I had to protect Laurette at all costs. So I would just leave out the part where she asked me to tail her husband and find out if he was a lying, cheating cad.

The blond woman, whom Juan Carlos finally introduced me to as Tammy, rushed outside to retrieve her pit bull, Badger. She flashed me a look of warning, as if I were the one who was growling at her precious four-legged soul mate. Badger snapped at my leg as she pulled him by the collar back into the house, and I heard her murmur under her breath, "Good boy."

That left me alone with Juan Carlos, who looked down at me from the kitchen window, not budging, frustration rising the longer it took me to offer up an explanation.

I let out a deep sigh. "The thing is, Juan Carlos, I love Laurette with all my heart."

"As do I," he said emphatically, a hint of defensiveness in his inflection.

"Well, I've known her a long time, and she can sometimes be impulsive, and well, when she rang me up to tell me she was marrying you after only knowing you such a short time, naturally I became suspicious of your motives."

Juan Carlos didn't flinch. His brown eyes, almost empty of emotion, stared at me. I pressed on. "And, well, I just wanted to make sure you're sincere about your feelings for her because the last thing I want is for Laurette to get hurt."

"I would never hurt Laurette. She's my life now, my whole life," he said.

"But surely you can understand where I'm coming from," I said.

Nothing. Not even a slight nod. Apparently he didn't understand.

"With your ex-girlfriend showing up at the wedding and a dead body at the reception, I mean those are pretty big red flags."

"I already told you and the police. It's over between Dominique and me. It has been for a long time. And I don't even know that man who died at the wedding."

"He didn't just die. He was murdered."

Finally. A slight reaction from Juan Carlos. His eye twitched and he shifted in the window, a little uncomfortable hearing the word "murder."

"Poisoned. Didn't you hear?" I said.

"How could I? Laurette and I just got home last night." His patience with me was waning. "Look, Jarrod, as you can see, Tammy and I are just scene partners, not secret lovers. Dominique is long gone. I have no idea where. And I had nothing to do with that man who died . . . excuse me . . . was murdered at my wedding. You should be talking to the hundred other people who were there that day."

"You're right. I'm sorry," I said. "I've been very foolish."

He softened a bit, and even offered me a slight smile. It wasn't sincere. He was just the kind of guy who liked to keep his enemies close.

"I accept your apology," he said, rather condescendingly.

I needed to ensure that he didn't suspect Laurette of any wrongdoing.

"Please, Juan Carlos, don't tell Laurette what I've been up to. She'd never speak to me again."

He paused, and thought long and hard. He really wanted to make me squirm while he decided my fate. Finally, he gave me a wink. "Fine. This will remain between us."

"Thank you," I said. "Thank you."

He waved me off, and returned to continue rehearsing his dramatic scene with Tammy. What a prick.

I walked back out to the street, where the blinding valley sun made my eyes ache. I squinted as I climbed back into my car and donned my sunglasses. Starting up the Beamer, I pulled out from the curb to make my way over the hill back home, when I passed a Mazda 626 with an Enterprise rental car sticker on the rear bumper that was parked on the west side of the street. A tiny woman was in the driver's seat, watching the pea green stucco house I had just left. It was Dominique.

I turned the corner and drove back out onto the main strip just east of Screenland Drive, a major street called Hollywood Way, where I immediately U-turned in a strip mall parking lot, and double backed. I rolled to a stop on the opposite side of the street from Dominique's rental car. She didn't notice me. She was too busy studying Tammy's house.

About twenty minutes passed before Juan Carlos and Tammy emerged from the house. Dominique sank low in her seat, not wanting them to spot her.

Tammy gave Juan Carlos a peck on the cheek, and he flashed her a smile before hopping into Laurette's SUV and driving off. Dominique jammed her Mazda into gear, and roared off after him.

I followed Dominique. Juan Carlos, ignorant to the fact he was leading a caravan, steered onto the Ventura Freeway West toward the ocean. It was still early in the day, so traffic wasn't heavy. Juan Carlos exited onto Topanga Canyon, a loopy, rustic road that eventually spilled out onto the Pacific Coast Highway and the vast beaches of Malibu. It took over an hour to get there, and Juan Carlos kept driving north, to a remote spot just past the Malibu Colony, home to many of Hollywood's elite. He parked on the side of the road, jumped out, stripped off his shirt and jeans to reveal a tight black swimsuit, and padded down the sand to the surf.

Dominique pulled off the road, the car rolling over gravel until she was about twenty feet from the SUV. She turned off the car and stared down at the beach, where Juan Carlos bravely ventured into the cold, numbing water. When he was knee deep, he dove into a small wave and disappeared.

I was so busy watching Dominique eye Juan Carlos that I almost tapped the rear end of the Mercedes in front of me that was stopped at a red light. I slammed on the brakes, jerking to a halt, nearly causing the motorcyclist behind me to do a double flip over my roof. He screamed a couple of obscenities at me as he swerved out around me and passed by. I shrugged, mouthed, "I'm sorry," and took the hint to get off the road.

The sun was assaulting and the temperature must have been upwards of ninety degrees. Sweat dripped down my brow as I kept my eyes focused on Dominique, who had lost sight of Juan Carlos in the surf, and was starting to get antsy. She got out of the car, and wandered down to the beach, keeping one hand above her eyes to block out the sun. I had a pair of minibinoculars in the trunk I used when I could only get nosebleed seats for a concert at the Staples Center. I popped open the trunk, unhooked the lens protectors, and peered through them. After a few seconds of searching, I caught a glimpse of a pair of arms splashing through the water, circling around a buoy, and then starting back for shore. It was Juan Carlos.

Dominique waited for him. After another fifteen minutes, Juan Carlos surfaced and, muscles tired from his workout, slowly made his way up the beach. He didn't spot Dominique at first, never even looked her way. She finally called out to him, startling him, and he jerked his head around to see her. She was smiling, hopeful, as if she was expecting some kind of warm reunion. He gaped at her for a few moments, trying to discern if it was really her. And then she ran toward him, arms outstretched, yearning for an embrace.

When she reached him and threw her arms around his neck, he stiffened. When she began smothering his face with kisses, he pushed her away. I was too far from them to hear the conversation, but it was heated. He yelled at her, berated her, but she held on to his arm, her lips trying to desperately caress his bronze skin. He wrenched his arm free, and shoved her again. Hard. She fell down, her face in the sand, humiliated.

Juan Carlos spat out a few final words, and stalked back to the SUV. He was livid as he yanked open the door, grabbed his shirt to wipe himself off from the water and the smell of his ex's desperation, jumped in, and peeled away. Bits of gravel flew in all directions.

I didn't follow him. I knew he was probably heading home to Laurette. Instead, I kept my eyes fixed upon Dominique, who had now climbed to her hands and knees and was sobbing. Her eye makeup smeared her face like a clown as she rose to her feet. The blustery wind almost knocked her tiny body down again. But she pushed forward, hands covering her face, and rushed toward the ocean before her.

It took me only a few seconds to figure out what she was going to do. She bounded into the surf, her arms stretched out, as if offering herself to the turbulent, dangerous waters of the

Pacific. Before I sprinted down to the beach, she was already up to her waist, and by the time I had reached the water's edge, she had disappeared below the surface altogether. I blocked out the freezing sensation as I dove headfirst into the water and swam out with bold, choppy strokes. I stopped, treading water, my arms, legs, and torso paralyzed with cold. There was no sign of her. Nothing. All I could see was a family of four—mom, dad, and two kids, with their dog—having a picnic lunch down the beach. I wanted to call to them for help, but what could they do?

I inhaled sharply, and dropped down underneath the surface, eyes open, trying to focus on anything. But it was dark and murky, and after only forty-five seconds, I had to shoot up to the surface again, and take another deep breath. I dove once again, and this time I caught sight of something. A fish? No, it was a hand. Just a few feet away. I shot forward and grabbed it, tugging it toward me. A face appeared through the shadowy depths. It was Dominique, her eyes wide open, her mouth agape, filling with water.

I wrapped an arm around her waist, and hauled her to the surface. With all my strength, I dragged her limp body toward shore. I coughed and sputtered from swallowing a mouthful of saltwater. I wasn't sure if she was dead, or unconscious, or in a state of shock. Finally, my foot touched bottom, and I was able to carry her out, setting her down in the damp sand out of reach of the tide. I gave her mouth-to-mouth, and after a few tense moments, she gurgled, throwing up a quart of seawater, and crying uncontrollably.

I helped her to sit up, and we sat in silence as she held my hand and whimpered, unsure if she was happy or sad to have survived.

"Why did you do it?" I said.

She looked at me, vaguely recognizing me from the bus trip up to the Hearst Castle. She gave me a quizzical stare, and then shook her head and quietly cried.

"He wants nothing to do with me," she said.

"Juan Carlos?"

Her eyes fluttered, surprised that I knew who had broken her heart. "Yes," she said. "He told me he didn't care if I was alive or dead, just that he wanted me to leave him alone. He loves *her* now."

I knew exactly who "her" was. This was going to be good news for Laurette. But for this fragile creature, who took Juan Carlos at his word and decided her best option was simply to drown herself, I felt sorry. She struck me as a wounded bird, fallen from the nest, alone and afraid. Although Juan Carlos may have proven his intentions, his treatment of Dominique only reinforced my opinion of his character. And the thought of him sharing a bed with my best friend made me shudder.

Chapter 8

Dominique was in a trance-like state as I led her back to her car. Fearing she was in no condition to drive, I offered to chauffeur her anywhere she wanted to go, especially if it was to the nearest psychiatrist's office. But quickly snapping out of it, she assured me she was feeling better, and before I could convince her otherwise, she was back behind the wheel of her rented Mazda, and merging into the heavy traffic on the Pacific Coast Highway. She definitely had no desire to open up anymore to a complete stranger.

So I was left standing on the dusty, dirt shoulder of the highway, secure in the knowledge that Juan Carlos was at least faithful. That still didn't leave him off the hook as a murder suspect.

I got back into the Beamer, and headed east on the 10 Freeway, exiting the commuter-clogged La Brea Avenue north, which led me straight to the Hollywood Hills, and finally home.

As I wound up to the English Tudor–style house I shared with Charlie, I saw his Volvo parked out front. He was home early. Definitely a welcome surprise. Snickers was running in circles when I entered the kitchen from the garage, and I scooped her up and followed Charlie's voice into the den, which was my favorite room in the house. The walls were covered with Hitchcock and Wilder movie posters and an impressive DVD collection, all positioned around the wide-screen TV. In other words, heaven. Charlie sat on the couch, talking on the phone. He winked at me as I ambled in, and patted the cushion next to him. I plopped down, sinking deep into the soft, intoxicating lushness of the cushions (we spare no expense when it comes to comfort). He slipped a muscular arm around my neck, pulling me closer, and I closed my eyes, nestling my head against his chest as he talked.

"So man, how long has it been?" he said, smiling. "Jesus, that long? No, things here are good. I've got a boyfriend now, going on three years." He gently kissed the top of my head and I couldn't help but smile.

"No, seriously. What, you think I was going to wait for you?" Charlie said.

My eyes popped open. Who the hell was he talking to? Going to wait for whom?

"Very happy. He's an actor," Charlie said. And then, after a moment, Charlie laughed. "I know, I know, but I love him anyway."

Charlie tousled my hair, and gave me another wink. I wasn't as receptive anymore. I shot up, and stared at him as he wound up his conversation.

"You too, man, and thanks. You've been a huge help."

He clicked off the phone.

"Hey," he said, as he leaned in and kissed me softly on the lips.

"Hey," I said flatly. "Who was that?"

"Friend of mine in Miami."

"I don't remember you ever mentioning a friend in Miami." I knew I was being the unreasonably suspicious boyfriend, but after snooping around after Juan Carlos all day, it was in my blood.

"We met in Michigan. At the Police Academy. Good guy."

There was a long silence as I considered dropping the whole subject. But a lot of people have learned not to bet on me dropping anything. "So were you just friends, or were you, you know, more than just friends?"

"Yeah, there was a flirtation for a while. Pretty innocent though. Never got past the groping stage. But then he dropped out of the Academy and joined the military. We kind of lost touch."

"So what brought about this big reunion?" I said, my eyes boring into him.

Charlie was so used to my drama, he never flinched or blinked or lost his cool. He just chuckled to himself, and took my hand.

"You."

"Me?"

"Yeah. You've been so caught up in finding out if Laurette's husband had anything to do with that Teboe guy getting poisoned, I decided to make a few calls. I heard this guy was living in Miami, doing some side work for the police, so I got his number from the South Beach precinct, and rang him up to see if he knew anything about the victim."

I perked up. "Did he?"

"Did he ever." Charlie snaked his hand behind my back, and yanked me across the couch until our faces were inches apart.

"Well, what does he know?" I asked.

"Later," he said, and lowered me down on my back. He lifted my head in the crook of his elbow, and jammed his lips over mine. Our tongues danced and probed together, and he wrapped his legs around mine and locked them into place. Charlie didn't demand much from me, but when he got hot and horny, he hated to wait. We weren't going anywhere.

He was the best lover I had ever known, and if I had been

smart, I would have just gone with the flow, and put my curiosity into neutral, but once my mind starts racing, there's no turning back, and I just couldn't help myself.

I reached up, kissing his cheek, his forehead, making my way over to his right ear. Charlie's anticipation was building. This was always the part where I talked dirty.

"So what exactly did your friend know about Teboe?" I said.

Charlie let out a sigh, but chose to ignore me. He ripped open my shirt, and started caressing my chest with his hands. I slipped mine up underneath his sweater and did the same. Then, he grabbed ahold of my zipper and yanked it down, cupped a hand below my genitals, and rubbed furiously. I gasped, lost in the pleasure of his touch. Charlie was certain this would do the trick. No more questions until we were through.

"Did your friend know whether Teboe and Juan Carlos worked at the same restaurant?" I said.

Charlie stopped and pulled away. I could see the frustration on his pained face. But he knew it was a hopeless cause.

"Yes," Charlie said. "He confirmed it. The two met working at the Nexxt Café. Teboe was a chef. Juan Carlos a waiter. My friend was keeping tabs on Teboe because he was investigating Javier Martinez."

I had no clue who that was, so Charlie enlightened me. "Big head of a Miami-based crime family. Into money laundering, extortion, weapons smuggling, you name it. They're bigger than some multinational corporations. Teboe's last gig was working as a personal chef on Martinez's yacht. He left under mysterious circumstances, though no one knows why."

I sat up. "What about Juan Carlos? Did your friend say he was connected with the family too?"

"No. Juan Carlos never worked for them. But Martinez sure as hell knows who Juan Carlos is, and isn't a fan, to put it mildly. There was a rumor that Martinez put a hit out on Juan Carlos, which might explain why he left Florida in such a hurry."

"Why would a bad soap actor piss off a big-time crime czar? And why would Juan Carlos lie about knowing Austin Teboe?"

Charlie shrugged.

"Anything else?" I said.

"Nope. That was it."

To Charlie's chagrin, I started buttoning up my shirt.

"What are you doing?"

"Going over to Laurette's."

"Now?"

"Don't you think she ought to know that her husband is mixed up with the Tony Soprano of South Florida?"

He couldn't argue with my logic. But that didn't make him any less perturbed.

I jumped up, zipped my pants back up, and grabbed my car keys out of my pants pocket. I halted, then turned back, leaned down, and kissed Charlie hard on the mouth. "I know I'm insane, and obsessive, and really hard to handle, but just know that I love you, and I really hope you're here when I get back."

Charlie saw right through my quick fix. He wasn't going to let me off so easily this time. "Maybe," he said. "Depends on whether or not I can get a flight to Florida tonight or in the morning."

This floored me. My mouth dropped open and we stared each other down. And finally, after an agonizing thirty seconds, he gave me another one of his adorable trademark winks. "Don't be late."

"I love you," I said, as I raced for the garage.

"Yeah, yeah, I've heard it all before."

Chapter 9

"So, Juan Carlos told Dominique that he loved *me* and not her, is that right?" Laurette said, clutching an apple martini in her recently renovated backyard, which now boasted a kidney-shaped pool, a blue-tiled Jacuzzi, and several bamboo trees and rosebushes.

"Yes, but he lied about knowing Austin Teboe. They did work together in Miami Beach. Now why would he lie about something like that?" I said.

Laurette took a generous sip of her martini. I thought she was considering my question, but then, after a moment, she leaned forward and said, "So it's definitely over between them then."

"Yes," I said, unable to conceal my exasperation. "But this Javier Martinez sounds like a real dangerous character, and Juan Carlos has somehow ticked him off, and at the risk of sounding melodramatic, I think your life could be in jeopardy."

Laurette's eyes brimmed with tears. I thought I had finally broken through. She threw her head back and exclaimed, "Thank God! Thank God he's not cheating on me! Oh, I feel *so* much better!"

She never heard a word I said.

I snatched the apple martini out of her hand, holding it hostage. This finally spurred a reaction. As her arm snapped out to grab it back, I wrenched it farther out of her reach.

"Honey, this is serious," I said. "Juan Carlos is in with some big-time bad guys, and you need to deal with that."

"Please, Jarrod, whatever past he may have had in Florida is over. His life is in LA now. With me."

"But what if it turns out that he did have something to do with poisoning Austin Teboe? What then?"

"We've been over this and over this. He's not a murderer. The only time Juan Carlos killed anyone was when he played Brutus in *Julius Caesar* at the La Hoya Playhouse. Now enough. Promise me you'll leave him alone."

Maybe it was me. Maybe I just didn't like the guy. I knew if I kept up this relentless pursuit of the truth, I risked losing my best friend. It was time to pull back.

"Maybe I'm just being overprotective," I said.

"And I love you for it." Laurette squeezed my hand and leaned over and kissed me on the cheek.

Out of the corner of my eye, I saw movement inside the house. It was Juan Carlos. He tossed his keys on a side table in the living room, spotted us having a cocktail hour out on the patio, and sauntered out to join us.

"How was your day, honey?" he said as he leaned over his wife and gently cupped her face in his hands, stealing a soft, brief kiss.

He completely ignored me.

"Busy," Laurette sighed. "Seems with all these reality shows featuring D-list actors, my whole client roster is working." She caught herself, gently touched my arm, and with apologetic eyes, said, "No offense, Jarrod."

"Don't worry about it. I may be D-list, but I still have my dignity."

Laurette turned to Juan Carlos, who just stood there, glaring at me. "We got a generous offer for Jarrod to do *Child Star Hotel*, this new MTV show where a bunch of has-beens move in together and run a business, but he just won't even go there."

"A job's a job," Juan Carlos said.

I shrugged. "Call me Pollyanna, but I just think there's something better out there for me on the horizon."

"There is, sweetie, there is. You just hang in there," Laurette said as she reached out and took her husband's large, bronzed hand and brought it to her cheek as she gazed lovingly up at him. "How did your audition go today?"

"Got a callback for tomorrow."

Laurette leaped up and threw her arms around him. "Honey, that's fantastic!"

Juan Carlos never took his eyes off me. "Funny, I thought Jarrod might have told you already."

"Jarrod?" Laurette said, with all the commitment of Meryl Streep in *Sophie's Choice*. Her husband was hoping to expose me to his wife. Little did he know that it was his wife who'd sent me out snooping in the first place.

"It was the strangest thing. We kept running into each other today," he said.

"Really? How odd?" Laurette said, with big, fluttery, innocent eyes. She was overdoing it. If she wasn't careful, Juan Carlos was going to figure out she knew more than she was letting on. Subtlety was one skill God never had time to bestow on Laurette.

"Yes, I saw him in Burbank. At Tammy's house."

Laurette turned to me. "What were you doing there?"

I couldn't believe it. In her panicked efforts to hide her own complicity, Laurette was selling me out. She didn't mean to, but she didn't want to upset her new husband.

I just stood there, with my mouth open and my mind racing. "My dentist has an office on that street. I was getting a cleaning." How lame.

Juan Carlos grinned. He loved watching me lie. And he didn't care. He just wanted to see me squirm some more.

"After we rehearsed our scene, I drove out to the beach to do a little body surfing," he said.

Laurette ran her fingers over his hardened, sculptured biceps. "He exercises all the time. But why state the obvious?" She was proud of him. And had every right to be. He was a good-looking, sexy man. For a manipulative, cocky son of a bitch.

"It's weird. I was all the way out in Malibu, by myself, and I swear I saw Jarrod's car. That fancy Beamer he likes to cruise around town in."

"Well, it couldn't have been his if you had just seen him in Burbank," Laurette offered.

"No, I guess that would mean he was following me or something."

I was through playing Juan Carlos's little game. I stood up. "But since I've already said I was getting my teeth cleaned, I guess it doesn't mean anything."

"I guess not," Juan Carlos said, folding his beefy arms. "So what have you two gossips been whispering about while I've been out?"

There was a long, agonizing pause.

"That's agent-client privileged information," Laurette said with a forced giggle.

"I thought that only applied to lawyers." He was dead serious.

"Jarrod's NBC pilot died, so we were discussing what's next for him."

It was a good save. But Juan Carlos wasn't buying. Any of it. It was time to make a graceful exit.

"I better get home to Charlie," I said, downing the last of my own drink, handing Juan Carlos the glass, and heading for the door.

"Call me tomorrow. Give my love to Charlie," Laurette said as she gulped down the last of her apple martini.

I hated leaving Laurette alone with that brute, but I had to respect her wishes. If at any time she got in over her head, I was confident she would call me.

I slid into my car, hooked the seat belt in place, and turned over the engine. Suddenly blasting through the car stereo speakers was the original cast recording of *A Chorus Line*. Track Three. "At the Ballet." Look, I never claimed to be straight. As I started backing out of the driveway, the front door of the house flew open, and Juan Carlos stalked out. He circled around the hood of the car, and marched up to the driver's side window. I put my foot on the brake.

He tapped lightly on the glass, and motioned for me to roll it down. I complied, wondering what it was he wanted.

"Before you go, I just want to say something," he said in a low, gravelly voice.

"What?" I turned down the volume until the cast of *A Chorus Line* faded into silence.

Juan Carlos closed his eyes, took a deep breath, and then slowly opened them again. They were full of loathing. A shiver went up my spine.

"I don't like you following me around, Jarrod."

"Look, I thought you might be sneaking around on Laurette, and I was wrong. I already told you that. End of story."

"No. That's not the only reason. You think I had something to do with that guy Teboe's death. Well, I didn't."

I didn't answer him.

He put his hands on his hips, the frustration rising in his voice. "Why do you think I'm hiding something?"

"I don't think you're hiding something," I said evenly. "I think you're hiding a lot of things. Good night, Juan Carlos."

Before I had a chance to take my foot off the brake, he grabbed a fistful of my shirt and yanked me forward. The window was only halfway down, so my head barely made it through. The tip of the glass pressed against my neck, cutting off my air, and I gasped. The more I struggled, the harder it was to breathe.

Juan Carlos pushed his face up close to mine until our noses touched. "If you don't disappear, you and I are going to have big problems. I mean it, Jarrod. Your NBC pilot won't be the only thing dead."

Between gasps I managed to get out, "Let go of me."

"When I'm good and ready," he said, spittle forming at the corners of his mouth.

I grabbed the door handle, wrenched it up, and swung open the door with all my might. It slammed into Juan Carlos's groin, and he instantly released me. He fell back, falling into one of Laurette's immaculately kept rosebushes. I tumbled out of the car, grabbing my throat with my hand, coughing and trying to catch my breath.

Juan Carlos was on his feet in an instant, wild with fury. I was on my hands and knees. He reared back and, with a sharp boot, kicked me in the solar plexus. I rolled over, clutching my throbbing gut and curling up into the fetal position.

He stood over me. I could hear him chuckling under his breath. That really pissed me off. I lay there, sprawled on the ground, just like Richard Dean Anderson in this one particular *MacGyver* episode in the late eighties when I guest-starred as the son of a tough, bull-headed Army general who was physically abusive to me. When MacGyver befriended me, and began a crusade to free me from my father's beatings, the general decided to teach MacGyver a lesson for interfering in his private affairs. It was one of those very special episodes with a message, and the climax unfolded on a mountaintop with the general (ably played by Dean Stockwell) kicking the shit out of adorable Richard Dean Anderson. With the hero curled up and barely conscious, the general leaned down to inspect his handiwork. He rolled him over to make sure he was out. That's when MacGyver's fist shot out and slammed Dean Stockwell square in the face. If it worked for MacGyver, it could work for me. So when Juan Carlos knelt down to see if I was ready to give up, the back of my hand connected with his upper lip with a loud smack, and he screamed, reeling back. As I've said many times before, there's nothing more brutal than smacking an actor in the face. It's like cutting off the fingers of a painter.

I thought it would bring this brawl to a halt. It only served to enrage Juan Carlos even more. He threw himself at me just as I climbed to my feet, and the two of us hit the freshly mowed lawn hard. The blows were fast and furious, and I raised one arm to block them as I nailed him like a punching bag with the other.

Suddenly I felt a sharp jab in my lower back. And then another. And another. Someone else was hitting me.

I heard Laurette shrieking behind me. "Stop it! Stop it, both of you!"

Juan Carlos let go of me first. Whatever was whacking me was walloping him too. We both looked up, dazed, to see Laurette hovering over us, a crazed look in her eye, armed with a broomstick. "If you two don't leave each other alone, I'm calling the police myself! If the neighbors haven't done it already!"

Juan Carlos and I, both smarting from the unrelenting blows, slowly and with great effort stood up. Neither of us helped the other. And we didn't raise our heads to face Laurette. We kept them down, like two dogs that have just been caught making a mess.

"I don't want to know what started it," Laurette said, "or whose fault it was. I just want you, Juan Carlos, to get your ass inside and go to bed, and I want you, Jarrod, to get in that car and go home."

We both did as we were told. As I got back in the Beamer, I saw Laurette standing motionless in the doorway as Juan Carlos brushed the blades of grass off his pants. She was there to make sure I didn't try running over her husband on my way out of the driveway.

As I backed out, Juan Carlos disappeared inside. Through the kitchen window I saw him grab a cold Diet Coke from the fridge and place it over one of the welts I had left on his right cheek.

I had no idea how things had gotten so out of hand. And with my friendship with Laurette already on life support, I was afraid this little altercation might be the deciding factor for her to pull the plug. But I wasn't sure. I was only sure of one thing. This scuffle with Juan Carlos was only the warm-up. It didn't take my psychic friend Isis to tell me we would clash again. And one of us probably wouldn't walk away the next time.

Chapter 10

"**W**hy didn't you call me? I would have been over in a flash and beaten the shit out of the bastard," Charlie said, popping a piece of chicken tikka into his mouth. We sat on the floor around our glass-top coffee table in the den surrounded by half-empty cartons of white rice, vegetable curry, and lamb vindaloo and crushed tin foil that had once been wrapped around meat samosas and onion bajji before we'd made short work of them. It was our weekly Indian food and DVD night. Just the two of us. We would unload our individual dramas of the week, make plans for the weekend, watch a popcorn flick, and more often than not, cap off the evening with some hot sex. Tonight was Charlie's turn to pick the movie so the James Bond movie *Die Another Day* starring Pierce Brosnan and Halle Berry played on our widescreen TV. After a week of chasing down LA's lowlifes, Charlie didn't want to tax his mind too much, so a light-action romp was the perfect way for him to unwind.

Halle had just wandered out of the surf in an eye-popping orange bikini revealing enough to stop even two gay men in mid-sentence. We stared in awe as she sashayed up the beach and began a conversation with 007.

Charlie finally tore his eyes off the TV and returned his attention to me. "It's not too late. I can go over there and haul his ass downtown for assault."

I shook my head. "No. Laurette's mad at me enough as it is. And it's not like he didn't have somewhat of a reason."

There was no point in hiding it from Charlie anymore. I told him all about the pact I had made with Laurette to find out if Juan Carlos was the dishonorable louse I feared him to be.

Charlie, ever the patient boyfriend, listened as I prattled on, and remained silent after I'd finished. I knew he was ticked off. But it was more out of concern for my well-being. It was always about that. And sometimes I felt I really didn't deserve such a catch.

"He could've really done a number on you," he said finally.

"I can take care of myself. Two years of scene combat classes, baby."

"That's fine if he takes a swing at you, but what if he decides to drop a little poison in your Diet Rite like he did with Austin Teboe."

"You know what?" I said. "We have no proof that he had anything to do with that. And for once, I'm going to let the police up in San Simeon do their job. I'm through with Juan Carlos. It's none of my business."

Charlie threw his hands up in the air and exclaimed, "Finally! A breakthrough!"

I playfully slapped him lightly on the cheek. "Bastard."

He tapped the back of my head with the palm of his hand. "Freak."

On the TV, Halle and Pierce were going at it big time. Lots of bare skin and thrashing about in a fluffy white bed somewhere in Cuba. That was all we needed. Charlie and I lunged at each other, both determined to try again after our aborted lovemaking attempt the night before.

Facing each other, both of us swelling with good old-fashioned lust, we ripped off our shirts as we locked mouths, anxious to make up for lost time.

The doorbell rang.

"Ignore it," I said as I worked to unhook my belt. "Probably just a Jehovah's Witness."

Snickers, who had been hovering near the coffee table, hoping one of us might drop a succulent piece of chicken tikka that she could snatch up in her teeth, tore out of the den, barking at the top of her lungs as she scampered to the front door.

This time, I pushed Charlie down on the couch, ran my fingers through his forest of chest hair, then tugged open the zipper on his jeans and set about devouring him.

The doorbell rang again. And again. And again. Snickers was in a frantic state, running back into the den to summon us, and then darting back to the front door. Between the unrelenting doorbell and our nearly rabid dog, we both knew our night of hot, passionate lovemaking was doomed to failure. Charlie zipped up. I threw on my shirt. We both headed for the door.

Laurette stood on the front stoop; her SUV was parked three whole feet from the curb and angled halfway into the street. She was obviously in a hurry.

"Laurette, I'm so sorry. I don't know what to say. Things just got out of hand," I said.

Charlie put a comforting hand on my shoulder from behind. "He feels terrible. Just now, we were discussing how he should apologize."

I glanced at Charlie, who stifled a smile.

"Oh, who cares about that?" Laurette said as she pushed her way in and headed for the kitchen. "You got any Scotch?"

After pouring herself a drink and settling down in the red

diner booth, Laurette got right to the point. "I got a call right after you left. From Larry Levant."

Nothing. Neither Charlie nor I had ever heard of him.

"The director. Made a big splash at Sundance last year for his documentary on the gay porn industry called *Give 'Em Head, Harry*.

"Sorry I missed it," said Charlie.

"Anyway," Laurette said. "He's been in preproduction on his new movie for months now. It's a low-budget horror movie. But smart, you know? Not one of those straight-to-Showtime pieces of shit. He had raised most of the money through independent sources, but was still about a million short, and just today the rest of the financing came through. Some big mucky-muck in South Florida who wants to be in the movie business."

"Is Larry Levant a client of yours?"

"No," she said, a teasing lilt in her voice. "I represent the actor who he desperately wants as his leading man."

My heart skipped a beat. I had been so down after my NBC pilot tanked in testing. Not one audition had come my way. Not even for an under-five-line bit part on *7th Heaven*. And now, was Laurette excited because she had finally done her job and snared me a leading role in a promising independent film?

"Me?" I said.

"No. Juan Carlos."

This was either a mean-spirited joke on her part or bitter revenge for brawling with her husband on her front lawn. "You came all the way over here to tell me that?"

"Of course not," she said. "Larry's a big fan of yours. And there's a supporting role we both think you're perfect for. Frankly, I think it's more interesting than the lead."

Agents always said that. I wasn't about to fall for it.

"You'd play a single dad camping with your son," she said. "Going through a bitter divorce. Fighting for custody. At your wit's end. Things couldn't get any worse. And that's when you're stalked by a homicidal maniac in the woods."

Actually it sounded like a meaty part. One I could make a meal out of if someone let me. "I've never played a wounded single parent."

"You die twenty minutes into the movie, but you're in almost every scene up to the point where you get an axe in the back of your head."

"Sorry, Laurette. He's not going to do it."

I froze. Who had said that? It sounded like my boyfriend Charlie. But he knew I would psychologically torture him senseless if he denied me a richly deserved acting gig.

Laurette and I both stared at Charlie, waiting for some kind of explanation for such a sweeping, dictatorial decision.

"You heard what she said, Jarrod," Charlie argued. "Juan Carlos is playing the lead, and I think we've strongly established that you two don't get along."

"In this business, that's not a deal breaker," Laurette said.

"Well, I don't think it's a good idea for you two to spend three months on a film shoot together."

"But you heard Laurette," I said. "I die after the first twenty minutes. I'll be there two, three weeks tops."

"Why put yourself through that?" Charlie said.

"Because it's a job," I said, pouring myself a Scotch. "And we both know how few and far between those have been lately."

"I just don't think it's a good idea." Charlie was adamant. But I had no intention of letting this opportunity slip through my fingers.

"But the director is a fan. He really wants me to play the part. How can I compromise his vision by saying no?" I was the King of Bullshit when I had to be.

Charlie chuckled. "Come on, babe. Can't you see Laurette is playing you? I think you're a terrific actor, but seriously, do you really believe this big director only wants *you* for the role? There's something else going on here."

Actors, especially former child actors, live to be the center of attention. And sometimes they can float above the realm of reality, and simply exist inside their own heads. As much as it angered me that Charlie was yanking me back down to earth from my blissful fantasy of being indispensable and one of a kind, he had a point. Larry Levant insisting I play an important role in his new film was akin to Steven Spielberg crowing that he could do *Saving Private Ryan* only with Corey Feldman. Laurette was scheming, and she had just been exposed.

Charlie and I looked at her, and she caved immediately. "All right, all right. Larry owed me a few favors, so I talked him into giving you a part in the movie."

"Why?" I asked.

"Because you haven't worked in a while, and I was feeling guilty about not getting you more work."

I was ready to buy it, but Charlie wasn't. "And?"

"And because Juan Carlos got a phone call while he was on the computer, and when I went into the office to get my checkbook so I could pay a few bills, there was an e-mail up on the screen from a woman in Florida."

"Dominique?"

"I don't think so. It was someone else. But obviously a woman. And they've clearly known each other awhile. She didn't write her name or anything, but the note had a very strong sexual connotation."

"What the hell does that mean?" I said.

"There was a lot of dirty talk," Charlie answered.

"Oh."

"This woman clearly has feelings for Juan Carlos," Laurette said. "And she's still very much in his life. But to what degree, I don't know."

"What does that have to do with me playing a part in Larry Levant's movie?"

"Isn't it obvious? She wants you to be on location to make sure Juan Carlos doesn't fool around behind her back with this mystery woman," Charlie said, folding his arms, satisfied the case was closed.

I turned to Laurette. She had no fight left in her. Everything was on the table, and there was nothing she could do about it. She was just betting on the fact that my ego would outweigh my common sense. Good bet.

"I'll do it."

"What?" Charlie said, stunned.

"A part is a part. And this is a feature. I haven't done a feature film since I was twelve years old and played Huck Finn in that hideous *Tom Sawyer* remake with Jason Bateman. Who knows what this could lead to? If I don't take it, I'll always wonder if it could have turned things around for me."

"I don't believe this," Charlie said. "You're actually going to do this."

Laurette knew to keep her mouth shut, and let me handle Charlie. I gently touched his arm, and smiled. "It's only for a few weeks. Besides, my parents have been bugging me to come see them, and they're only a couple hours north of Miami. And don't worry about Juan Carlos and me. I'll buy him a beer, make nice, we'll be buddies by the end of the first day. Besides, it'll make it easier for me to babysit him when we're not shooting."

"You're going to be great, Jarrod. And this is going to do wonders for your career," Laurette crowed. "Larry Levant is hot, hot, hot."

Charlie stood there, steadfast in his resolve. But even he knew this was a no-win situation. In the end, I would go where the work took me. He knew that about me on the first day we met. But he still didn't have to like it.

"Fine," he said, and stalked out of the kitchen to the den, where he resumed watching *Die Another Day*.

"I didn't mean to cause a fight," Laurette said.

"Don't worry. He'll be fine."

Easier said than done. This was going to take more political wrangling and sensitive diplomacy than the Israeli-Palestinian peace talks. But I was up for the challenge. Charlie would come around. Eventually. And as for me, I was excited about working again. Despite the gnawing fear that Juan Carlos might slit my throat in the wilds of South Florida.

Chapter 11

The only way I could convince my shopping buddy and personal clairvoyant Isis to drive me to the airport for my flight to Miami was if I promised to make a pit stop at a Costco discount warehouse on the way. Isis was one of those extreme bargain hunters, willing to bungee-jump off the Golden Gate Bridge if it would save her a few pennies on a refill bottle of Ivory Liquid Soap. She had lost her membership card, and while she was waiting to get issued a new one, she needed my Costco card in the interim to gain access to Mecca.

When Isis arrived in her weathered, dented, smoke-billowing 1986 Chevy Caprice Classic, Charlie and I were in the middle of a terrible row. We rarely fought, but somehow the tension surrounding my imminent departure to Florida had ignited an inferno that was burning holes through the fabric of our once fireproof relationship.

Charlie was already late for a court appearance downtown where he was testifying in the trial of a two-hundred-and-twenty-pound Latina gang member named Tiny who had hurled an empty bottle at one of his fellow detectives when they were dispatched to investigate a homicide in the neighborhood. But I guess his boyfriend costarring in a low-rent shocker with a real-life suspected murderer took precedence.

"Sometimes I get the feeling you take your career far more seriously than you take me," Charlie said, arms folded, hovering over me in the kitchen as I tossed a few candy bars in my carrying case for the flight.

"That is not true, and you know it, and I'm tired of you always making me choose between the two," I said.

"Just once I would like to see you make a decision based on what's best for us, as opposed to what's best for you."

I zipped up my bag, stood erect, and threw the strap over my shoulder. "If that's what you really think, then maybe me going away for a while isn't such a bad idea."

There was a loud honking from outside. It was Isis in her Caprice. I glanced out the kitchen window that overlooked the street in front of the house. She was checking her watch, and craning her neck to see how ready I really was. I could tell she was calculating just how much time we would have to buy Green Forest toilet paper in bulk before we had to head on to the airport for the tightened security checks.

I started for the door. Charlie gripped my arm, stopping me. "Look, babe, I know things haven't been perfect between us lately, and maybe I just need to blow off a little steam, but you're not thinking straight."

"I never have," I said, unable to resist a little humor.

Charlie didn't smile. Hell, he didn't even smirk. He always found me funny. This was not good. "Maybe I'm just a little pissed off that you're not respecting what I think."

"What do you think?"

"I think Juan Carlos Barranco is bad news, and he's got it out for you, and buying him one beer is not going to smooth things over between the two of you. And . . ."

"And what?"

"And I'm worried I'm not going to be there to make sure he doesn't try to harm you in some way."

I should've dropped the bag right there and threw my arms around him. I should've said, "Screw the movie. I want to stay right here in LA and be with the man who loves me more than anyone else in the world." I should've said all that. But I didn't.

"Just because I don't have a badge like you doesn't mean I can't take care of myself," I said.

More honking. It was as if Isis's left hand was surgically attached to the car horn on the steering wheel. She could see us arguing in the kitchen, and with her right hand clutching the four-page shopping list, she wasn't going to indulge us with her patience.

Charlie threw his hands up in the air. "Fine." He grabbed his wallet and holster off the table, and walked to the door off the kitchen leading to our two-car garage. He turned his head slightly, barely making eye contact. "Call me when you get there . . . if you find the time." And then he opened the door, marched through, and closed it with a big slam.

I almost went after him. But Isis was now hitting more notes on her car horn than Beethoven's Fifth. With only three hours until my flight, and heavy traffic building on the 405 Freeway, Isis's time at Costco was limited. I grabbed my bags and headed out the front door.

As we bombed down the hill toward Franklin Avenue, Isis sat behind the wheel, her tiny body slumped down in the seat, her eyes barely making it over the dashboard. Her foot was pressed on the accelerator, and she continually flicked her eyes to the digital clock in front of us. We had gotten a late start, and she was not happy about it.

We sat in silence for a few minutes before I cleared my throat and decided to say something. "I'm afraid Charlie and I might break up."

"Don't be ridiculous," she said, slamming on the brakes, hurling us both forward as we stopped in the middle of an intersection for a red light. "It's just the seven-year itch. All couples go through it."

"But we've only been together for three."

"Oh," she said quietly.

More silence.

"So tell me. Do you see us breaking up?" Isis was my psychic. My spiritual guru. Like the Egyptian gods of her homeland she studied so prodigiously, Isis had adopted ancient Eastern philosophies and possessed many mind-blowing powers of acute observation, many of which were astounding glimpses into the future. Even though lately the farthest east she'd ever been was to a Bruce Springsteen concert outside of Boston.

Isis hit the gas when the light turned green, and we sprang forward.

I sat in the passenger seat, watching her, as her mind kicked into gear, and a torrent of psychic energy washed over her. I couldn't stand it anymore.

"What do you see? What are you thinking?" I said.

"I'm thinking that maybe La Cienega might be faster at this time of day. I don't want to get clogged up in traffic on Fairfax. As it is, we'll only have twenty to thirty minutes at Costco."

"What about me and Charlie?"

"I see a lot of conflict."

You didn't have to be a psychic to pick up on that.

"But the power lies within both of you to weather it and move on together," she said. "There are worse things than to be with someone who worries about you, Jarrod."

She was right. And I was feeling guiltier than the time I told Charlie I borrowed three hundred dollars from our Alaskan cruise vacation fund to buy a new suit for a callback for a recurring role on *The West Wing* when I actually used the money on a deluxe treatment at the Burke Williams Day Spa in West Hollywood.

I rummaged through my bag for a cell phone to call and apologize, but Isis put a gentle hand on my thigh. "Give yourselves some breathing room. Take some time to think about what you're going to say. Call him when you get to Florida." She was right again. I was never in top form when I impulsively spewed a stream of apologies and reasons for my sometimes abhorrent behavior. It was best to rehearse the speech, work on my character motivation, and deliver such a tour de force performance that Charlie would find it utterly impossible not to forgive me. God, it's no wonder some people can't stand us actors.

When I thought about it, it dawned on me that Isis's sound advice had its own hidden motivations. She was afraid if I called Charlie down at the courthouse, and we got wrapped up in a conciliatory conversation, I would seriously cut into our shopping time at Costco.

When we reached the Costco on Washington Boulevard in Culver City, a scant twenty minutes from Los Angeles International Airport, the parking lot was jammed. Isis hurriedly did a few loops, before she spotted one narrow space, and squeezed her Caprice between the lines reserved for compact vehicles. We both had to squeeze out our respective doors so as not to bang into the cars parked on either side of us.

Isis immediately snatched my trusty Costco card out of my hand, grabbed a cart almost twice as big as her tiny frame, and rolled it inside. I did everything I could just to keep up. She was like a NASCAR racer, speeding through the meat and produce section, squealing into a sharp turn that led her to the mass quantities of boxed cereals and cans of coffee. Her eyes blazed with determination as she filled one cart, and dispatched me to round up another.

When I returned with a second cart, she was carefully scanning her list to see what else she needed.

I was still hung up on my fight with Charlie. "Do you think Charlie is right to worry? Should I be concerned about working in such close proximity to Juan Carlos?"

Isis sighed. I was starting to irritate her. She was on a mission and I was hampering her efforts. "Of course he's right," she said. "You said yourself that the two of you duked it out on Laurette's lawn like a couple of middleweight boxers. Juan Carlos isn't going to forget about all that just because you're now acting together in a movie."

"So do you see me in physical danger down in Florida?"

Isis studied the prices on two brands of paper towels, not satisfied with either. "They've both gone up four cents since last month," she muttered to no one in particular. "Unbelievable. This place is supposed to be a cheaper alternative."

I stepped forward, grabbed the cheaper of the two brands, and tossed the eight-roll package into the empty cart. "I'm going to miss my flight if we don't get through your list faster."

Isis tore the list in half, and handed me one of the pieces. "Here. You get the items on this, and I'll concentrate on these. We'll get out of here a lot sooner."

"Deal," I said, checking my list. Lots of soaps and detergents. Isis spun around, and pushed her cart toward the next aisle. I called after her. "You didn't answer my question. As my psychic, tell me, am I in danger?"

She stopped her cart, and spun back around. She nodded. "Yes, you are. There's danger everywhere. It's around you right now. Now leave me alone so I can concentrate."

Not the most comforting observation. But good to know nevertheless.

After stockpiling enough provisions for another Waco standoff, Isis was ready to check out. She sent me back for one more extra large package of Pillsbury cookie dough while she found a place in the checkout line.

When I returned, I saw her immersed in an argument with a big, lumbering man who had obviously cut in front of her. His back was to me, so I couldn't make out his face. Even though he towered over her, Isis was spunky and aggressive, and she was not going to back down.

"I would've let you go ahead of me if you had asked politely," she said. "But you just pushed me aside." The man was unresponsive. For a minute I thought he might be deaf.

I decided diplomacy was the best tactic since time was of the essence. My flight was in a little over an hour and I had bags to check. "Excuse me, sir, normally we wouldn't mind you going through first, but we're in a bit of a hurry. I have a flight to catch. So we'd appreciate it if—"

The man slowly turned to face me. And my blood ran cold. It was Wendell Butterworth. He broke out into a wide smile. "Of course, I'm sorry. Go right ahead." He yanked his cart back, giving Isis enough room to move ahead of him in line. With a huff, she positioned her cart at the belt, and started unloading her groceries.

I stood frozen. I didn't want to take one step nearer to Butterworth. He waved me forward, as if taunting me. He wanted to know if I had the guts to step closer to him.

Isis, who had never seen Wendell Butterworth, had no idea who he was. And her psychic powers were not suggesting he was anything but a rude shopper lacking people skills.

We stared at one another for what seemed like an hour, but it couldn't have been more than a few seconds. Finally, a frizzy-haired Irish lass with a cherubic smile and wearing the traditional Costco uniform of a red vest and blue pants logged on to her cash register and called out to Wendell. "Excuse me, sir, I can take you over here."

Wendell grinned from ear to ear as he maneuvered his cart around mine and wheeled it over to the open register.

Isis, completely clueless and having given up on me helping her, pulled my cart forward and started unloading the items herself.

Wendell Butterworth was stalking me again. And I felt powerless to do anything about it.

Just a few feet away from me stood the man who tried to kill me. To the naked eye, he appeared harmless enough. Just a big cuddly bear of a middle-aged man out stocking up on a few canned goods. But to me, he was a living nightmare.

He glanced over at me, and gave me a wink as he plunged his hand into his cart and withdrew a twelve-pack of Reese's Peanut Butter Cups. When I was ten, I told Johnny Carson that was my favorite candy, and the following day Wendell had four giant boxes delivered to the set. He made sure I got a good look at what he was buying. And then he started whistling. The tune was instantly recognizable. It was the theme song from my long-running sitcom, *Go to Your Room!*

Chapter 12

After leaving Costco, I had my eyes fixed on the side-view mirror to see if Wendell Butterworth was following us. After hustling through the checkout line, and loading up Isis's Caprice, I spotted him waving at us as we peeled out of the lot. I was convinced he was following us, and would book a ticket to Miami to join me on my film shoot. Isis, having learned how to drive from her parents, who were used to maneuvering through the suicidal highways of Cairo, zipped in and out of traffic with the precision and focus of Paul Walker in the *Fast and Furious* movies. If anybody could lose Wendell, she could. But there was no sign of him as we slid into the steady stream of cars filling up the departure lanes leading into the airport. I thought about contacting the parole board and updating them on Wendell's recent activities. But what could they do? They had already granted him parole.

Once Isis had deposited me in the white loading zone at United Airlines, I took one last look around at the sea of travelers lined up with their bags for curbside check-in. I half expected to see Wendell's eerily serene yet maniacal face staring at me. I walked into the terminal, momentarily disoriented by the late-morning chaos, and dragged my bags to the endless line of economy passengers waiting for their boarding passes. Since this was a low-budget production, first-class travel was not an option, especially for a supporting player in the cast like me. The last time I had done a feature film I hadn't even started shaving yet.

I stood there, people watching to pass the time. And then I saw him. Wendell. He was in a wheelchair being pushed by an airport employee. No, wait. He was over to the right. In a USC football jersey and cutoff jeans. No. Behind the counter in a blue jacket and tie, checking in first-class passengers. Wendell Butterworth was everywhere. In my head. I needed a sedative, or at the very least, a stiff drink.

What I really needed was my boyfriend. I needed Charlie. And it finally dawned on me that I could not get on that plane without clearing the air. I didn't want to give us both some breathing room as Isis had suggested. No. I wanted to see him now. I gathered up my bags, left the line, and bustled back out to the curb, where I glimpsed a cab dropping off another traveler. Wendell stepped out of the back. Or it could've been Wendell if he'd had gray, wispy hair pulled into a bun, a hunched back half concealed by a bulky blue overcoat, and was a four-foot-eight-inch-tall grandmother. I was really losing it.

After helping the old woman deliver her bags to a curbside check-in attendant, I hopped into the cab and instructed the driver to take me downtown to the Los Angeles County Courthouse, where I knew Charlie would be just about finished testifying at the gang-related assault trial.

As we raced along the 105 Imperial Freeway, connecting to the 110 Harbor Freeway that stretched north toward the shiny, pristine skyline of downtown LA, I imagined the perfect movie moment ending with me showing up in the courtroom in a surprise last-minute appearance. Charlie would be sitting on the stand, relating the events of the night in question. I would sweep in, momentarily distracting him. He would fumble in his testimony, fight back a smile, and continue on, ever the consummate professional police officer. Once the judge allowed him to step down, we would meet outside in the hallway for an embrace, and then retreat to an empty courtroom for some hot, passionate sex on top of a hard wooden table usually reserved for the defendant and his attorneys. I was flushed just thinking about it as I sat in the back seat of the taxi.

When I arrived at the LA courthouse, the line to pass through security took forty minutes. I had to take off my belt, shoes, and jacket, and my three pieces of luggage I was hauling had to be carefully sorted through. Who showed up at the courthouse with a month's wardrobe? Once cleared, I took the elevator up to the fifteenth floor of the criminal courts building and to the room where Charlie had mentioned he would be testifying.

I opened the room, and quietly entered, expecting to slide into an empty seat off to the side and wait for the judge to call a lunch break. But to my surprise, the room was empty. This was odd. It was a four-day trial that had just begun yesterday. I couldn't understand where everybody had gone. I looked around for a stenographer, bailiff, anybody to enlighten me. But nobody was around. I walked back out into the hallway, where a tiny woman in her late twenties, wearing a suit jacket with a matching short skirt, her face hidden in a massive array of light brown curls, jotted furiously in her notebook. I glanced down and recognized Charlie's name in her scratchings.

"Are you one of the lawyers for the assault trial that's supposed to be going on in there?" I asked.

She nodded, not bothering to even look up.

"I'm looking for Charlie Peters."

"We're on a break. Judge Yellin asked to see him in his chambers."

"Could you tell me where I can find Judge Yellin's chambers?"

"Down the hall to your right," she said, and then snapped her notebook shut, annoyed at my intrusion. She stood up and clicked down the hall in her high heels. Definitely a big fan of the canceled *Ally McBeal* show.

"Thank you," I called after her, but she didn't respond. She just disappeared around a corner. I followed her directions, and found a door marked JUDGE YELLIN. I knocked softly, but got no answer. I tried again. I pressed my ear to the door, hoping to hear if he was on the phone or something, but all the commotion in the hall made it impossible to hear anything. I tried the door. It was unlocked. Should I just barge into a judge's chambers unannounced? I should've tried Charlie's cell phone instead, but I didn't want to cheat myself out of all the bells and whistles of an emotional reunion. Alerting him by phone would diminish the impact. So I opened the door and stepped inside.

It was dark. The shades were drawn, blocking the sunlight from the gorgeous day outside. I turned to leave, when I heard a rustling sound across the room. And heavy, intense breathing. I reached over and felt for a light switch. When I flipped it up with my index finger, I had a sinking feeling I was in the wrong place at the wrong time. And as the fluorescent lights struggled to reach maximum capacity, I knew I had made a tragic mistake. On the couch, off to the right side of the door, I saw a man in a judge's black robe, lying on top of another man. They were making out on the couch. The sudden flood of lights startled the judge, who despite being well north of fifty, was impressively distinguished with an immaculate head of silver hair and a tanned, handsome face. He leapt to his feet, in a state of shock and confusion.

"I'm sorry," I said, embarrassed and mortified. "I didn't mean to . . ."

My eyes fell on the man still sprawled out on the couch. His tie was askew, his dress shirt ripped open, his slacks had been hurriedly unzipped and wrenched halfway down to his lower thighs. It was Charlie. My Charlie. Detective Charlie Peters. Sucking face with a judge and about to do a whole lot more. As they used to say on *Laugh-In*, "Here cums da judge!"

"Ladies and gentlemen, we have begun our descent to Miami. Please make sure your tray tables are in the upright position, and that all portable electronics have been turned off. We will be landing in approximately ten minutes."

The soothing female flight attendant's voice stirred me out of a deep sleep. Another flight attendant, this one male with a severe look and a prissy demeanor, scooped up the knocked-over plastic cup that sat wedged between my legs. I yawned, and the spittle caked onto both corners of my mouth cracked. Catching Charlie in a compromising position with a judge had just been a dream. But I knew if I didn't make amends soon, it could become my reality.

I hadn't rushed to the courthouse. Like the good SAG member I was, I had boarded my plane to Miami. With makeup and hair tests scheduled for the morning and wardrobe fittings in the afternoon, I didn't have a choice if I wanted to keep in good stead with the independent film community.

After we landed and I retrieved my bags, I stepped out into the balmy air of south Florida and looked around for my ride. I immediately spotted a maroon van with a cardboard sign jammed into the dash that read, CREEPS—TRANSPORTATION CAPTAIN. A bouncy, chatty production assistant rolled down the window and called out to me, "Jarrod Jarvis?"

She didn't wait for me to answer. She jumped out and threw open the back doors of the vehicle. She was short and had a cute little body tucked into an aqua blue T-shirt with *Creeps* emblazoned on the front and tight jeans that accentuated every delicious curve of her hips and legs.

"I'd recognize you anywhere," she chirped. I knew it was coming. "Baby, don't even go there!" She exploded with laughter. "God, that cracked me up when I was a kid."

"You seem a little young to have been a fan of the show," I said, guessing she was no more than nineteen or twenty.

"TV Land. They play all those moronic shows," she said, and then caught herself. "Not that your show was moronic. I mean, it wasn't Shakespeare or anything, but it had its moments." She wisely chose to change the subject. "I'm Amy Jo."

"Hi, I'm Jarrod," I said. She grabbed my bags and tossed them in the back, and then was behind the wheel in an instant. I was winded just trying to keep up with her. As we drove south toward Miami Beach, Amy Jo decided I was due to hear her long-range career goals in the film business. Despite her knowing the trademark line from my long-running sitcom, Amy Jo insisted she'd never watched much television growing up. Her parents had raised her as an artist, and after a brief stint at the Academy of Dramatic Arts in New York (she wasn't asked back for vague reasons best described as political), she decided her future was behind the camera, and this gig as a PA would be the perfect way to kick off her foray into writing and directing and composing and editing. I loved the misguided idealism of youth. It just made me feel better about myself, being a bitter old pro in my thirties.

When Amy Jo began a dissertation on her life-long devotion to Quentin Tarantino and how his films affected her on a deeply fundamental level, I whipped out the cell phone, begged my driver's pardon, and tried to call Charlie. I got his voice mail. Maybe he really was banging the judge. No, I wasn't going to go there. It had just been a silly, ridiculous dream. So we fought, and whenever we fought, Charlie always had to go blow off some steam, and what better way to blow off steam than to . . . No. I had to stop it. Otherwise, I was going to have Amy Jo turn the van around and drive me back to United, which would leave my career in tattered ruins. Or at least in more ruins than it already was.

Amy Jo dropped me off at the Ritz Plaza, one of the many hotels lining Miami's historic South Beach. Although the film was shooting in a small wooded park in Coral Gables, the production was putting the cast up in downtown Miami Beach. I was ecstatic. There were lots of diversions here, and the Latin-heavy population was just gorgeous to look at. Unfortunately the hotel, surrounded by the more opulent and ornate establishments such as the Delano and the Marlin, was a decidedly lackluster affair. The box-like rooms with scuffed white walls and simple, uninspired furniture did nothing to excite one's aesthetic sense. In fact, it downright depressed it.

I debated switching rooms, but I didn't want to cause a fuss. I understood that I was not part of a Warner Brothers multimillion-dollar production starring Jennifer Lopez. So I kept mum and unpacked my clothes.

Amy Jo told me she would be back at 7 A.M. to pick me up for makeup and hair tests, which left me the rest of the evening to grab some dinner and stroll along the boardwalk of Ocean Avenue, which boasted dozens of outdoor cafés, shops, and bars. I showered, shaved, and changed into a light white shirt, white pants, dark blue blazer, and sandals, which seemed appropriate for a night out in South Beach.

When I stepped off the elevator into the lobby, I recognized the man checking in at the reception desk. It took me a moment to place him out of context, but then it came to me.

"Rudy? Rudy Pearson?"

He turned and looked at me. Sweat poured down his chubby cheeks. His skin was ruddy and pale. His linen suit was stained with sweat. Rudy, the soap journalist who had been ejected from Laurette's wedding, had suddenly popped up in Miami.

Rudy knew exactly who I was, but in an attempt to put me on a more level playing field, he feigned ignorance. "I'm sorry . . . you are?"

"Jarrod Jarvis. We met at Laurette and Juan Carlos's wedding."

"Oh, right. I had to leave early that day for another appointment," he said, rewriting history and completely blocking out the fact that he was tossed out of the Hearst Castle on his ass.

"What are you doing here in Miami?" I said.

"Officially, my magazine sent me down to cover a *Days of Our Lives* fan convention being held here this weekend," he said, his eyes darting back and forth. I didn't need a lie detector to tell that wasn't what had brought him here.

"So if that's the official reason, is there an unofficial reason?"

This caught him off guard. But he went with it. "Yes," he said. I wasn't expecting him to elaborate, but Rudy was a soap journalist after all, and all journalists are shameful, relentless gossips. "I've come across some interesting information about someone who is down here shooting a movie, and I'm going to make sure it gets out so the whole world knows."

"I'm down here shooting a movie, so I sure hope it isn't about me," I said, nudging him gently.

He stepped back, surprised. Rudy apparently wasn't used to people touching him. And from where I was standing, I'm sure they're weren't a lot of takers anyway. He just stared at me and then, in a soft voice, replied, "No, it's not about you."

This guy had not hit the jackpot in the lottery of social skills.

"What the hell are you doing here?" a voice bellowed behind us.

We both spun around to see Juan Carlos charging toward us.

"I'm . . . I'm in the movie," I said. "Didn't Laurette tell you?"

"Not you," he barked, pointing a thick finger at Rudy. "I mean him!" If it hadn't been obvious before, the subject of Rudy's hatred was painfully obvious now.

Rudy, his ire up, straightened his drenched linen coat and lifted his nose as high as it could go. "It's a free country. I can be wherever I want."

"Not here," Juan Carlos said, pushing me aside, and towering over the much shorter Rudy. "I want you out of here right now."

"Make me," Rudy squeaked, as he had probably done countless times on the playground when harassed by one of the many bullies who'd undoubtedly paraded through his miserable life.

Juan Carlos shrugged, then bunched up his fingers into a fist and let it fly smack into the middle of Rudy's fleshy, pockmarked nose. Rudy stumbled back, his eyes wide with astonishment.

The hotel staff began congregating behind the reception desk, quietly debating on whether or not they should call the police, or handle the situation themselves.

Rudy rubbed his nose. A stream of blood trickled down his left nostril.

Juan Carlos took a step closer to him, and pointed to the door. "I'm not telling you again! Get out of here!"

Rudy, humiliated, tried sniffing the blood back up into his nose, but to no avail. It kept flowing. His hand was smeared with it, and some more had wiped off on his light-colored suit. But instead of retreating, Rudy let out an anguished roar, and with arms outstretched like an angry bear, he rushed at Juan Carlos. Rudy had at least a hundred pounds on him, so when they collided, I could feel the air whoosh right out of Juan Carlos's body. I felt like I was watching a repeat of my own altercation with the fiery former soap star.

But what Rudy had in size, Juan Carlos made up for with street smarts. As I had already learned, Juan Carlos had a whole repertoire of dirty tricks at his disposal. He gouged Rudy's right eye with one of his fingers, and bit hard into one of his fat cheeks.

The concierge grabbed the phone and punched in 911. My hand shot out to stop him. "No! I'll take care of this!" This was not a heroic act on my part. I just didn't want an arrest to hold up production on my big comeback movie.

I jumped in between Rudy and Juan Carlos. "Stop it right now, both of you!" But they were in the zone, too immersed in their battle to even realize I was attempting to pry them apart. Which was why I could never blame Rudy for socking me square in the right eye.

I sank to the ground. The room spun around me like some bad AFI student's opening shot in his first short film. My eye throbbed with pain, and I managed to look up to see both Rudy and Juan Carlos, staring down at me as if noticing me for the first time. At least I got them to stop fighting.

Chapter 13

"Hi, this is Charlie Peters. You've reached my voice mail. You know what to do."

Beep. This was the fourth time in an hour I had tried calling Charlie. Why wasn't he picking up his messages? Was he embroiled in a big case I didn't know about? Was he really screwing the judge presiding over the trial he was involved in? I couldn't let my paranoia consume me. I returned to the matter at hand.

Stella, a gloriously big-boned, brassy blond makeup stylist, was applying some pancake base to the corners of my right eye as I sat still in a director's chair in the tight quarters of the makeup and hair trailer. It was obvious she was using the cheap stuff, because no matter how much she rubbed onto my face, it wasn't enough to cover the dark bruise that made me look like half a raccoon.

Stella stepped back and inspected me. "Oh, honey, we're going to need a little more."

"But you've used almost the whole jar already," I wailed. "We're never going to be able to cover it up. Do you have something else?"

"This is all the budget allowed me to buy. Hell, this production is so cheap, I had to bring my own brushes and eyeliner pencils."

"Maybe I can run out to the nearest Sav-On and find something," I said, starting to stand up.

Stella pushed me back down in my seat. "There's no time. They're nearly done with the lighting out there. You're probably going to be called to the set any minute now."

The door to the trailer flew open and Larry Levant, the documentary wunderkind who was about to shoot his first narrative feature film, stuck his head in. He had obviously read his "How to Look Like You're an Up-and-Coming Hollywood Film Director" handbook. He had taken great pains to dress the part. A baseball cap, T-shirt, brown leather jacket, blue jeans, and Reebok sneakers. He was a small guy, not much over five and a half feet, had a hawkish nose and tiny hands, and the cap covered what I was sure was premature balding.

"Hey, Jarrod, how's the eye?"

"Can't even tell," I said hopefully, knowing full well I looked like a battered Farrah Fawcett in *The Burning Bed*.

Larry inspected me closely, unable to hide his obvious revulsion, and thought for a moment. He pressed a fist to his chin, and lowered his head like a Rodan statue. After a few painfully long seconds, he raised it again and this time had a twinkle in his eye.

"Why don't we write it into the script?" he said, snapping his fingers for emphasis.

"Brilliant idea," said Stella, an obvious kiss-up who wanted to be hired on future Larry Levant films.

"We've already established that your son Stevie is a troubled kid. Gets into lots of fights on the playground and that kind of shit. Where does he get it from? Dad! You're a drunk who gets into all kinds of bar brawls, and one of the reasons you went on this camping trip was to recover from getting the shit kicked out of you by some yahoo redneck you mouthed off to when you were liquored up!"

He looked at me for a reaction. I paused. "I thought Stevie and I were on the camping trip to get over the fact my wife deserted us to go find herself."

"Yeah, yeah, I know. I stole that from *Kramer vs. Kramer*. Great movie! Changed my life! I *was* that kid. But this is far more fucking original, don't you think?"

"Um, sure," I said, not wanting to argue with my director on the first day.

"I love it!" Stella chirped as she started scraping the mounds of makeup off my face. "It totally works with his black eye."

"Perfect. I'll get you some rewrites by tonight. See you on the set," he said as he flew out of the trailer.

As Stella worked her magic on my face, I wondered if Juan Carlos had arrived yet. After I had been knocked down in the lobby of the Ritz Plaza, Rudy Pearson had beaten a hasty retreat. He was afraid I might press charges or something. Juan Carlos watched him scurry away, and then reached down and hauled me to my feet. He looked at the swelling around my eye.

"Jesus, that's gotta hurt," he said. Not exactly a warm truce, but at least he didn't sock me in the other eye so I'd have a matching set. Juan Carlos steadied me, and then strolled out the glass door toward Ocean Avenue to kick off his own night on the town. Dizzy and disoriented, I swayed a bit as the concierge, a tall, slim Colombian, raced to my aid and escorted me back up to my dismal and depressing room. A bellman arrived with an ice pack, and I crawled into bed, calling it a night.

It seemed as if only a few seconds had passed before Coldplay was blaring through the CD alarm clock. I stumbled back downstairs, where the impossibly perky Amy Jo quickly greeted me and then, before I could request coffee, whisked me out to her maroon transport van, and we began our twenty-minute journey to the set of *Creeps* in a wooded park just outside Coral Gables.

Stella finished dabbing up the sweat that had formed on my brow, and then wheeled me around so I could get a good look at her handiwork. I was pale, haggard, my hair was matted and dull, and my eyes were bloodshot. But none of it was noticeable because all attention was drawn to the large purple-and-black shiner that was now taking up a quarter of my face, and was getting bigger by the minute.

"I look terrible," I said weakly.

"Well, you heard Larry. You're a mess. Your wife just ditched you and you were in a bar fight."

"But don't you think this might be overkill? Maybe you went slightly overboard with the whole death-warmed-over look."

Stella bristled at my pointed criticism of her artistry.

"Honey, I didn't do a damn thing," Stella said. "This is the real you." She saw the horror in my face and decided to mollify the situation by adding, "Besides, this is an independent film. We want to go for realism."

I pulled myself up out of the chair and left the trailer. Outside, the mood was a bit ebullient as the crew prepared for the first shot on the first day of production. People were a lot more cheerful on Day One when inclement weather, blown-out klieg lights, injured actors, and overexposed film were still days, perhaps even weeks, away from having to be dealt with.

The first scene on the schedule was a simple-enough one to kick off the five weeks of principal photography. At this point in the story, the intrepid hero, a park ranger played by Juan Carlos, has gathered a group of campers to warn them that a homicidal maniac may be loose in the forest, and that it is vital we stay together as a group until he is caught. Of course, in the following pages, various circumstances occur that split us all up so the methodical killer can pick us off one by one.

In addition to my character and the boy playing my son, the other endangered campers included college students paired off into three couples, a retired Army general and his son, and the script's leading lady, a psychoanalyst, who would later prove useful in providing a disturbing psychological profile of our adversary. With her was her mother, a doctor, who would later on offer medical assistance to those lucky few who escaped the killer with their lives but nevertheless nursed dangling limbs and knifed torsos.

My only line in the scene, which I had already committed to memory, was, "Forget it. I'm going to take my chances and try to get out of here with my son!" At which point, the ranger (Juan Carlos) would shake some sense into me, and impress upon me how important it was we all stick together, or risk certain death. I refuse to listen until my son, a child with wisdom well beyond his years, looks at me with his big brown eyes and says, "Daddy, please. Do as the nice man says. I don't want to die." I stop cold. Look at everybody. And then my eyes fall back down to meet my son's pathetic gaze. After a long beat which I planned to milk of every last ounce (and to ensure extra screen time), I muss my son's hair with a smile, deeply affected by his words, and nod silently. The boy throws his pudgy little arms around my waist and sobs, "I love you, Daddy." Not a bad scene for a first day.

I spotted Larry hugging a brunette, presumably our leading lady, who had just arrived on the set. My involvement with this picture had happened with such speed, I still had no idea who my costars were besides Juan Carlos. When the brunette pulled away, I was in for a big bombshell. It was Dominique.

Larry clutched her hand and dragged her over to me. "Jarrod, I want you to meet Dominique. She's playing Sarah the psychoanalyst."

Dominique looked at me with empty eyes. She had no memory of who I was.

"We've met," I said.

"We have?" she said incredulously.

"Twice. Once at the Hearst Castle and once out in Malibu," I said, refraining from adding, "When I fished your ass out of the surf following your attempted suicide drowning."

Her eyes flickered at bit, trying to come to life, like a pair of waning headlights sucking the last juice out of a dead car battery.

"Oh, right," she said.

"I have to set up the master shot with the DP. I'll let you two get acquainted," Larry said as he hustled off toward his Panavision camera, the one top-of-the-line piece of equipment on this shoot.

"I didn't know you were an actress, Dominique," I said, studying her face for any signs of animation.

She nodded.

"So, are you doing well? The last time I saw you, you were a bit . . . down." That was putting it mildly.

She perked up ever so slightly. "I'm fine. I've put the past behind me, and I'm moving on. I want to put my career first for a while."

I was ready to believe her until I saw her notice something. Her face fell, and she let out an audible gasp. I turned to see what had caught her so off-guard, and spotted Juan Carlos sweep in, his arm around a stunning older beauty in her mid-forties. She carried herself like a queen and was blessed with a porcelain face, immaculately styled hair, and a slim, statuesque figure. She was in a smart white pantsuit, and laughed while resting her head on Juan Carlos's broad shoulder. They were sharing a private joke.

The stunning woman's eyes met Dominique's, and she gave her a halfhearted wave. Juan Carlos, barely able to contain himself, bussed the older woman's cheek with his hot passionate Latin lips. And then he slapped her playfully on the behind as she scampered over to the hair stylist and commandeered a hand mirror to check her appearance.

Juan Carlos managed to give me a half smile as he sauntered over to the craft service table for a bagel. He gave a quivering Dominique even less attention.

"First team in, please," bellowed the first assistant director through a bullhorn as the stand-ins who filled in for us while the lighting was set up filed off the set. I had one last chance to call Charlie. I hit the speed dial. It rang twice.

"Hi, this is Charlie Peters. You've reached my voice mail. You know what to do."

put on the warmest, most welcoming smile I could muster. Juan Carlos wasn't the only actor in Laurette's life.

"Hi, you must be Juan Carlos. I'm Jarrod." I wanted to add, "And Laurette's best friend who will hunt you down and gut you with a knife if you hurt her in any way," but it seemed too early in the evening.

"I've heard a lot about you, Jarrod." There wasn't a trace of a Spanish accent. Maybe he was second or third generation. Or maybe he had been working with a voice coach to pound it out of him.

Despite my suspicions based on Annabelle's stories, I couldn't help but be impressed upon first glance with Juan Carlos. He was, just as Laurette promised, gorgeous. About six feet, broad shoulders, jet-black hair, and smoldering brown Spanish eyes that glistened in the light from the lamp just outside the front door. He was wearing a Hugo Boss suit, but the tie had been undone and the shirt was open, giving me more than a hint of his toned muscular smooth chest. He looked even better in person than he did on *90210*.

"Sorry I'm late," he said as he shook my hand and entered before I had a chance to invite him inside.

Laurette ran into the entryway from the kitchen and threw her arms around him. She smothered him with kisses on his face, ears, and neck. Whatever was in reach of her lips. I noticed him tense slightly as she hugged him. It was just for a split second, and then he relaxed and allowed her to maul him. Finally, he gently pulled away and smiled. His teeth were fluoride white and perfect.

"I nailed it, honey. I'm pretty sure I got the part," he said.

"Oh, honey, that's wonderful. I'm so happy for you," Laurette said, before turning to me. "See, I told you he was good."

Charlie was the next to amble out of the kitchen, and stride over to Juan Carlos with an outstretched hand. "I'm Charlie. Nice to meet you, Juan Carlos."

Juan Carlos gripped Charlie's hand, and looked him up and down. It was subtle, barely detectable in fact, but I caught it. If I didn't know better, I'd swear he was checking Charlie out.

"I better head out to the backyard and check on the steaks. How do you like yours done, Juan Carlos?" Charlie said.

Juan Carlos smiled and slipped his hand behind Laurette, lowering it until his palm was firmly clamped on her butt. "Blood red."

Charlie nodded and walked away. I thought I saw Juan Carlos peek at Charlie's ass as he strolled off, but he instantly averted his eyes when he felt me watching him. I had to be imagining this. Laurette had excellent gaydar. She of all people would likely know if the man she was planning to marry was straight or not. But it did depend on how good an actor Juan Carlos was.

"So, sweetie, what did you bring us for dessert?"

Juan Carlos frowned, and then gave us both an apologetic look. "In all the excitement about the audition, I forgot to pick something up."

"That's all right, darling," Laurette said. "I have to lose twenty pounds in six days anyway if I want to fit into my wedding dress."

They embraced again, and Laurette mouthed the words, "Isn't he fabulous?" over his shoulder to me.

That's when it hit me what she had just said. "Did you say six days?"

"Yes. You don't already have plans or anything, do you? We just didn't have time to send out formal invitations."

"No, we don't have plans. But six days? I had no idea you were going to get married so soon."

Juan Carlos flashed me a self-satisfied smile. "We both know this is it, the real deal. What's the point in waiting?"

Laurette took his hand and gazed longingly at him. I had to snap her out of it somehow. I didn't have time to get the full story on Juan Carlos in only six days. "But there's so much to plan. You have to pick out a venue, a dress . . ."

"It's done," Laurette said. "You know I've always wanted to be married at the Hearst Castle. There was a last-minute cancellation next weekend. It cost me most of my savings, but I got it. My dress is being altered as we speak. I've booked a band. Invited everybody I want to be there. There's not a whole lot left to do."

My head was spinning. I knew Laurette was a freight train when she decided to do something, but I didn't expect her speed to rival a space shuttle.

"There is one problem, though," she said with a scowl.

Finally, something I could work with to stop this madness.

"I could only afford the Hearst Castle for three hours," she said. "With setup and cleanup, that leaves approximately one hour and seven minutes for the ceremony and reception. It's going to be tight."

I was speechless. There was a momentary silence before Juan Carlos picked up the slack in the conversation. He beamed at his blushing bride. "Oh well," he purred. "More time for the honeymoon."

And then the happy couple proceeded to suck face right in front of me, devouring each other like a pair of five-year-olds chowing down on their first hot fudge sundae.

I felt sick to my stomach.

La Cuesta Encantada, or the "Enchanted Hill," is located in San Simeon, midway between Los Angeles and San Francisco, and is situated sixteen hundred feet above sea level on a sprawling two hundred and fifty thousand acres. Housing one hundred and sixty-five rooms, two spectacular swimming pools, and an astonishing collection of art and antiques, the magnificent compound was built by publishing magnate William Randolph Hearst over a twenty-eight year-period. Since Hearst and his longtime mistress, the comedy actress Marion Davies, loved hosting Hollywood royalty, including Charlie Chaplin, Jimmy Stewart, Greta Garbo, and Cary Grant, the camp value alone made it the ideal spot for Laurette's nuptials. Ever since her parents carted their wide-eyed eight-year-old daughter on a bus up to the grounds for a tour, Laurette had been fascinated with the history and beauty of "the ranch," as Hearst liked to call it, and felt it was destiny that she be married among the ghosts of the Hollywood elite. Since her first wedding was a Vegas quickie so her husband could jet off to Prague for an obscure film festival, Laurette decided to arrange a more formal affair at the Hearst Castle upon his return. But when he did arrive home six weeks later, he kept putting her off until she finally gave up on both a San Simeon wedding and her ill-fated marriage.

Juan Carlos was an entirely different animal altogether. The thought of an expensive party at a sprawling hilltop retreat looking down on the blue sea and up at the blue sky was not only a good thing, but a God-given right. Despite having no financial resources of his own from what I could see, this charmer certainly had cultivated tastes. He was more excited about getting married at this exotic location than his blushing bride was.

Charlie didn't share my suspicions about Juan Carlos's character. He felt I was being overprotective of my best friend, and should just lay off and be happy for her. So naturally my persistent suggestions that he run an ID check on Juan Carlos using his police sources fell on deaf ears.

The drive up to the tiny seaside hamlet of San Simeon took about three and a half hours, not counting the hour-and-a-half stop at the Biltmore Hotel in Santa Barbara for their remarkable all-you-can-eat Sunday morning brunch. Charlie tried reminding me that there would be food at the reception, but since Laurette could only afford to rent the Castle for such a limited actors, practically orgasmic over Dominique's performance as he mouthed the dialogue along with her.

As they neared the end of the scene, a lone tear streaked down Dominique's face. She shyly wiped it away and said, "If we don't get him before he gets us, I want you to know, even if that mad killer carves out my heart with a hunting knife like he did to those other campers, it will still belong to you."

Okay, really bad dialogue. But she sold it. And a euphoric Larry screamed, "Cut! That's a wrap for today! Everybody have a nice weekend!"

Larry sprinted over to embrace Dominique. She accepted his accolades with graciousness, but kept one eye on Juan Carlos, who bounded off the set and over to Viveca. Juan Carlos, though obviously wanting to shower the older woman with affection, restrained himself when he realized I was watching. The last thing he needed was his wife's best friend calling her to report his on-set shenanigans. He settled for a soft sweep of his lips across Viveca's still beautiful but aging and definitely pulled-back face.

Dominique excused herself from Larry, who was still fawning over her, and dashed off to her trailer. Once she was gone, Viveca was less apprehensive about where she put her hands. Right on Juan Carlos's butt. She yanked him closer, whispered something in his ear, and then with a flourish, grabbed her fur coat, threw on her oversized Christian Dior sunglasses despite the fact that it was already dark outside, and said her good-byes to the crew.

Juan Carlos watched her go with an adoring smile on his face. It faded when he noticed me watching the whole scene. With a scowl in my direction, he grabbed his leather jacket, tossed it over his shoulder, and marched off the set and down a trail to the parking area, where his Kawasaki motorcycle awaited him.

I gathered up my things, and followed him. I figured since Juan Carlos and Viveca had made such a production of leaving

separately, then they were undoubtedly planning a secret rendezvous later. When I'd reached the end of the trail leading to
the large paved lot at the foot of the park, Viveca was not there
to greet him. But Dominique was. He marched up to her and
enveloped her in a hug. They spoke softly, completely oblivious
to me. I walked nonchalantly toward the Ford Taurus that Amy
Jo had so kindly rented for me the day before in case I wanted to
do some sightseeing over the weekend.

Juan Carlos brushed aside some of Dominique's hair to get a
good look at her face. He smiled, and then kissed her gently on
the lips. She quivered at his touch. This girl had practically been
stalking him, and now he was acting as if she was on *The
Bachelorette* and he was the last guy holding a rose. What was
going on here? It was clear to me that Juan Carlos was two-timing
Laurette. But I just couldn't figure out whom he was cheating
with. Viveca or Dominique? Or both? That was too much to
think about.

I slipped behind the wheel of the Taurus, and shut the door as
quietly as possible. I didn't want Juan Carlos to know I was
watching. He held Dominique in his arms, and they rocked back
and forth, her head resting on his broad chest. He seemed to be
whispering gentle apologies in her ear.

Finally, when Larry and his assistant director loudly pounded
down the trail to the lot discussing the dailies from yesterday's
shoot, Juan Carlos pulled away. He kissed the tip of his right
index finger, and then pressed it to Dominique's lips. As she ran
off giddily to her car, Juan Carlos peeked around to make sure
there had been no witnesses, then put on his shiny black helmet
and straddled his Kawasaki. Revving it up, he squealed out of the
lot, heading, from what I was guessing, straight toward a hot
night of unbridled sex with Viveca. I turned the ignition key,
threw the Taurus into drive, and peeled out behind him. He
headed straight for the 95 Freeway north, hit the on-ramp, and

at that point I almost lost him. He effortlessly weaved the cycle in and out of traffic, getting farther and farther ahead of me.

Luckily, as we hit the Fort Lauderdale exits, traffic slowed and he cut down on the fancy maneuvering. Once past the city, the highway opened up, and it was easier to hit the gas and keep him in my sights while maintaining a safe distance.

We drove on 95 for over two hours. Where the hell was he going? Was he so afraid of getting caught that he had to drive to a remote part of the east coast of Florida? Or did Viveca have a quiet little getaway on the Sebastian River? She had a few minutes' head start, so she was probably putting on a little mood music and pouring a couple of glasses of Merlot. I could still see the bright red glow of the Kawasaki's taillight as it veered right off the freeway, ten minutes past the town of Vero Beach. It dawned on me exactly where I was. The little hamlet of Sebastian situated roughly midway between Orlando and Miami. I had been here many times before. This was the home of Clyde and Priscilla Jarvis. My parents. Like many Florida zip codes, Sebastian was populated primarily by East Coast retirees who had discovered the joys of golfing and square dancing. For my parents, it was paradise. They had bought a quaint two-story riverfront house at an affordable price after I turned eighteen and no longer needed them to manage my career. They had despised the Hollywood scene, and were more than happy to leave it behind. They had both grown up on the East Coast, and were blessed with grounded East Coast sensibilities. They loved the simple life of Florida, where they could lounge with a cocktail on their deck that overlooked the river and watch the space shuttles take off from Cape Canaveral a short distance away. Viveca was just shy of their age range, so it didn't surprise me that she had bought in the area as well.

Juan Carlos sped down Highway 111, and for a brief disquieting moment, I thought he was heading straight for my parents' house. But just a mile short, he pulled into the parking lot belonging to a flat, plain-looking structure. In front, a weathered hanging sign barely illuminated by a dull street lamp rocked in the heavy wind. It said SAND DRIFT MOTEL. Viveca had certainly presented herself as a woman of means with her fur coats and flashy jewelry. This was well beneath her. Maybe I was wrong. Maybe Juan Carlos was meeting Dominique, and at any moment, she would pull in behind me. As Juan Carlos pressed the kickstand of his bike down with the heel of his boot, I drove pass him so as not to raise any suspicion. I parked on the far end of the lot, facing him, turned off my engine, and shut down the lights.

Juan Carlos checked himself out in the rearview mirror of his Kawasaki, straightened his jacket, and popped a breath mint into his mouth. He ambled down the row of doors lining the one-story motel. When he reached door number six, he rapped on it twice with his fist. After a moment, the door opened, and I saw a young man step out. He was about Juan Carlos's height and slender of frame, with dark olive skin and wavy jet-black hair. He broke out into a sexy, winning smile when he saw Juan Carlos. The kid was about twenty-four. He had on a ripped pair of jeans, no shirt, and he was barefoot.

I had expected Viveca or Dominique and was surprised by this new character in the picture. I was even more surprised when he grabbed Juan Carlos's jacket and drew him close, covering Juan Carlos's mouth with his lips. They stood there, devouring each other, before Juan Carlos got self-conscious, glanced around to see if they were being watched, and then pushed the kid back in the room, following him inside and slamming the door behind him.

I sat motionless in my Ford Taurus. The question was no longer, "Who is Laurette's new husband sleeping with?" The question was, "Who *isn't* Laurette's new husband sleeping with?"

Chapter 15

Istaked out the Sand Drift Motel for the whole night. Juan Carlos and the young shirtless stud who had greeted him at the door never left the room once. When the sun rose hours later, I sat in the Taurus, bleary-eyed and exhausted, knowing full well that the night hadn't been nearly as satisfying for me as it had been for the occupants of room six. My scratchy throat ached for hot coffee, my mind imagining the jolt of caffeine that would help spring me to life. But if I left my post, I risked missing something that could shed some light on the salacious secrets of Juan Carlos Barranco.

With overwhelming proof, I was certain at this point that Juan Carlos was a stinking, lying cheat who never really loved Laurette, and used her heart and kindness to get ahead as an actor. But a murderer? With the San Simeon police not any closer to handing out an indictment in the murder of Austin Teboe at the Hearst Castle, my firm belief that Juan Carlos was somehow behind it all was a shaky proposition at best.

My cell phone battery was dead, so I plugged the jack into the cigarette lighter and started the car to give it some juice. Luckily I was on the Verizon America's Choice plan that gave me unlimited calling access anywhere in the country. I hit the speed-dial button for home, and waited for a grumpy, groggy Charlie to pick up. I got our machine. It was eight-thirty in the morning in Florida. That meant it was only five-thirty on the West Coast. Where the hell was he? Why couldn't I reach him? Was he on some all-night stakeout like me? I tried his cell number and got his voice mail. I was beginning to regret accepting the job in Florida. Charlie and I always worked things through, but maybe this time I had gone too far. Maybe he had reached his limit with me, and there would be no coming back from this one. As I pondered the state of my relationship, I spied a sleepy, long-haired desk clerk in his late twenties stirring inside the registration office. Since the shirtless kid in room six had arrived before Juan Carlos, chances were he had registered himself.

I stepped out of the Taurus, stretched my legs, and bounded across the parking lot, keeping one eye on the door to room six to make sure no one came out while I was in plain view.

The bells above the door clanged as I entered the office and startled the laconic clerk with the half-closed eyes.

"Can I help you?" he said with a slow, Southern drawl, barely offering me a cursory glance.

"Yes," I said, mustering up a chipper, friendly voice. "I was wondering if you could tell me who is in room six?"

"Can't. It's like a rule or something." His gaze suddenly caught mine, and his half-closed eyes popped opened all the way.

"Oh," I said with proper disappointment. I reached behind for the wallet tucked into the back pocket of my jeans. I was not above a little bribe since it looked like the kid, wearing a torn, stained Counting Crows tour T-shirt and faded cutoffs, barely made enough for beer money.

He was still staring at me. "You're . . . you're that guy. From the TV show."

Sometimes my past proved to be an invaluable asset.

"*Go to Your Room!*" I offered with a smile.

"Yeah, I watched you all the time when I was just a rug rat. You had that saying, the one that was on all the T-shirts," he said, straining to remember. "What was it?"

"Baby, don't even go there!"

He shook his head. "No, that wasn't it. It was something like 'Baby, don't you be messing with me.' "

I wasn't going to correct him. Let him think he was right if it got me what I needed.

"That's right," I smiled.

"Man, you've gotten old."

My smile faded.

Oblivious to his social faux pas, the kid prattled on, "So what the hell are you doing way out here in the boondocks?"

"I thought I spotted a friend of mine from the good old days. One of the kids from *Head of the Class*."

"You're shitting me, man! No way! Which one?"

I had to think fast. I had gone clubbing with pretty much all of them at some point during the heyday of our various sitcoms. There was one in particular, though, I had always thought was adorable. I went with him. "The one who played the preppy, snooty kid."

"Fuck, yeah! I remember him! That show was awesome, man!"

"Totally awesome," I lied. When my show was canceled, my agent tried to float the idea of adding me as a new student in the show's third season, but they didn't bite so I forever hated the show.

"So where did you see him?"

"Right here. At the Sand Drift."

I thought the clerk was going to drop dead from shock. Not one, but two big stars at this obscure, crumbling motel were almost too much for him to take. He snatched up the registration book off the desk, and began skimming through the pages.

"I saw him go into room six," I said, praying he wouldn't ask me the actor's name because I was drawing a blank.

The clerk ran his finger down the page and studied the name. He looked up at me hopefully. "David Miller?"

I shook my head and sighed. "Nope. Not him. Damn. He looks just like him."

"Fuck, man, what a bummer. I was going to offer him a free continental breakfast and get him to be the first one to sign our VIP guest book."

I glanced out the window and saw David Miller heading straight for the office. I turned to the clerk and said quickly, "Oh, well. Thanks anyway."

"Hey, would you sign it?" the clerk said. "I know you didn't stay here or anything, but who the fuck's gonna know?"

I figured it was quicker to do as he asked rather than argue, so I scribbled my name illegibly in his scuffed blue notebook, dropped the pen, and held open the door as David Miller swept inside.

"I'm here to check out," he said gruffly, tossing the keys down on the desk. He never looked my way and I took the opportunity to slip outside.

Juan Carlos stood by his bike and put on his helmet. I turned my head the other way as I passed him, hoping he wouldn't recognize me, but he was lost in his own thoughts.

As I crossed the parking lot, I noticed a black Lincoln Town Car situated across the street and facing the motel. Two giants, one Caucasian, one Hispanic, were stuffed into the front seat. The one in the passenger seat held binoculars up in front of his face and watched me as I headed toward the Taurus. When he noticed that I was watching him watch me, he quickly turned and spoke to the driver. The Town Car roared to life, spun out of the gravelly road across from the motel, and sped off down Highway 111.

I hopped into my car just as David Miller ambled out of the

registration office. Juan Carlos sat on the bike, twisting the handlebar accelerator so the bike's engine revved loud enough to accentuate his macho posturing. Juan Carlos was obviously proud to have such a powerful machine wedged between his muscular, toned thighs.

David stopped, caressed Juan Carlos's cheek with the back of his index finger, whispered a good-bye, and then headed to his own car, a sleek red BMW from the five hundred series. Whoever this kid was, he had money. So why meet at the dumpy Sand Drift?

Juan Carlos zipped out of the lot and headed back toward the 95 Highway. I knew he was returning to Miami. He had already gotten what he'd come for, and there was no reason to hang around on this desolate stretch of road anymore. I debated following the kid to find out more about him, but I was afraid someone in the area might recognize me. And if it got back to my parents that I was in town and didn't at least stop in to say hello, Jarvis family relations would undoubtedly be dealt a severe blow.

It was a five-minute jaunt to River Oak Drive, and as I pulled up to the white two-story house with its breathtaking river view, I saw my father, Clyde, fussing in his tiny vegetable garden that sprouted one cucumber a year if he was lucky. Oh, well, it gave him something to do between golf games and square-dancing competitions.

The Ford Taurus pulling into the small paved driveway caught his attention, and as I waved with a bright smile, his face lit up. My father was a retired Navy captain, who'd spent most of his life touring ports around the world. He cut a striking figure at six feet four inches tall, and had a barrel chest that would have made him physically intimidating were it not for his sweet, kind demeanor. His silver hair was thinning, and he wore thick glasses that suggested his age, but his broad face darkly tan from nine months a year in the Florida sunshine was nearly wrinkle-free. Although seventy, most people would put him somewhere in his mid-fifties.

When Dad retired from the Navy, I had just landed my first commercial. I was five years old, and it was a thirty-second spot for Cap'n Crunch cereal. Although all I had to do was salute a cartoon character and say, "Ahoy, matey!" before diving into a bowl of cereal, seeing me on television made him cry. For a Navy captain, my dad cried a lot. He cried when I got my sit-com. He cried when I guest-starred on his favorite show, *JAG*, as a Navy admiral's homicidal son. He cried when I broke up with my first boyfriend. He was always proud of me no matter what I did or whom I was dating. His years of military service did little to diminish his loving acceptance of me. I was his son and I was gay. Big deal.

As I stepped out of the Taurus, he rushed at me and enveloped me in his big, comforting, tanned arms. "Well, hello, stranger!"

"Hi, Dad," I said breathlessly as he squeezed the last gulps of air out of me with his bear hug.

"How's the movie going? How's Charlie?"

Before I could answer, my mother, Priscilla, came sauntering out of the house. A foot and a half shorter than my father, she was your typical fiery redhead, a ball of energy and full of uncensored attitude. She carried a crossword puzzle and pen, and pushed her husband aside to steal a quick hug for herself. "He just got here, Clyde. Don't hit him with so many questions!"

Although my mother had once run my career, she was not a fan of Hollywood. She was much happier now, mingling with real people outside of the spotlight. And although she'd lived among the gays while residing in LA and counted many of them as her close friends, in a stunning twist of irony she was not as accepting as my Navy dad. Her reaction was similar to Cher's when her only daughter, Chastity Bono, had her coming-out party. "I love the gays, they've made my career, but please God, not *my* kid!" She cried, too, when I broke up with my first boyfriend, although upon closer inspection, I was able to identify them as tears of joy. In the early days of our relationship, Charlie had worked his magic, and she instantly adored him, treating him like her own son. She chose to ignore what went on between us behind closed doors and loved us both unconditionally. But she made it very clear she didn't understand what had made me this way.

Mom and I decided to keep our relationship on a superficial yet loving level. She didn't ask questions about my personal life, nor did I offer up any answers unprompted. Dad, on the other hand, would have drawn his own PFLAG posters to march in a gay pride parade if he'd felt it would bring us even closer. The bottom line was, however, that I loved them both. And to see their happy faces at my surprise visit dispelled any issues I had with the depth of my relationship with my mother.

After the initial flurry of kisses and hugs and updates on all of our activities, we piled into my parents' Roadtrek motor home, which they'd purchased for a cross-country excursion that never happened, and drove to the nearest Olive Garden for an early lunch. Over pasta, garlic sticks, and the famous bottomless salad, my mother asked about Laurette's wedding. She had heard through my sister in Maine that someone had died at the reception and she was champing at the bit to hear the details.

"He was a chef. He worked for some kind of mobster based out of Miami. Javier Martinez."

"I've seen that guy on the news," Dad said. "Feds have been trying to nail him for years," he added gleefully, thrilled to be discussing something other than which restaurant chain they were going to target for an early-bird special later. "You think Laurette's husband poisoned him?"

"I don't have any proof of that, but I've got a gut feeling he's involved somehow."

"Motive?" Dad could barely contain himself. When I became embroiled in the murder of former child star Willard Ray

Hornsby last year, my notoriety reached new heights. My Dad, a huge fan of *CSI: Crime Scene Investigation*, reveled in my involvement. He was a closet detective and an avid reader of mystery novels. He yearned to discuss the fine points of police work with Charlie whenever he could corner him in a room, and now that I was this amateur sleuth who'd cracked a real case, he found it harder and harder to suppress his own desire to be the next Lieutenant Columbo.

My mother wasn't very tolerant of her husband's fascination with murder. She preferred lighter topics such as the latest movie releases and what kind of salary I was pulling down for this small independent film shoot in Miami. Even though her time in show business was peripheral and now a distant memory, Priscilla Jarvis loved talking money.

"Just give me a hint. Is it at least five figures?"

"It's not about the money, Mom," I said defensively. "Sometimes it's about the art."

"I thought you said it was a cheap horror movie," she said, her eyes raised with suspicion like most mothers who are on the brink of catching their child in a lie.

"That's right. And sometimes it's not about the art, it's about just working on something. The director is really hot right now, and if I do well, he could use me again when he gets his first big job at a studio. This could be an amazing opportunity."

"What does Charlie think?" Dad asked innocently.

I should have at that point confessed that my relationship was teetering on the edge of extinction, and that I hadn't been able to reach him by phone from the moment I arrived in Florida, and that I feared he was banging a judge, but instead, I popped the last garlic bread stick into my mouth and, between chews, replied, "He thinks it's great."

After a brief tussle over who was going to pay the whopping twenty-two-dollar bill, we piled back into the Roadtrek, and drove north toward the senior center where my parents square danced every afternoon at one o'clock sharp. My father pulled off Highway 111 and zipped along a narrow back road, the motor home taking up most of the pavement. I prayed we wouldn't collide with a car coming from the opposite direction.

Gripping the wheel, Dad glanced back at Mom and me as we sat at the tiny kitchen table booth in the back of the vehicle. "So, you want to know what I think?"

"No," Mom said emphatically. But Dad was years beyond listening to her.

"I think Juan Carlos has somehow crossed this gangster Martinez, and Martinez sent this Teboe fella to the wedding to rub out Juan Carlos. But before he had the chance, Juan Carlos spiked his drink with a fast-acting poison. How does that sound?"

My mother rolled her eyes, and jabbed a finger at Dad. "Keep your eyes on the road!"

Dad grimaced, and then swiveled back around.

"I swear he's going to get us killed someday. If it's not from poking his nose where it doesn't belong, it'll be from his driving," she said.

Dad sat quietly in the RV's captain's seat. He desperately wanted a response to his theory, but he didn't want to ask me for fear of another tongue-lashing from his wife.

"Sounds like a reasonable scenario, Dad. Except for the fact that the poison was something called monkshead. Very rare and not indigenous to California. Someone had to bring it to the wedding with the intent of using it. It was pretty clear Juan Carlos wasn't expecting Austin Teboe to show up."

"Damn. I thought I had the case wrapped up." He thought some more. "How about this? You said Juan Carlos is cheating on Laurette. What if she found out and was wild with fury, and decided to take him out at the wedding. But instead, she poisoned Teboe by accident—"

"Oh, for heaven's sake, Clyde. Shut up! You don't know what

you're talking about! Laurette is not a murderer!" my mother screamed, whacking him on the back of his head with her crossword puzzle book.

"They say it's always the least likely suspect," he said softly.

"Well, then you might as well accuse Jarrod. Or what about me? I was down here in Florida with you. Thousands of miles away from the wedding. That makes me the least likely, wouldn't you say?" She was mocking him now, and he hated it.

I was about to intervene when I noticed a black Lincoln Town Car behind us. I left my mother at the table and walked up to sit next to Dad. I casually glanced out the side-view mirror for a better look. It was the two linebackers I had seen earlier scouting out the Sand Drift Motel. And they were closing in on us.

Chapter 16

"I don't want anyone to panic," I said quietly and evenly. "Don't turn around."

"What?" my mother said, spinning her head around faster than Linda Blair in *The Exorcist*. "Is it the police? How fast are you going, Clyde?"

"Jesus, Mom, what did I just say?"

"What is it, son?" Dad asked, an excited lilt in his voice.

"We're being tailed."

My mother's face fell.

Dad's eyes danced with glee as he tightened his grip on the wheel and broke out into a wide smile. "Want me to outrun 'em?"

"For crying out loud, Clyde, we're in an RV!" my mother wailed before grabbing my shirtsleeve in desperation. "Do they have guns, Jarrod? Are they going to shoot us?"

"I don't know," I said. "I have no idea who they are."

"Then that settles it," said Clyde Jarvis, former Navy captain and hero of the high seas. "They're going to eat my dust!"

And with that, Dad slammed his foot down on the accelerator.

As the Roadtrek shot forward, the sudden jolt sent my mother and me flying to the back of the RV, and we both landed on the plush plaid comforter decorating the queen-size bed just off the narrow kitchen area. After untangling our limbs, I glanced out the back window to see the Town Car speeding to catch up with us.

I studied the license number and committed it to memory as my mother grabbed the wood-trimmed dining table for support, and hoisted herself forward toward her husband.

"For God's sake, Clyde, slow down before you get us all killed!"

Ignoring his wife's pleas, my dad could barely suppress his euphoria over his first experience with a real-live car chase. "Those fuckers still on my ass, son?"

I wasn't used to hearing my dad swear. He was usually such a gentleman, but the adrenaline of the moment was turning him into his favorite macho movie star, Clint Eastwood. Dad was suddenly in his own *Dirty Harry* movie and loving every minute of it.

"Still there, Dad," I said.

Dad jerked the wheel, and the Roadtrek screeched into a sharp turn off the paved road. My mother and I collided, and fell to the floor as dishes and glasses from the cupboards rained down on us, smashing and shattering all around us.

"Clyde, my Fiestaware!"

But Dad had tuned her out, and was intently steering the RV down a narrow dirt path through a wooded area. The vehicle shook and rattled as it plowed over the bumpy terrain and managed to drown out my mother's own colorful language.

I grabbed the steel handle on the utensil drawer and used it to regain my balance and climb to my feet. But Dad threw us into another sharp turn, and the drawer flew completely out of the cupboard. A hail of forks, knives, and spoons fell clattering to the floor, much to my mother's horror.

Dad checked on us through the rearview mirror to make sure we weren't bleeding or unconscious. Then, with another gleeful smile breaking out on his face, he gripped the wheel of the RV tighter and barreled forward through the woods.

"Dad, where are we going?"

"Don't worry, son. I know these roads like my own backyard. Those ass wipes won't be able to keep up with us for long!"

The Town Car had fallen a bit behind but we were still in its sights. How we were going to lose them was a big question mark in my mind.

My mother was on her knees, carefully picking up the broken shards of her dinner plates and silently cursing my father.

We broke through a thicket of trees, and hit a gravel road that stretched across an empty field. In the middle were some train tracks. And a red light in front flashed at us to stop. But we didn't.

"Dad, I think you better slow down."

"Clyde, a train's coming," my mother said, her voice trembling, knowing in her heart he had no intention of stopping. After thirty-five years of marriage, she had developed an instinct.

A train approached from the east, clocking in at close to sixty miles an hour. The Town Car didn't see it. Dad slammed down on the accelerator until his foot pressed against the floor. We hurtled onward, and careened over the tracks just as the black-and-white-striped guard pole came down fast within an inch of our taillight.

I looked out the back window to see the two goons in the Town Car erupt in panic. As the driver hit the brakes, the car spun to the right, its passenger side door crashing into the metal guard pole. The mile-long Amtrak train zipped by, serving as a wall to separate us, and ensuring our escape.

Dad let up on the accelerator and, with a big, broad grin on his face, turned around and said, "Everybody okay back there?"

My mother was so filled with fury, she couldn't even open her mouth to yell at him.

I, on the other hand, was duly impressed. "Nice going, Dad. Thanks," I said.

"No problem, son." He tried to stay cool, but he couldn't stop beaming. The guy was proud of himself for making short work of the bad guys.

My cell phone rang. I checked the caller ID. It was Charlie. Finally. I hit the talk button, and sounding a bit too much like my mother for comfort, I said, "Where the hell have you been?"

Charlie's voice was calm. "Been working on a new case. I haven't been home much."

"I've been trying to call you. You're never home."

"I've been working a stakeout. It's been brutal," he said, and then after a long pause, added, "Isis has been nice enough to come over and walk Snickers while I've been at work."

Uh-oh. Isis was a talker and I knew what was coming next. "How come you didn't tell me you saw Wendell Butterworth again at Costco?"

"I tried, but I couldn't reach you."

"You could have called me at the precinct and left a message. I can't protect you from that psycho if you keep things from me."

"Well, I'm thousands of miles away from him now, so it's a moot point."

"I hate when you get like this. You don't want to face the fact that this guy is stalking you again, so you slip into a state of denial."

He was looking for a fight. He was still angry with me. I had two choices. Engage or retreat. It was better to retreat. At least for now. "You're right. I'm sorry."

He wasn't used to me backing down so quickly. But if we lapsed into a fight, then I wouldn't have been able to sweet-talk him into securing me some information.

"So I was wondering if you could run a license plate for me," I said.

"Why? What's going on down there?"

"Oh, it's nothing, really. Just a car I've spotted a couple of times while I've been out. I just want to make sure Wendell didn't find out I'm in Florida and follow me here."

My mother's ears perked up at the mention of Wendell. I had tried to keep Wendell's recent parole under wraps for fear they would be sick with worry.

"He's out?" she said, her voice tense.

I nodded, and then cupped the phone with the palm of my hand. "Yes, but it's nothing to worry about."

I took my hand away and said into the phone, "Florida plate. CASA CON 6."

"Hold on," Charlie said. "I'll run it through the computer."

While I waited, my mother stopped picking up her broken Fiestaware and hovered over me with a worried look on her face.

"When was he released?" she said.

"A few weeks ago," I said as nonchalantly as possible.

"You see him skulking around any?" my Dad asked, glancing through the rearview mirror as we barreled back toward my parents' house on the Sebastian River.

"Oh no," I lied. "He knows to keep his distance."

"I should hope so," my mother said.

"I'm just playing it safe," I said.

"I got a good look at those goons in the Town Car," my dad said. "Neither one looked anything like that creep Butterworth."

I instantly clamped my hand back over the phone's mouthpiece and prayed Charlie didn't hear.

"But you never know. He may have made some friends in prison," Dad said.

My mother shuddered at the suggestion.

Dad was still in Clint Eastwood mode. "I'll mow those fuckers down if they dare try anything."

"I'm probably just being paranoid," I said.

Charlie came back on the line. "Car's registered to a building contracting company in Fort Lauderdale. Casa Construction. It's one of twelve company cars."

"Why would somebody from a construction company chase us?"

"Chase? I thought you said you just spotted it a couple of times?" Charlie said.

All my little white lies inevitably came back to haunt me. "It followed us for a bit, but Dad lost them."

"I didn't know you were visiting your parents," Charlie said, his voice brightening. He was a big fan of Clyde and Priscilla.

"Just for the day. I have to get back to Miami for shooting on Monday."

"Promise me you'll call if anything weird happens," Charlie said.

"I will."

There was another long pause before I said hesitantly, "I miss you."

"I miss you too. Bye, babe."

Click. He was gone. And even in the company of my loving parents, without Charlie, I felt very alone.

Chapter 17

When I returned to the set on Monday, the cast and crew were abuzz over the reputed affair between Juan Carlos and his much older costar, Viveca. As Stella applied a pound of makeup to the slowly fading bruise on my right eye, she could barely contain herself.

"I heard they spent all weekend locked in a room at the Delano. I'm sure she paid. He couldn't afford a place like that on what he's making on this movie," she said.

I could have clued her in to the fact that Juan Carlos was also screwing around with a handsome young lad two hours north of Coral Gables, but decided it was wiser to play my cards close to the vest.

A mousy PA armed with a walkie-talkie poked her head into the messy makeup and hair trailer. "We're ready for you on the set, Jarrod," she said tentatively.

"Okay, thanks, Lucy," I said.

Furrowing her own brow, Stella studied my face and shrugged. "About as good as it's going to get, I'm afraid."

I yanked off the paper bib protecting my freshly pressed

wardrobe, and stood up. "You sure know how to talk to actors," I said.

Stella guffawed, and slapped my behind as I headed out of the trailer.

The outdoor campground set was bustling with activity as I made my way to my mark. A lighting technician gauged the shadows in the shot, and then repositioned a klieg light set up just outside of camera range.

Larry was engrossed in conversation with his director of photography, while over at the craft services table, Viveca picked up a Payday candy bar, unwrapped it, and playfully stuffed it into Juan Carlos's mouth. He let his hand slip down until it cupped her still firmly toned butt.

Caitlin dragged her devil child Simon onto the set, and spoke to him in urgent hushed whispers. I assumed she was bribing him. If he completed the scene without a tantrum, she would indulge his sweet tooth with all sorts of goodies. It was a pointless effort. Even if he did cry and make demands, she'd still give the little bugger anything he wanted.

"Good morning, Simon," I said with as much cheer as I could muster.

He snorted. No real words. Just a short, derisive snort. I hated him so much. It was going to take every last ounce of my acting ability to portray this little shit's loving father.

Larry bounded on the set. "Okay, this is a pretty straight-forward scene," he said, talking with his hands. He turned to Simon. "You're pretty scared at this point. There have been rumors around the campground that four tourists have been found brutally slaughtered just half a mile away. You want to go home. But you know how much your dad's been looking forward to this quality time with you, so at the last minute you decide to stick it out. Serial killer be damned!" Larry then turned to me. "Jarrod, this is basically Simon's scene so just react accordingly."

Great. I was a glorified extra to this tiny terror. But I smiled and nodded enthusiastically. No one could ever accuse me of not being the utmost professional.

Larry ran back behind the camera, leaned over the shoulder of his DP to check the shot, took his seat in the director's chair with his name embroidered on the back, and yelled, "Action!"

Simon launched into his monologue, and as much as I loathe admitting it, he was pretty good. The kid had talent. I stayed in the moment, playing the doting parent who took great pains to understand what his frightened son was trying to tell him. Just as Simon reached the climax of his speech, making the choice to stay in the woods and risk a run-in with a madman, someone's cell phone rang.

"Cut!" Larry screamed, hurling his baseball cap to the ground in frustration. "Who the hell forgot to turn off their phone?"

Of course this time I knew it couldn't be mine. Since that disastrous first day, I had always left my cell phone in my gym bag, which I kept stored in the wardrobe trailer. The ringing continued. It was very close by. Everyone looked around frantically, trying to locate the source of the disturbance.

"It's coming out of his ass!" Simon screamed, pointing at the back pocket of my jeans. Oh God! I had taken it out to check my messages when I'd arrived on the set, and got so interested in watching Juan Carlos and Viveca paw each other at the craft services table that I had completely forgotten to put it back in my bag.

"Larry, I'm so sorry," I offered weakly.

"Just answer the goddamned phone! It's driving me nuts!" he said. "Everybody, take five!"

Simon glared at me and then ran after Larry. "I can't work like this, Mr. Levant! That was my best take on the whole picture and he ruined it!"

I was mortified, and looked around at everybody with an apologetic smile, but they scattered to keep their distance as if I were a walking virus.

I finally answered the phone. "Hello?"

"It's me," said Charlie. "Can you talk?"

Glancing around at the deserted set, I shrugged and said, "Sure. I've got five whole minutes."

"I did some digging on Casa Construction. Found out it's a legitimate business owned by none other than Javier Martinez."

"The Miami mob boss?"

"Yeah. I called my friend in South Beach and he said it's probably a front for all sorts of illegal activities. The question is why has a guy like Martinez suddenly taken an interest in *you*?"

I should have told Charlie that Martinez's henchmen probably spotted me staking out Juan Carlos, who was busy hooking up with a young stud at a dilapidated motel, and decided to find out if I was somehow connected to whatever business it was that had soured Martinez on Juan Carlos. But instead, I simply said, "Beats me."

"I don't like this one bit, Jarrod," Charlie said. "Martinez has a history of making people disappear, and if you're suddenly on his radar, that can't be good."

"I agree. So don't worry. I'll be really careful."

"Maybe I should book a flight down there."

"Charlie, I'm around people all the time on the set. I'm completely safe." Charlie wasn't a fan of my amateur sleuthing, so I didn't want to raise any hackles by confessing my recent Hardy Boy adventure.

"All right. But I have a very bad feeling, so if you get the slightest hint that someone's following you . . ."

"I'll call the police and then call you."

"Okay. What about Juan Carlos? Laurette's been calling three times a day to see if I've heard from you, and if you have any news."

I wasn't ready to fess up to the fact that Laurette's new husband was shacking up with more Floridians than the number who voted in the state's ill-fated 2000 presidential election. I needed to find out more about Juan Carlos's illicit affairs, his relationship with Austin Teboe, and the deadly business he had gotten mixed up in with Javier Martinez. The last thing I needed was Charlie reporting back to Laurette.

"I haven't seen much so far," I said. "But I can say he's got his fingers in a whole lot of pies."

Larry stalked back onto the set, his face covered in powdered sugar from the half-eaten donut in his hand. If looks could kill.

"Charlie, I've got to go. We're about to start shooting again."

I shut off the cell phone and was about to stuff it back into my jeans pocket when the mousy PA ran up to me, stuck out her hand, and said, "Larry wants me to hold on to your phone." Her eyes pleaded with me not to make a fuss.

I surrendered the phone without a word.

Caitlin brought her son back onto the set as an exasperated Larry screamed, "Are we finally ready to do this again?"

Trying my hardest to be contrite, I turned to Simon, who stepped on the piece of black tape designating his mark. "I'm really sorry I disrupted the take, Simon," I said.

He just snorted. And I clasped my hands behind my back until the urge to strangle his fat little neck subsided.

My scene with Simon wrapped just before lunch, and after grabbing a turkey and Swiss sandwich and a Diet Coke to go, I jumped in the Taurus and drove to Fort Lauderdale in just under twenty minutes. If I was ever going to unearth the mystery of why there was such bad blood between Juan Carlos and Mr. Martinez, the best course of action was to talk to the Miami mobster directly. After placing a call to Casa Construction, I was told by the very curt receptionist that Mr. Martinez was on-site today supervising an oceanfront construction job. She refused to disclose the exact address, but since the city's downtown area was relatively small, I decided to just drive around until I spotted a couple of guys in orange vests and a few cement trucks.

A viable alternative to the glittery, fast-paced South Beach, the city of Fort Lauderdale had reinvented itself by pouring over twenty-six million dollars into refurbishing its dreary and dated oceanfront. Now completely revitalized, the city was thriving in the tourist trade. And no doubt companies like Casa Construction were reaping the benefits.

It took all of ten minutes to lock in on a building under construction. And before I could even find a parking space across the street, I saw a big sign posted out front boasting the newest job by Casa Construction and a telephone number to call if you needed the city's number one building contractors.

I stepped out of the Taurus, locked it up tight, and made my way across the street to the site. There were a few workers sitting in folding chairs eating takeout from Taco Bell. I started to approach them when I spotted the two goons pull up in the familiar black Town Car. I ducked behind a giant green earthmover that had been parked about a hundred feet from the half-constructed building. They walked toward a white aluminum trailer that had been set up to serve as a makeshift on-site office. They rapped on the door, waited a few moments, and then entered. Just as the bigger one went to close the door behind him, I spotted Javier Martinez sitting behind a desk, sipping a Starbucks coffee. He had a strikingly handsome face marred by a scar down his left cheek. He was in his late forties and very fit from what I could tell. The door closed. I knew his goons Laurel and Hardy would never let me get close to the boss, so my best point of attack would be to sneak around to the back of the trailer, wait for his henchmen to leave, and then talk my way in, pretending to be some kind of representative of a company interested in acquiring the services of Casa Construction. That would only work, of course, if Martinez had yet to see a picture of me. I was banking on him knowing I was out there following Juan Carlos, but not knowing what I looked like.

I left my earthmover cover and circled around behind the

workers on their lunch break. I tiptoed behind the trailer, carefully making sure not to step on any rocks and debris that littered the site. Once I was positioned in the back, I picked up a discarded pail and set it down underneath a window. Stepping up on it, I raised my head high enough to peer inside. The two goons were both talking at once, presumably filling in their boss on their own surveillance activities. I had little doubt I was a part of the discussion. Martinez's back was to me, so I had no idea what his reaction was. After a few minutes, Martinez put down his Starbucks cup and waved Laurel and Hardy away. They both nodded, and then turned to leave, bumping shoulders in the small, enclosed space. They both tried going through the tiny door at the same time, almost crushing each other in the process. Finally, with a big sigh, the white guy allowed the Hispanic to pass through first. I couldn't tell if Martinez had even noticed this little comedy sketch.

Now was my chance. Martinez was alone. I stepped down off the pail and moved quickly to the edge of the trailer. I peeked out and spied Laurel and Hardy getting back in the Town Car. They drove away. I had to move fast. I thought up a fake name for the company I worked for and a nonexistent building project to bluff my way into Martinez's office, but before I could take a step toward the small aluminum door, a beefy hand clamped tightly over my mouth and yanked me back behind the trailer.

Chapter 18

Whoever it was who grabbed me spun me around and shoved me hard up against the chain link fence that separated the office trailer from the construction site. He kept his hand pressed firmly over my mouth as he hissed in my ear, "Not a word, or we're both dead."

When he was confident I was going to keep quiet, he removed his hand and stepped back so I could finally get a good look at him. He was a big guy, well over six feet, with a shaved head and a dragon tattoo on his left bicep. He looked like a studly action hero cut from the Vin Diesel mode, and even wore a tight Army green tank top, camouflage pants, and black scuffed boots. His handsome stubbled face was dark and tan, a perfect testament to his obvious Latin heritage. He was the sexy, strong, silent type, and boasted a killer body underneath his casual military attire. If I hadn't known better, I would have sworn I had just walked into the middle of a gay porn video.

"Who are you?" I whispered.

"Later. Right now I'm going to get you out of here."

"Not until I talk to Mr. Martinez."

He looked at me as if I were an idiot. And at the moment, that was exactly what I felt like.

"You say the wrong thing to Martinez," he said, "and you might wind up on a one-way cruise to Cuba as fish food."

I had heard that line before. It was probably from when I'd guest-starred on *Miami Vice* in the eighties as a child prodigy chess champion who competes in a high-stakes international tournament against the thirteen-year-old son of a Havana-based drug dealer Crocket and Tubbs were investigating.

"Trust me," he said. "Not a smart move. Now come with me."

I wasn't used to being told what I could or could not do. Charlie would certainly attest to that. But my instincts told me to trust this guy.

He gripped my arm with his enormous, thick hand and steered me toward an alley leading away from the site and to a vast empty parking lot on the other side of a neighboring building. He pulled a set of keys out of his pants, clicked a button, and unlocked a custom-made sleek blue van that was more buffed and built up than he was. He released my arm and crossed to the driver's side door.

"Get in," he said in a gruff, impatient voice.

"What about my car?"

"Forget it. Martinez's meatheads recognized it parked across the street when they came out. They're just waiting for you to come back so they can pounce. Now are we going to stand here and jabber all day or are you going to get in my van?"

I stopped just short of climbing in the passenger's seat. "You're not some serial killer, are you? I just had this vision of you knocking me over the head with a crowbar, and me waking up in some carved-out ditch in your basement handcuffed to a water heater."

He treated me to a barely perceptible smile. "Relax. You're safe with me."

I decided to go with it and jumped in the van next to him. As he thrust the key into the ignition and fired the van up, he turned and added with a swift wink, "Of course, if you don't stop looking at me with those ocean blue eyes of yours, I may have to pounce."

I was starting to like him. A lot.

We pulled out and drove south toward Hollywood, Florida, a tiny hamlet wedged between the two larger, more famous cities of Fort Lauderdale and Miami. We drove in silence for a few minutes. I was still reeling from his flattering remark regarding my eyes. Maybe it was a tactic to throw me off balance so I wouldn't give him any more trouble. I guess the *Hairspray* T-shirt I was wearing, from the Broadway show, had given my loosely guarded sexual orientation away.

"So what were you doing sneaking around Martinez's site?" I asked.

"Same as you," he said, keeping his eyes fixed on the road. "Trying to find some answers. I'm a private detective. Name's Bowie. Bowie Lassiter."

I wasn't sure how much I should reveal. He could be lying. He could be on Martinez's payroll and just pretending to be on the same side to find out how much I knew about Martinez's illegal operations. And once he had drained all the necessary information out of me, he would just slit my throat with the hunting knife that was sheathed in the leather pouch tied to his belt. Man, he was butch.

"I'm not pulling your chain. Check the glove box," he said.

I twisted the knob, and the compartment popped open, revealing a Florida private investigator's license with a laminated photo. It was definitely him. The picture didn't begin to do him justice. I tossed the identification back in the box and snapped it shut.

"Your turn," he said.

"I'm Jarrod Jarvis. I'm here working on a movie, and I have

reason to believe that one of my costars on the picture has somehow gotten mixed up with Javier Martinez."

"Too bad for him," Bowie said.

"I think he's crossed him in some way."

Bowie shook his head slowly. "Man, pissing off Martinez is like contracting a fatal disease. It's not a question of if you die, it's a question of when."

"How do you know so much about Martinez?"

"I grew up in the area. Everybody knows the family. They're famous for outfoxing the police, the lawyers, the city, and whoever dares to stand up to them. Javier controls half the businesses in South Florida. I've managed to stay out of his way until recently," he said.

"Why poke your nose into his business now?"

"A cousin of mine, Calvin, met Martinez's daughter at a night club about six months ago. Had no idea who she was. They started dating. She fell hard for him. But then, it slowly dawned on him who her father was, and it scared the hell out of him. He didn't want to be dragged into the mob, so he pulled back. And it broke her heart. Once Daddy found out that some local kid upset his only daughter, he made it his mission to be damn sure he'd never do it again."

"You mean he had him killed?"

Bowie shrugged. "Don't know. Calvin just up and disappeared one day. That was three months ago. But there's a long list of unsolved homicides that the cops are convinced are tied to Martinez's operations. So it's a good bet."

"I guess your family is counting on you to give them some closure," I said.

Bowie nodded, but didn't say anything else.

When we arrived in South Beach, I was about to instruct Bowie to drop me off at the drab Ritz Plaza where I was staying, but he veered off to the right and headed down the congested Ocean Boulevard and finally to a dock housing several retro houseboats from the swinging sixties. He pulled the van into a reserved parking space in front of a wide, flat, white houseboat in desperate need of a paint job. There was a deck on top for sunbathing. Stenciled on the bow was QE3. If his gratifying comment about my eyes hadn't betrayed him, a houseboat named after Queen Elizabeth would have certainly clued me in that all was not completely butch in boy land.

"Come on in," he said, waving me inside. "I'll make us a drink."

I dutifully followed, and once I crossed the threshold into the unknown, I found a messy, disheveled, old-fashioned bachelor pad with an unmade pull-out couch bed, empty pizza boxes and beer bottles, and a wide-screen TV that had been left on ESPN. As he crossed to the wet bar, Bowie scooped up the remote and hit the mute button so he could check out the scores while making us cocktails.

"Scotch okay?"

"Sure," I said, looking around and spotting a weathered, creased manila folder that rested on top of the worn, stained couch bed. On the front, someone had scribbled MARTINEZ FILE in pencil that was now smudged. I picked up the folder, flipped it open. There was a small stack of surveillance photos of Martinez leaving his various properties and businesses, dining out at some of South Beach's finest eateries, meeting with a few prominent city officials. When I reached the bottom of the pile, one picture caught my eye. I froze. A man and a woman in their early twenties playfully frolicked in the Miami surf, blissfully unaware of the shutterbug in their midst. Pulling it out of the folder, I crossed to the bar and shoved it in front of Bowie as he diluted the scotch with a splash of soda and then stirred the drinks with his index fingers.

"Who is this?" I asked.

Bowie studied the picture for a second and looked up at me. "That's Calvin. My cousin."

I pointed at the young woman. "And her?"

"That's Martinez's daughter."

I stared at the picture. There was no mistaking it. Martinez's daughter was Juan Carlos's fragile, emotionally distraught ex-flame Dominique.

Chapter 19

After three more scotches, the shock of Dominique's family tree began to wear off, and I was swimming in a sea of confusion. I may have uncovered some dirty secrets involving Juan Carlos's ill-fated love affair with the daughter of a Miami crime czar, but I still wasn't any closer to solving the murder of Austin Teboe. Charlie's friend had told him Teboe was once a chef on board Martinez's yacht, but had left his employ under a cloud of secrecy. Juan Carlos and Teboe met working at the Nexxt Café on Lincoln Road. Was it just a coincidence that Juan Carlos's coworker had worked for the father of his one-time girlfriend? Was it Teboe who had introduced them? The only thing I was pretty sure of at this point was the reason behind the rumored hit Martinez put out on Juan Carlos. Dominique was an emotional powder keg, and the blame for her recent breakdown rested squarely on Juan Carlos's shoulders. If I were Martinez, I'd hire an assassin to rub him out too.

Bowie folded up his mess of a sofa bed, and the two of us sat side by side on the dusty, worn, patched-up converted couch, our feet resting on the cracked and scuffed coffee table. I polished off the last of my scotch.

"So why would Juan Carlos be stupid enough to accept a movie role down here in Florida knowing Martinez and his men are just lying in wait to off his ass?" Bowie asked.

"Someone must be protecting him," I said.

"Dominique?"

"Maybe. But one minute he's made her suicidal and the next they're cooing and kissing like newlyweds. It's hard to get a good read on her. Although he's certainly got some kind of guardian angel looking after him," I said. "Actually, he's got a lot of little angels around him. The guy gets more action than the backroom of a Bangkok massage parlor."

Bowie laughed, drained the last of his own scotch, and grabbed the nearly empty bottle of Johnnie Walker Black Label off the coffee table. I covered the rim of my glass with my hand.

"Please," I said. "One more and I won't be responsible for my actions."

"Works for me," Bowie said as he playfully tried to fill up my glass again.

He was smart and swarthy and funny and sexy, and I knew it was time for me to get the hell out of there. I set my glass down and stood up. "Think it's safe to go retrieve my car now?"

A disappointed look flashed over Bowie's face, but he quickly replaced it with a smile. "Should be. But I'll take you there just to make sure everything's cool."

"You okay to drive?" I said.

Bowie nodded, grabbed the keys to his van off the cluttered wet bar, and we headed out.

I felt a pang of guilt as we drove north back to Fort Lauderdale. Bowie and I had hit it off, and I could tell there was some simmering chemistry between us. He was definitely interested. So why didn't I mention I was already involved with a terrific guy back in Los Angeles? Charlie and I had been enjoying a wonderful, fulfilling monogamous relationship for the past three years, and I never once had the urge to jeopardize it in any way. But it gnawed at me that I didn't bring him up. Not once. What did that mean? Fortunately I was sober enough not to do something stupid that I would live to regret despite the not-so-subtle hints from my handsome, musclebound host.

I was paralyzed by my attraction to Bowie and how bad it made me feel, so he did most of the talking on the twenty-minute drive back to my car. I learned that he'd been born into a large Cuban family in the heavily Latino-populated city of Coral Gables. He figured out he was gay when he was fifteen and on the football team and wasn't too anxious to let go after tackling an opponent. When he got out of high school, he dabbled in a couple of careers before joining the Navy to ease some of the burden his parents had in supporting such a big brood. He wound up joining the Seals and partook in a number of top-secret missions worldwide before he fell victim to the military's "Don't Ask, Don't Tell" policy. He got involved with an officer and felt no obligation to hide it from anybody. The officer, though, turned out to be married with four children, a fact he kept hidden from Bowie. To save himself from a discharge, the officer reported Bowie as a homo, and he was promptly drummed out despite a stellar record. So much for a wobbly, ineffective policy to protect our gay military personnel. Most critics claim it's even worse now than before "Don't Ask, Don't Tell." Bowie moved back home, got his private detective's license, sank his life savings into buying the QE3, and opened up his own shop. His gumshoe work had been paying the bills for five years. Except when he took on cases for free like finding his cousin Calvin, who may or may not have fallen victim to Martinez's dirty doings.

When we reached Fort Lauderdale's oceanfront, Bowie shut off the headlights as we rolled to a stop half a block from my rented Taurus. It was dark and windy with just one lone street lamp illuminating the quiet and deserted construction site.

Bowie and I sat quietly scanning the area for any sign of Laurel and Hardy. They had obviously long given up on me returning to my car. It seemed pretty safe now.

"Thanks for everything, Bowie," I said and reached for the door handle.

"You know where to reach me if you need anything," he said, and then patted my knee with his hand. "I mean it. Anything."

He let his hand linger a moment on my knee. I froze, having no idea what to say. So I giggled. Like a damn schoolgirl. God, I hated when I did that. It was a nervous response and I did it all the time. Some casting directors used to call me "Dr. Giggles" after an obscure horror flick starring the actor who played the retarded office boy on *L.A. Law* in the eighties. It was a humiliating name, and I learned fast to control my annoying little giggle fits during auditions. But during moments like this, when a hot-looking ex–Navy Seal had his hand on my knee, well, there was just no holding back. It was like a bad case of the hiccups.

"Good night," I said, practically diving out of the car. He watched as I unlocked the Taurus and got behind the wheel. Before I turned the key, I imagined a stack of dynamite strapped to the bottom ready to blow me up at the turn of the ignition, but decided Martinez wouldn't try something like that before he found out my connection to Juan Carlos. I took a chance. The car roared to life before settling into a steady hum. I waved to Bowie, who sat in his van watching me, and hastily peeled away, heading straight for the Ritz Plaza in South Beach.

When I arrived back in the Ritz's "desperate to be as hip as its neighboring hotels" lobby, I took the elevator to my own floor, the same floor Juan Carlos was on. I marched down to his suite and rapped on the door. It was just after midnight. After a moment, I heard a familiar voice answer from inside.

"Who is it?"

"It's me, Juan Carlos, Jarrod. I'd like to talk to you."

"It's late. Can't it wait until tomorrow?"

"No. I'd really like to say this now."

I heard him unhook the safety latch and open the door halfway. He was naked except for a white cotton towel draped around his waist. He had a half-eaten green apple in his hand and a sharp pocketknife to slice it with.

"What?" he said huffily.

"I know who she is."

"Who?"

"Dominique. I know she's Javier Martinez's daughter."

I turned to go.

"Wait. Who's Javier Martinez?" His face feigned innocence.

"Don't," I said.

"Don't what?"

"Don't pretend you don't have a clue what I'm talking about. I know you have a history with Austin Teboe at the Nexxt Café. I know you had an affair with Dominique and broke her heart and pissed off her father, who unfortunately for you is a violence-prone mob boss. And I know you're cheating on Laurette with both men and women."

His face darkened. I was becoming more of a problem than he had anticipated. He took a big bite out of his apple and let the juice run down the corners of his mouth. Then he casually waved the pocketknife in front of me as he spoke.

"You think you know everything, don't you?"

"No. I still don't know why you killed Austin Teboe."

"How many times do I have to tell you? I didn't kill anyone!" he said, gripping the handle of his knife so hard, I thought his knuckles would pop out of his skin.

"Well, then who did?"

"I don't know. I'm as much in the dark as you."

I nodded, not saying a word, wanting to let the deafening silence hang in the air. Juan Carlos, ever the actor, couldn't let the silence go for too long. It might force him to reflect on his actions.

"I don't know who is gossiping about who I may or may not be sleeping with, but it's bullshit, you hear me? Bullshit!"

"I saw you at the Sand Drift Motel. He was a cutie."

His face went pale.

"And I wasn't the only one," I said. "A couple of guys on Martinez's payroll were there for the show too."

I thought he was going to faint. He fell against the door, and grabbed the knob to steady himself.

"They . . . they saw me with . . . him?"

"Yeah, they did," I said with a twinge of insincere sympathy. "Bummer."

Juan Carlos dropped the apple, and his hand shot out and grabbed my arm, pulling me closer to the door. In the other hand, the sharp tip of the pocketknife was a quarter of an inch from my belly.

"Don't mention any of this to anybody, do you hear me?" Juan Carlos said, his voice full of desperation. "Promise me, Jarrod."

"Laurette is my best friend," I said as I kept my eyes focused on the knife's blade. I now felt it straining against my skin just to the right of my belly button. It was about to puncture through and draw blood.

I looked up into his eyes. They were wild with fear. He was on the edge. And for a minute I was afraid I had overplayed my hand. As the knife pressed into my gut, I suddenly had the sick feeling I was about to befall the same fate as Austin Teboe.

Suddenly a woman's voice came drifting out from the bathroom inside Juan Carlos's room. "Darling, is it room service? Did you order more wine?"

It was Viveca. I caught just a glimpse of her as she strolled toward the door in a Victoria's Secret red lace bra and panties. For a woman in her late forties, she still looked like she could easily grace the cover of their summer catalog. I was impressed.

Panicked, Juan Carlos withdrew the knife and seethed, "Good night, Jarrod." He slammed the door in my face.

I just stood there. The more I baited Juan Carlos, the more nervous he got. And with Juan Carlos ready to snap under the pressure, there was no telling whom he would take down with him. As I lifted my *Hairspray* T-shirt to see a trickle of blood slide down my belly and stain the elastic band of my Calvin Klein briefs, I was pretty sure I would be the first one on his list.

Chapter 20

After sticking a Band-Aid on my slight flesh wound in my room, I checked my messages on the cell. I only had one, from my parents. My mother cooed about how nice it was to see me if only briefly, and my father offered a few more well-thought-out theories in the Austin Teboe murder. I picked up the TV remote and started channel flipping. I was restless and couldn't sleep, and finally after shelling out twelve bucks for a pay-per-view showing of the Martin Lawrence stinker *Big Momma's House*, with Martin in drag, I was able to catch a couple of hours of sleep before the phone startled me awake. I reached out from under the covers, snatched the receiver from its cradle, and grunted.

"Good morning, Jarrod! Rise and shine!" a cheery voice chirped. It was Amy Joe, the perky production assistant.

I rubbed my eyes, shook my head, and tried focusing on the clock: 5:32 A.M.

"Amy Jo, it's really early," I said, trying to maintain my cool, even though I wanted to rip into her for waking me up after I had finally gotten to sleep.

"I know. We're running late. I'm waiting for you downstairs in the van."

"But I don't shoot today."

"Yes, you do. Today's your big death scene."

"No. I'm pretty sure that's tomorrow," I said.

"I think you better check your production schedule, Jarrod," she said.

"Hold on." I put the phone down, crawled out of bed, and crossed to the cheaply made acrylic desk near the window. I had laid out the week's production schedule sheets. I picked up the first one and examined it. Just as I had thought. Today was a few simple exterior scenes with the extra they had hired to play the homicidal maniac. Underneath it was tomorrow's schedule, which listed my last scene in the movie. A particularly bloody affair involving a meat cleaver and my skull.

I walked back over and picked up the phone off the night table. "I'm looking right at today's call sheet, Amy Jo, and I'm not scheduled to work."

"Check the date."

"March fifteenth."

"That's tomorrow's date, Jarrod. Look at the other page. The one where you *are* scheduled to work."

"March fourteenth."

"Bingo!"

My heart stopped. I had somehow inverted the pages when Amy Jo had slipped them under my door. Today was my most important day on the entire shoot, and I was operating on two hours' sleep. Not to mention the fact I hadn't even memorized any dialogue. I was screwed.

"Well, what do you know? You're right. Um, I'm going to need a little time up here," I said with a nervous giggle.

There was a long pause on the other end. And then, with just a hint of panic in her tone, Amy Jo said, "Are you trying to tell me you're not ready? Your call time is in ten minutes and it's a twenty-minute drive to the set."

"I'll be right down."

I slammed down the phone and raced into the shower, suppressing a scream as the ice-cold torrent hit my bare skin. I washed as fast as I could with some cheap no-brand soap supplied by the Ritz Plaza, scrubbed a dollop of Nioxin Bionutrient Scalp Therapy into my locks (an aging actor in his thirties needs a good hair stimulant), and quickly dried off. As I bolted for my closet, I jammed my left foot into the sliding glass door and howled like a three-year-old at Disneyland who didn't get his picture taken with Ariel. But I didn't slow down. I pulled on some jeans, threw on my soiled *Hairspray* T-shirt, stepped into a pair of Docksiders, and was good to go.

When I bounded out of the lobby and spotted Amy Jo's maroon van, I could tell from the look on her face that the hint of panic I had detected in her voice had now grown into a full-blown meltdown.

"Hurry up! Let's go! Let's go!" she barked.

I hopped into the passenger's seat, and we squealed away before I had a chance to even buckle up.

"I'm really sorry, Amy Jo," I said.

"No problem," she lied. "But if I get fired over this, would you put in a good word for me on your next movie?"

"They're not going to fire you. I'll make sure they know this is my fault," I said, knowing full well that at the bottom of the totem pole, she would bear the brunt of everybody's wrath. I kept thinking, "They can't fire her, because after this movie I'll probably never work again so I won't ever be able to give her any kind of recommendation."

We broke speed records to reach the Coral Gables campground set. Amy Jo was impressive maneuvering expertly in and out of traffic. As we pulled up to the makeup and hair trailer, I noticed Stella standing outside, sucking on a Virginia Slim and tapping her foot angrily.

"You are so fucking late," she bellowed.

"I know, I know. Don't blame Amy Jo. I didn't know I was shooting today," I said.

She hauled me into the trailer and started slapping globs of base on my face as I picked up some sides off the counter and read them over. Luckily there wasn't a lot of dialogue in my pivotal death scene. Just a lot of screaming and lines like, "Run, Joey, run!" as I sacrifice myself to save my son. I wondered if the "Run, Joey, run!" line was an homage to that old seventies ballad by David Geddes. That was before I realized there would actually have to be a modicum of depth required in the script, and depth was one thing this opus sorely lacked.

Amy Jo poked her head inside the trailer. "They're ready for you on set, Jarrod," she said.

"Jesus, I haven't even done your hair," Stella said. "Forget it. I'll do it in final touchups. You better go, Jarrod, before Larry starts yelling."

I dashed out of the trailer and over to the campground set, where the crew waited for me. Viveca, in a flattering yellow sundress, flirted with the crew as I said my good mornings and walked over to my mark. The lighting technician and a couple of his assistants immediately buzzed around me to make sure I was lit properly.

Viveca turned and offered me a bright smile. "Good morning, Jarrod."

I was sure this was the first time she had ever deigned to speak to me. "Good morning."

"Sleep well?" she cooed.

"Not really, no."

"Me neither. I was up *all* night," she said with a playful wink. We both knew where she was last night, and she seemed mighty proud of it. I guess it was our little secret. I didn't know much about Viveca, nor was I anxious to find out more. She struck me as too flighty and girlish for a woman in her late forties or early fifties. Her behavior annoyed me, and it took every last ounce of self-control not to offer her my opinion. But I wasn't about to start yet another feud with a costar. I was in enough trouble already.

So I plastered a conspiratorial smile on my face. "That's too bad you didn't get any sleep. Must have been something you ate," I said, returning her wink. "You go, girl."

She erupted in laughter. "You're so naughty. I love you." I had called her a "girl" so in her mind we were now the best of friends.

Larry ambled onto the set, gave me the once-over, and then turned his head and yelled, "Stella, get over here and do something with his hair! And can we get some drops for his eyes? They're all bloodshot. He looks like shit." Larry looked back at me suspiciously. "What's the matter? You just get up?"

"Of course not. I just thought after the turmoil and trauma my son and I have been through up to this point in the story, I would be looking awfully run-down and exhausted."

"Christ, don't tell me you're one of those method actors," Larry said, making a big show of rolling his eyes. Stella was all over me now with her eyeliner pencil and a wooden brush that she wrenched through my hair.

"No," I said, "I just want to be truthful."

"Okay. Whatever. Let's shoot this." Larry left momentarily to inspect the shot.

Stella gently placed her hand above my eyes and let loose with a shot of Alberto VO5 hairspray to hold my freshly combed locks in place. "You sure pulled that one out of your ass," she said, smirking.

"Do you think he bought it?"

"For him not to, he'd have to stop thinking about himself for one second. And we both know that's never going to happen."

Stella stepped back and nodded, satisfied with her handiwork.

We were ready to roll. I looked around for the tiny terror playing my son, but he was nowhere to be seen. "Where's Simon?"

Larry shuffled back over to me. "We don't need him for this scene. We'll have Maggie, the script coordinator, read his dialogue off camera. This is all about you and the killer, finally face to face." Larry glanced around the set. "Where is he, by the way?"

A grip pointed to a large man sitting in a spare director's chair. He wore a red and black plaid hunting jacket, Army-issue green pants, and a pair of black boots. A cartoon mask of Elmer Fudd covered his face. That was a last-minute touch added by Larry. He didn't want the killer's identity to be revealed until the end, but he didn't want the headache of hiding his face throughout the movie. So in the tradition of *Friday the 13th* and *Nightmare on Elm Street* (a couple of Larry's childhood favorites), he gave the killer a mask. And Elmer, in Larry's mind, was an inspired choice. After all, Elmer Fudd was a hunter who spent most of his time chasing after Bugs Bunny. But he was never able to catch him. Larry explained to us all in the hotel bar one night early on in the production that all of our characters represented all the other rabbits in the woods, and Elmer Fudd, who had spent years unsuccessfully hunting Bugs, was now going to take his frustration out on all of us. He'd kill and kill again, skin a whole slew of bunnies, but he would never be satisfied because none of us was truly Bugs Bunny, the elusive prey he could never beat. Larry saw the mask as the perfect symbol for the story he wanted to tell. I saw it as too many Jell-O shots after a long day of shooting.

"You ready to do this, big guy?" Larry called to the masked actor.

He nodded, stood up, and lumbered over to us. He carried a machete made of rubber. Larry turned quickly and whispered frantically in my ear, "The guy we hired in LA went AWOL on us, and we just hired this guy yesterday locally, but I can't re-member his name, so I just call him big guy, okay?"

"Okay," I said as I reached out to shake Elmer Fudd's hand. "Hi, I'm Jarrod. Nice to meet you."

"I'm Elmer Fudd," he said in a deep, scratchy voice. Everyone laughed appreciatively. Larry slapped him on the back.

"You feeling confident about what we're going to do here?"

Elmer nodded. Larry clasped his hands together and ad-dressed us both. "Good. Now, your son's been lost in the woods for almost a day. The whole campground has risked their lives searching the area, knowing a maniac is loose somewhere out there. You finally find him. Kneel down to hug him. Big reunion. Blah, blah, blah. The kid screams bloody murder. You turn to see Elmer standing over you. You tell the kid to run. He does. Elmer pushes you down on the ground with his boot. You do your "No, please, no!" line, and then he starts whacking chunks off your face with the machete. Everybody cool with that?"

"Sounds simple enough," I said.

"Excellent. We can wrap this scene up by lunch," Larry said as he jogged back over to the camera and slid into his director's chair. As the makeup and hair people rushed in for final touchups and the cameras began rolling, I tried again with my new costar.

"I'm sorry, I didn't catch your name?"

He didn't answer me. The goofy face of Elmer Fudd simply stared at me. And the open slits in the eyes weren't big enough for me to see anything behind it.

"Quiet on the set, please!" said the assistant director.

"We're rolling," said the cameraman.

"And action!" roared Larry.

Maggie the script coordinator, a been-there, done-that, bored veteran in her late forties, who had worked on countless produc-tions, read Simon's lines.

"Daddy, look out, he's right behind you," she said flatly, with all the enthusiasm and dedication of a DMV lifer.

Looking at empty air in front of me since the boy playing my son was absent, I shot out my hand and shrieked, "Run, Joey, run!"

"No, Dad, not without you," Maggie read directly from the script. A coma patient would have given more of a performance.

I turned to see Elmer Fudd raising the rubber machete over his head.

"No, please don't!" Shoot. As the words came out, I realized the correct line was "No, please, no!" and I hated disrespecting the writer's words, but Larry didn't yell "Cut!" so I kept going.

Elmer pressed the heel of his boot on my chest and shoved me down so I was on my back, struggling and wriggling like an upended cockroach. The guy pressed harder with his boot to the point where I could barely breathe. Either he was truly in the moment or he just didn't like me. I did what the script called for and covered my face with my hands and released a guttural wail. Elmer slashed down seven times with his rubber machete. He was supposed to stop a couple inches short of my head, but instead he managed to whack me five out of seven hits. Since this was a master shot, Larry had decided not to use the blood squibs that would illustrate my head coming apart. He was saving those for the close-ups.

"And . . . cut!" Larry said. He leapt up and excitedly ran over to us. "Beautiful! Just beautiful."

I was happy he was pleased. It would make up for some of my blunders so far, such as my disruptive cell phone and my call time tardiness.

Larry threw his arms around Elmer Fudd. "I love you, man. You're so fucking scary."

I waited for Larry to compliment me, but he was too preoccupied showering praise on my costar. "Man, I believed you were a nut job. I really did. You're a natural."

I tugged on Larry's sweatshirt. "Need me to make any adjustments for the next take?"

Larry threw me a cursory glance, suddenly aware of my presence. "No, Jarrod, that was fine."

I had come to the set totally unprepared so it shouldn't have bugged me that I was all but ignored. But it did. Actors live with so much rejection they crave any kind of positive reinforcement. We want everything we do to be adored and we have a need to be constantly showered with accolades as if every day we were the special guest on James Lipton's *Inside the Actor's Studio* series.

"I want to watch the playback on the monitor and then we'll go again," Larry said as he hustled back over to the phalanx of cameras and film equipment.

I turned to Elmer. "Nice job."

"Thanks," he said in his low, barely audible, raspy voice.

"For a minute there, I thought you were really having fun killing me."

Elmer removed his mask to finally reveal himself. Wendell Butterworth stood there, leering at me. His grotesque face was decorated with a sick, disturbing smile.

Chapter 21

Wendell Butterworth just stood there grinning as I sent all the furry little creatures of the forest scattering with my yelling. The startled crew descended upon us, and after I explained just who the man in the Elmer Fudd mask was, Larry marched up to him, poked a finger in his face, and with a quiet authority said, "You're fired. I don't ever want to see you near this set again, or I'll call the cops."

A couple of burly grips escorted him off the set.

"Can't we have him arrested?"

"For what?" Larry asked.

"I don't know. For impersonating an extra or something."

Larry put a comforting arm around my shoulder. "I don't think so, Jarrod. He gave us his correct name and social security number when we cast him."

I nodded, completely shaken. Now that he was sprung from prison, Wendell was never going to leave me alone.

"Jarrod, I'm so sorry," Larry said. "I thought he was a local. I hired him because of his intimidating bulk."

"It's okay, Larry, you couldn't have known."

Juan Carlos had arrived on the set just in time to witness the whole messy scene. He took great pleasure in watching my melt-down. Not even Viveca's little kisses on his shoulder or playful butt squeezes could draw his attention from me. After the initial flurry of drama had died down, Juan Carlos sauntered over and said with a self-satisfied smile, "Well, well, well. Jarrod has a stalker." He took a long sip of his coffee. "Maybe now *you'll* get a little taste of what it feels like to have someone following you around, watching your every move. How ironic."

"You know what amazes me the most, Juan Carlos?" I said, red-faced but remaining calm.

"What's that?" he said.

"That you actually know the definition of ironic, and can use it in a sentence."

He didn't like that one. He almost hurled his cup of coffee in my face. But he thought better of it, and strutted off in a huff.

Larry declared the campground a closed set for the duration of the shoot, and security guards were hired to patrol all access routes into the wooded park. Shooting resumed without incident, I finished my death scene with a strapping young grip filling in as Elmer Fudd, and we were wrapped by five-thirty in the afternoon. Larry was impressed with my performance (I didn't have to dig deep to find a lot of fear to play), and as the cast and crew dispersed for the day to various restaurants and bars, I was left alone in my trailer to change clothes and head back to the Ritz Plaza alone.

My cell phone rang. I pressed the talk button and cradled the phone between my left shoulder and ear as I stuffed my script and spare shirts into a gym bag.

"Hey, babe, just checking up on you," Charlie said. "Have a good day?"

I didn't want to run crying to Charlie every time something scared me. I had been standing up for myself since I was a little kid on the playground cornered by a gang of bullies, and I certainly was not about to become one of those whiny, victimized boyfriends who always rely on their better half to get through everything. On the other hand, this was the third time Wendell Butterworth had shown up, and I couldn't take it anymore.

"He's here, Charlie. He's here in Florida."

"Who?"

"Wendell Butterworth."

"Are you kidding me?"

I told him the whole ugly scene on the set with Wendell pretending to split my head open with a rubber machete while wearing an Elmer Fudd mask.

"Christ, Jarrod, why didn't you call me the minute it happened?"

"Because I didn't want to disrupt shooting. We're half a day behind schedule as it is."

"Where is he now?"

"I don't know. They tossed him off the set immediately. He could be anywhere."

Charlie took a deep breath, and then said, "Okay, I don't want you going back to that hotel by yourself. I want you to stay with someone tonight."

I wasn't sure who that someone could be. I had been so single-minded in my mission to expose Juan Carlos as a philanderer and connect him to the Austin Teboe murder that I hadn't exactly made a lot of burgeoning friendships on the set. Amy Jo was ticked off at me for being late this morning. Stella had already mentioned she was going up to Palm Beach to pal around with some friends. Juan Carlos despised me so it was safe to assume his two female lovers, Viveca and Dominique, were in the same camp. Larry was my boss, and not about to do me any favors after I'd mucked up two takes of his movie with my cell phone. And Simon was the spawn of Satan and more dangerous in my mind than Wendell Butterworth. My parents were too far away. After racking my brain, there was really only one person whom I would feel safe staying with tonight and who would be open to putting me up.

"You got somebody you can crash with?" Charlie asked.

"Yes," I said. "Yes, I think I do."

"Good. I want you to call me when you get there so I know you made it."

"Okay."

"The chief is on the other line. I've got to go. Call me."

"Charlie . . . ?"

But he was gone. And I was alone again.

I finished packing up my gym bag, and hurried down the wooded path toward the parking lot. The Taurus was the last vehicle left. I was surprised no one had offered to stay with me until I was ready to leave given the dramatic events that happened earlier, but I wasn't about to win any popularity contests on this job.

I jumped behind the wheel and drove straight into the glittery lights of South Beach. I didn't stop until I reached a parking space marked VISITOR in front of a boat slip off Ocean Avenue occupied by the *QE3* houseboat.

As I approached the front door, I suddenly felt foolish. What was I doing? I was a grown man who could take care of myself, and here I was about to ask a complete stranger to put me up because I was too afraid to spend the night alone. Despite Charlie's orders, I wasn't going to be some kind of damsel in distress. No. I would go back to my hotel room, order a nice big juicy steak so I would have a sharp knife to defend myself with, and tough it out. I walked back to the Taurus and was about to get in when the door to the houseboat flew open. Bowie stood there wearing a pair of shorts and nothing else. The lights from the marina illuminated every contour of his muscular torso. Damn. It was going to be a lot harder to leave now.

"I thought that was you. I was making some dinner and saw

you through the kitchen window," he said, a warm smile on his face.

"I . . . I don't want to bother you. Go back to what you were doing."

"I've made enough for two. Why don't you come in?"

I wanted to. I really did. But it didn't feel right. No. I had to leave now.

But then again, I would just be doing what Charlie wanted me to do. Right? He was adamant. He didn't want me by myself tonight. I would be openly defying the wishes of my boyfriend. And what would that say about our relationship? I had gone against Charlie enough lately. It was time I started to listen to him. At least that was how I convinced myself it would be okay to spend the evening with Bowie Lassiter.

"Thank you," I said. "I'd love to."

Bowie opened the door wide, welcoming me inside.

After a feast of seafood pasta, spinach salad, and warm chocolate cake, Bowie and I settled down on his couch to polish off the last of our third bottle of Chardonnay, our bellies stuffed and our eyes drowsy. Over dinner I had told him about the Wendell Butterworth drama, and he was happy to know I trusted him enough to put myself in his hands. Figuratively, of course.

As we sat on the couch, our knees slightly brushed against each other's. I felt woozy and naughty and none of that was good. I had to go to bed. Alone.

"Bowie, I really appreciate you letting me stay here," I said, as I yanked my knee away from his so they were no longer touching.

"I have to admit," he said with a sly smile, "I was pretty stoked when I saw you loitering outside the houseboat."

"Loitering?" I said, feigning indignation. "I wasn't loitering."

"Yes, you were. You were debating with yourself about whether or not you were going to come in."

How humiliating. He was completely aware of my attraction to him.

"But I'm glad things worked out the way they did," he said as he reached out and planted a hand on my knee, drawing it back closer to his. Then, using my knee to steady himself, Bowie leaned in slowly. His lips were about to touch mine when suddenly I jerked back, spilling my wine all over his couch.

"Oh, damn, I'm so sorry," I said, wiping the already stained upholstery with my hand.

"Don't worry about it. It's white wine. And the couch is pretty much trashed already if you hadn't noticed," he said with a chuckle.

Our eyes met, and he took my hand. "Hey, I'm sorry if I was moving too fast for you. I just really like you a lot."

"Bowie, I'm so sorry. But I have to tell you, I'm in a relationship."

"Oh," he said.

"I'm not going to say you got the wrong impression. I gave you the impression I wanted you to have. I didn't mention it before on purpose, and I feel lousy about that."

"It's cool. Don't worry about it." He was trying hard not to look disappointed, but was having a difficult time of it.

My cell phone chirped from inside my coat pocket.

"Excuse me," I said.

"Sure." He stood up and carried the empty bottle of Chardonnay into the kitchen. I fumbled through the pockets of my coat before finding the one storing my cell phone.

"Hello?" I said.

"Hey, babe," Charlie said. "Did you get to your friend's safely?"

"Yes," I said. "I'm here now."

"Good. You don't know how much better that makes me feel."

"I'll call you tomorrow from the set."

"No need to do that. I'll be there by then."

"What do you mean?"

"I'm at the airport now," Charlie said. "I'm taking an overnight flight to Miami that arrives in the morning. I'll be there by six."

"Charlie, really, you don't have to—"

"I know I don't have to," he said. "I want to. I want to see you. And I want to be there with you if that freak pops up again."

I glanced over at Bowie. He was scraping a few stray noodles from the seafood pasta off our plates into the garbage can before stacking the dirty dishes in the sink. He caught me looking and I swiftly averted my eyes.

"So where are you?" Charlie asked. "I'll just come there to pick you up."

"No," I said much too quickly. "Let's meet back at the hotel. The Ritz Plaza. You have the address."

"Okay, sounds good, babe. Sleep well."

"Good night, Charlie."

I was about to hang up when I heard his voice pipe up again. "Wait. What's the name and number of your friend so I can call in case the flight's late or something?"

I hesitated, but in the interest of full disclosure, I said. "Bowie Lassiter."

"Are you serious?" he said.

"Yes. He lives off Ocean Avenue—"

"On a houseboat called the *QE3*."

"How did you know?"

"Jarrod, that's my friend. The one in Miami who I've been calling for information."

I could almost hear God laughing.

Chapter 22

"You're *that* actor? Charlie's boyfriend?" Bowie said as he grabbed his wineglass, swished the last of his Chardonnay around, and then swallowed it in one big gulp.

"Small world, isn't it?" I said, instantly embarrassed by the lameness of my response.

I was still reeling from the shock. So was Bowie. After hanging up with Charlie, I knew I had to disclose everything. I didn't want any secrets coming back to haunt me. Secrets inevitably have a way of doing that.

"It makes sense now that I think about it," Bowie said. "Charlie called me to find out the dirt on Martinez, and then I run into you spying on him. Kind of funny we didn't figure it out before."

"Yeah, it's a laugh riot," I said. I wanted to get out of there. I was so consumed by guilt and confusion, and now with Charlie winging his way south, I had a desperate need to regroup. "Bowie—"

"Hey," he said, stopping me. "No worries. You were up front with me. You told me you were involved before anything happened. Everything's cool."

"So you and Charlie are old friends?"

"Yeah," he said with a smile. "*Just* old friends."

"He's on his way to Florida," I said. "I told him I'd meet him at the hotel when he gets here in the morning."

"What about this Butterworth dude?" he said.

"If I'm lucky, right now he's waiting for me in my hotel room with a loaded pistol, ready to put me out of my misery."

Bowie chuckled. "Seriously, you want me to escort you back there to make sure it's safe?"

Handsome *and* chivalrous. Charlie was on his way. Charlie was on his way. I had to keep telling myself that. "No. I'm a big boy. I can take care of myself." Yeah, right. The first sign of trouble, and I hightailed it over to a Navy Seal's houseboat to hide out. "Thanks for dinner. I had a great time."

"Me too," he said.

He walked me to the door. I resisted the urge to give him a hug good night. Hugs can lead to a kiss. And one kiss can lead to more kisses. And kisses can lead to . . . well, then you're screwed. Literally.

"Good night," I said.

"Good night, Jarrod."

I slipped behind the wheel of the Taurus, and as I drove back up Ocean Avenue toward the Ritz Plaza, I glanced through the rearview mirror and saw him standing in the doorway of the houseboat, watching me. He was still there when I turned right onto a side street, heading for Collins Avenue.

I got back to my hotel room without incident. Apparently Wendell had suspended his stalking activities for the night. Even delusional nutcases need their beauty sleep.

I climbed into bed, picked up my *Creeps* script off the night table, and turned to an earmarked page a third of the way through it to study the scene of me arriving at the campground with my son. We were scheduled to shoot it the day after tomorrow, and I needed to memorize the dialogue. Movie scenes are

almost always shot out of sequence. The order is designed to accommodate a wide variety of considerations such as location
availability and actors' schedules. So it was not unusual that my
death scene was in the can before my first appearance in the
movie. After reading it through a few times, my eyelids became
heavy, and I fought to keep them open, but within moments I
had drifted off to sleep.

I shot up at the sound of the phone ringing. No. It couldn't be
Amy Jo to pick me up. I had gone over the production schedule
five times to make sure I wasn't shooting today. "Please, God,
don't be Amy Jo!" I thought as I reached across for the phone.

"Hello?"

"Hi, babe, it's me," said a reassuring voice. Charlie.

"Hey, how was your flight?"

"Good. We're downstairs. What room are you in?"

"Eight-oh-six," I said.

"Okay, we'll be right up."

Click. Wait a minute. "*We'll* be right up?" Charlie wasn't
alone? Had he gone to his old pal Bowie's place first to pick him
up? Were we going to be the happy threesome sightseeing
around South Beach? I felt queasy, and those lingering pangs of
guilt only exacerbated my upset stomach.

I threw on a black and white *Creeps* sweatshirt that Larry had
handed out to the cast and crew on the first day of production,
and slipped on a pair of gray sweatpants just as there was a knock
on the door. When I opened it, Charlie stood there beaming,
and then enveloped me in a big bear hug.

"Man, it's good to see you," he said, squeezing so hard I
thought my bones would crack. He let up on his grip and then
kissed me gently on the lips. Maybe there was something to that
whole "absence makes the heart grow fonder" theory.

"Surprise!"

It wasn't Bowie. The voice was decidedly more feminine. And
more direct than a bulldozer. It could be only one person.

"Laurette!" I said, with as much fake enthusiasm as I could muster. This was not good. The jig was up for Juan Carlos. With his multiple affairs the talk of the set, it was only a matter of time before Laurette got wind of them.

She pushed her way into the room, inspecting the décor. "What a dump."

"Maybe you can get a suite or something that has better furniture," I said.

"Oh, please, I'm not staying here. I'm a couple of doors down at the Delano. Five stars. Very chic. Somebody saw George Clooney in the lobby checking in about a half hour before I did." It would only be a matter of time before Laurette befriended the entire staff and would know Clooney's room number.

Laurette plopped down on the bed, her purse in her lap. "I'll have Juan Carlos's things moved over. What room is he in? I want to surprise him."

Bad idea. Very, very bad. "I don't know," I lied. "But I'm sure he's already left for the set. I think he had an early call."

"Well, let's all drive over there. I want to see my husband," Laurette said.

Charlie noticed my visible hesitation. So did Laurette.

"What?" she said. "What aren't you telling me?"

"I think . . ." I wanted to spill everything. Dominique. Viveca. The young stud at the Sand Drift Motel. Possible mob ties. But I froze up.

"Come on, Jarrod," she said, clutching her purse tightly. "I can take it."

"Juan Carlos has gotten himself in some trouble. A dangerous guy named Javier Martinez wants to see him dead."

"Do you know how many people in Hollywood want to see *me* dead?" Laurette said.

"Martinez makes Tony Soprano look like Mr. Rogers. And his daughter is Dominique."

"The actress? The one from the wedding? The one who . . . ?"
I nodded.

Laurette's eyes brimmed with tears. Charlie put a comforting hand on her shoulder.

"And that's not all. There are more. Another actress in the movie. An older woman . . . and . . ." I really hated divulging all the sordid details. Laurette was so strong, but she sat on the bed, speechless and shaking. "And there's somebody else. A . . . a man . . ."

Laurette slapped her hands over her face and cried. I dashed over and threw my arms around her. Charlie's hand remained on her shoulder.

"I'm so sorry, honey," he said.

Laurette hunched over, sobbing, and said, "I don't believe it . . . I just don't believe it . . ."

"I know, I know . . ." I said.

"He told me I was the only older woman he's ever been attracted to. He made me feel so special."

"Laurette," I said softly, "didn't you hear what I said? He's also been sleeping with a man."

Wiping away her tears, she sniffled and said, "Oh, please. Half my boyfriends have been bisexual. You have to expect that when you date actors. But an older woman? That's such a betrayal!"

Laurette stood up, threw the strap of her purse across her shoulder, and marched for the door. "Come on, we're going over to the set right now to confront him."

"But, Laurette, he's shooting today. We can't disrupt the production."

"Movies come and go, Jarrod. This is my life we're talking about."

I glanced over at Charlie to garner some support, but he just shrugged. We both knew there was no stopping Laurette once she'd made up her mind.

* * *

When we arrived on the set, we were greeted by complete pandemonium. Juan Carlos was a no-show, and nobody knew where he was. The entire day had been structured around him, and now with him AWOL, Larry had nothing to shoot. As Juan Carlos's manager, Laurette was instantly embroiled in the controversy, and had to kick into her business mode in order to deal with the crisis. The production company was threatening to sue for the cost of the lost day, and Laurette was on the horn to her team of lawyers back in LA, keeping them apprised of the situation.

I was worried that Javier had made good on his promise to wipe Juan Carlos off the face of the earth. And deep down, I wasn't too distraught over it. But with Juan Carlos gone, any hopes of finding Austin Teboe's killer would probably disappear with him.

Charlie and I went to Juan Carlos's trailer to see if we could drum up any clues as to his whereabouts. It was locked up tight. I told Charlie to wait by the door while I fetched the keys from a production assistant. As I rounded the back of the trailer, I ran smack into a giant of a man, in a familiar plaid hunting jacket and wearing an Elmer Fudd mask over his broad face. I stood before him, paralyzed, my mouth open.

The big guy flipped the mask up. A kind face with an eager smile was underneath. And it didn't belong to Wendell Butterworth.

"Hi, I'm Eddie. I'll be playing the killer."

A rush of relief washed over me as I stuck my hand out and shook his. "Nice to meet you, Eddie."

My cell phone rang. I excused myself from Eddie, pulled it out of my pocket, and flipped it open. "Yeah?" I said impatiently, my eyes scanning the campground set for anyone who would have a key to Juan Carlos's dressing room trailer.

"Jarrod, it's Bowie. I think you better meet me."

"Why?" I said.

"It's Juan Carlos."

"Is he . . . dead?"

"No," Bowie said, his voice low and serious. "But I think you better see this for yourself. Can you meet me at the houseboat in twenty minutes?"

"Sure," I said and hung up. I grabbed Amy Jo as she scuttled past me. We were both in our matching *Creeps* sweatshirts.

"Amy Jo, I need to get into Juan Carlos's trailer."

She looked at me blankly. "I can't let you in there. It's against the rules."

"Look, he's missing and we're all going to lose our jobs if we don't find him. The best way to do that is to search his dressing room for some answers."

She stared me down defiantly. After all, I was the loser who slept late and almost got her fired. But the set was a madhouse because of Juan Carlos's disappearance, and if I did manage to find him, she'd be a hero for helping me get inside his trailer. She pulled it off her bulky ring of keys and handed it to me.

"Don't lose it," she said.

"Thanks," I said and ran back to find Charlie.

I searched around the set but didn't spot him. I asked around but nobody could tell me where he was. He was probably looking for Juan Carlos somewhere in the woods. Bowie was waiting, and it seemed important, and I had to make a quick decision.

So against my better judgment, after scanning the set one more time and not seeing my boyfriend, I hustled off to meet Bowie, the hot Navy Seal.

Chapter 23

Iknew if I had found Charlie and told him where I was going, it would open a floodgate of questions. And right now I had my hands full enough already with Austin Teboe's murder, Juan Carlos's extramarital escapades, and psycho Wendell Butterworth's sudden appearance in Miami. As I drove the Taurus through heavy midday traffic toward the boat slip housing Bowie's home, I knew it was only a matter of time before I would have to deal with the inevitable reunion between just old friends Charlie Peters and Bowie Lassiter.

When I reached the *QF3*, Bowie was waiting for me out front. He was decked out in a tight black tank top, khaki shorts, and a pair of sandals. A cheap pair of sunglasses shaded his eyes from the oppressive glare of the sun. I jumped out, and before I could even open my mouth to speak, he waved at me to follow and said, "Boat's ready. Let's go."

I decided not to ask him where we were going. I figured I'd find out soon enough.

I padded behind him silently as we circled around to the back of the houseboat, and walked down some metal steps to a small floating dock connected to the slip. Waiting for us was a sleek white 1990 Hydrostream Vegas XT twenty-one foot speedboat. Really cool. Bowie jumped in, turned the ignition, and the boat roared to life. I had barely stepped down inside of it before we were pulling back from the dock and hurtling out to the open sea. Sea spray splashed against my face, and I kept wiping it away to see where we were heading. Just ahead, only a few minutes from South Beach by boat, was the luxurious, world-famous Star Island. Rosie O'Donnell lives there. So does Gloria Estafan. It's a jetsetter's paradise boasting expansive, stunning multimillion-dollar homes, with tropical punch-colored flowers and towering palm trees swaying in the soft breeze and white caps from the electric blue-green ocean crashing gently onto the immaculate sandy beige beaches.

We circled around to the north side of the island until we were about two hundred feet out from a large mansion nestled into the foliage. Much of the property was hidden safely behind the trees and gardens, but wide picture windows gave the inhabitants a magnificent view of the bay.

Bowie cut the engine, and we floated up and down, riding the curve of the waves.

"So who lives there?" I asked.

"Javier Martinez. At least some of the time."

"You think Juan Carlos is in there? That maybe Martinez is holding him prisoner?"

Bowie shook his head. "No. Martinez and his wife are staying at their penthouse in the Delano. Except for a few of the household staff, the place is supposed to be empty. But it's not."

He picked up a pair of binoculars and handed them to me. "Go ahead. Check it out."

I peered through the binoculars. It took a few seconds for my eyes to adjust to the powerful lenses. I located the picture window on the back of the house and saw Juan Carlos inside, lying flat on a plush white leather couch. He was on his belly, totally nude, his left arm stretched out as his fingers mechanically stroked the fur on an enormous yellow-striped cat curled up on the floor.

"What's he doing there? Is he on some kind of suicide mission? What if someone catches him?"

"Keep watching," Bowie said.

Dominique. He must be there with Dominique. He was still seeing her. Mafia Daddy be damned. I had to admit, the guy had balls.

I saw a pair of hands slither down over the top of the couch and begin to massage Juan Carlos's shoulders, moving south down to his lower back and butt. Juan Carlos stopped patting the cat, wriggled happily at the sensuous touch, and smiled.

I steadied the binoculars. As the hands kneaded deeper into Juan Carlos's flesh, the mystery masseuse's face finally lowered into view. It wasn't Dominique. It wasn't even a woman.

I spun around to Bowie. "That's David Miller, the kid from Vero Beach who Juan Carlos has been sneaking around with!"

Bowie nodded evenly. "His name's not Miller. It's Martinez. That's Javier Martinez's son. Dominique's younger brother."

Oh . . . my . . . God.

I was drawn back to the scene inside the mansion. Looking through the binoculars, I saw Juan Carlos roll over on his back, reach up, and wrap his hands around David Martinez's neck, pulling him down over the couch on top of him. They laughed playfully, David hoisting himself up just enough to strip off his T-shirt. The two men locked lips, and began devouring each other before sliding off the couch and falling out of my eye line.

"They've been at it all day," Bowie said.

"But there are servants around," I said. "Won't they see? What's stopping them from telling their boss what's going on?"

"Are you kidding?" Bowie snorted. "Would you want to be the guy who tells a mafia kingpin that his only son is screwing around with another guy? The same guy who broke his daughter's heart?"

"I guess there's that risk of him wanting to kill the messenger," I said.

"He'll want to kill more than the messenger if he finds this out. And everybody in that house knows it."

I was awestruck by Juan Carlos's outright brazenness. He knew Javier Martinez had it out for him, and yet he openly and quite publicly returned to Miami to shoot this movie. He was practically flaunting himself right in front of the mobster's face. Even using the guy's own home as a little love pad. Maybe he was just insane. Or maybe he had someone high up in the Miami mafia protecting him. But who? And why?

In any case, Juan Carlos didn't appear to be the least bit concerned about his safety. At the moment, he was clearly more concerned about how long it would take for him to climax.

If Dominique found out that Juan Carlos was sleeping with her own brother, she would have been inconsolable. That might have been what brought her out to California. The reason she crashed the wedding at the Hearst Castle. She wanted to confront him with what she knew. Maybe even threaten him. Or threaten to tell her father. But she also wanted him back. So there was also the possibility that she tried to blackmail him. She could have told him she would keep quiet if he dumped her brother and came back to her. But Juan Carlos must have flatly refused. He knew Dominique loved him no matter how badly he treated her, and she would never knowingly put him in any kind of danger. Distraught, she tried drowning herself in the Pacific Ocean.

It all seemed plausible. But there was one big fat nagging question. What did Austin Teboe have to do with this whole scenario? Dominique obviously knew him. He worked for her family as a chef for years before he mysteriously quit. Had he and Juan Carlos met earlier than when they both worked at the Nexxt Café? Had they been introduced when Juan Carlos got romantically involved with Dominique? And what was the nature of their relationship? Maybe somehow things went sour between the two of them and Teboe sprung up in California with the intent of causing some kind of harm to Juan Carlos. Dominique found out about it and poisoned him to protect the man she loved. But where would a mafia princess get a lethal hit of monkshead? All I really knew was that Juan Carlos was playing a very dangerous game of Russian roulette, and sooner or later his luck would run out.

Chapter 24

Bowie shifted the gear of the Hydrostream Vegas XT, and we cut through the waves heading back toward Biscayne Bay and the dock housing the *QE3*. As we circled back around Star Island, I spotted another dilapidated boat with its motor off, bobbing up and down in the choppy water. A tanned, chubby fisherman with no shirt and wearing a Miami Dolphins baseball cap sat at the stern, chugging the last gulp from a bottle of Corona. Up front was another man, much heavier, his red flowery Magnum, P.I.–like Hawaiian shirt drenched from sweat. He clutched a Fujifilm digital camera and vigorously snapped pictures of the Martinez compound. I signaled Bowie to pass around in front of the boat so I could get a good look at the photographer. As we roared up and around the old wooden fishing vessel, the obese man at the bow stumbled back, startled by the sudden appearance of another boat, almost dropping his camera into the surf. It was Rudy Pearson. I ducked down fast, and Bowie powered us past the old barge before he had a chance to recognize me.

Why was Pearson so single-minded in his determination to dig up dirt on Juan Carlos? And for whom exactly was he working? *Soap Opera Digest* or the *National Enquirer*? Pearson's hatred for Juan Carlos was palpable, and there was obviously more history between them than either was willing to admit. I doubted Pearson was behind Austin Teboe's murder simply for the fact that neither acted as if they had ever met when I first saw them on the bus together driving up to the Hearst Castle. Still, my curiosity about this vengeful soap journalist was peaked, and I decided it was time to find out what his role was in the *Juan Carlos Show*.

When Bowie and I pulled up to the dock housing the *QE3* houseboat, it was going on four o'clock in the afternoon.

Bowie tied up the Hydrostream to a brass rail, and gently placed a hand on the small of my back. "Want to come inside for a drink?"

"No, thanks," I said, forcing a smile. "I better get back to the hotel. Charlie is probably there waiting for me."

Bowie raised an eyebrow. "Charlie's here in South Beach?"

I nodded, trying to conceal the flicker of guilt that undoubtedly flashed across my face. "I left him behind when you called. He's not too keen on me playing Mike Hammer."

"Well," Bowie said, swallowing hard. "I'd love to see him while he's down here . . . if you two have the time."

"I'm sure he'll want to see you too."

There was a long silence. Neither of us knew what to say next. The chemistry was crackling. Bowie finally took the lead. "Okay then. I'm going to head back out and keep a watch on the Martinez compound. I'll let you know if I see anything interesting."

Good. Back to the case. "Man, do you Navy Seals ever take a break?"

"I got a call from my uncle today. He was desperate for any news I might have about Calvin. It was tough telling him I had a big fat nothing. I've got to keep at it until I can give the poor guy some peace of mind about his son." Bowie averted his eyes to hide a show of emotion. His missing cousin was having a big impact on him, but he wasn't about to advertise it.

When I got back to the Ritz Plaza lobby, I picked up a house phone and dialed the reception desk. I watched as a lovely Cuban girl in a blue blazer answered my call.

"Reception, may I help you?" she said in a cheery voice.

"Yes, I'd like to leave Rudy Pearson a message, please."

"I'll connect you to his room right away," she said as her hand went down to transfer me.

"No! I know he's out covering a *Days of Our Lives* convention. I'm his editor at *Soap Opera Digest*."

She was probably wondering why I was offering so much information, but I was afraid if I stopped talking, she'd transfer me anyway.

"Just tell him to call the office when he gets a chance," I said, watching as she typed the message into a computer and hit the print button. It spit out into a tray, and she handed the piece of paper to an equally cute young Cuban male bellhop, who carried it toward the elevator.

"I'll be sure he gets it," she said.

"Thank you." I hung up the phone and dashed across the lobby to the bank of elevators where the cute bellhop was stepping into an available car. I joined him just as the doors closed.

"How are you today?" I said, smiling.

"Fine, sir. And you?"

Sir? Sir? I wasn't *that* much older than him. I suddenly liked him a lot less.

"What floor?" he said, finger poised.

I glanced at the floor numbers. Ten was lit up. I turned and nodded. "I'm going to ten too."

"Very good, sir."

When we reached the tenth floor, he stuck a hand out to hold open the door for me. I didn't want to go first. The plan was to follow him.

"After you, sir."

Okay, enough with the damn sirs.

This guy wasn't going to budge. So I stepped off first. I could go left or right. There was a fifty percent chance of getting it right. I went left. After walking a few feet, I didn't sense him behind me so I glanced back to see him heading down the opposite end of the hall. I should've gone right. I walked briskly to catch up with him, but slowed down as he stopped at a room and slipped my phone message under a door. Room 1032. He stood back up and saw me approaching. There was a slightly confused look on his face. I knew I had to offer some explanation.

"Dyslexic. Takes me an hour just to find the right room," I said, laughing.

"I see. You have a good day, sir."

Bastard.

After he turned the corner to get back on the elevator, I loitered outside the room until I saw a tired, overworked maid in a drab gray uniform complete with white apron slowly push a housekeeping cart up the hall. I marched up to her.

"Excuse me, I'm Mr. Pearson in room 1032. I've locked myself out of my room and was wondering if—?"

She looked up at me, and her mouth dropped open. "Sweet Jesus!"

"What?" I said.

"You're not Mr. Pearson! You're that little white kid from *Go to Your Room!*"

Sweet Jesus.

She howled and poked me in the ribs with a sausage-like finger. "Baby, don't even go there! I loved when you said that! I busted a gut every time!" She then swiveled her head around. "Is this one of those hidden camera shows?"

"You caught me . . . what's your name?" I said.

"Estelle."

"You caught me, Estelle. No, this isn't a hidden camera show. I just wanted to play a joke on my friend Mr. Pearson. I haven't seen him in a while and—"

"You know, I always had a crush on you. I wrote to that show on E! called *Star Dates*, where they hook you up with some has-been loser celebrity from way back. I told them if they ever tried to get a date for you, I was their girl! I wouldn't make fun of you afterwards like some of them do."

I was close to crying. Talk about hitting where it hurts. But I had to get in that room so I couldn't just walk away and lick my wounds.

"You know, I've thought about going on that show," I said.

"No shit. Really? You'd be a hell of a lot better than some of the jackasses they get. I mean, Eddie Munster? Come on! No. They need bigger names like you and Urkel. You know, real stars."

"Well, I'll make sure they contact you if I go on," I said.

Her eyes nearly popped out of her head. "Oh my word. Are you serious? Me on *Star Dates*?" I think she was more enthusiastic about being on TV than actually going out on a date with me.

"You're my pick. *If* I go on."

"You like to bowl?" she said, brimming with excitement.

"Love to."

She clapped her hands, envisioning our night together. And then, almost absent-mindedly, she pulled out her passkey and opened room 1032. "What about Italian food. You eat spaghetti?" she said.

"Every chance I get. Thanks for letting me in my friend's room."

"Please. You're a big star. I don't suspect you'll be stealing anything," she guffawed. I guess she hadn't seen the rap sheets of several of my fellow child stars.

"You're a peach, Estelle," I said as I headed in the room.

"You smooth talker," she said and she pinched my ass. Hard. I liked Estelle. A lot better than the bellhop who called me sir.

Once inside Rudy's room, I shut the door and looked around. I heard a hissing sound. No, more like the sound of running water. It was coming from the bathroom. Someone was in the shower. It couldn't be Rudy. There was no way he could've beaten me back to the hotel. No, Rudy was probably still floating out in the bay, snapping pictures of Juan Carlos and the Martinez boy in a wide variety of X-rated poses. Someone else was in the shower. I figured as long as I heard the water running, I had time to search the place. I went about opening suitcases and drawers in search of clues.

On the desk were two large scrapbooks. I opened the one on top. It was chock full of clippings and press photos of Juan Carlos. Soap articles written by Rudy about Juan Carlos. Any shred of news related to his comings and goings. A couple of candid photos of him leaving the studio. For all his obvious contempt of the soap actor, Rudy was acting like a fan. I picked up the second scrapbook and opened it. My heart stopped. This one wasn't a shrine to Juan Carlos. It was a shrine to me. Every page was filled with *TV Guide* articles, *People* magazine profiles, and Polaroid pictures of me when I was twelve years old, holding my mother's hand as we walked along the street in our neighborhood. There was one of me signing autographs for my adoring fans outside the sound stage where we taped the show. There was a signed script from *Go to Your Room!* that had been auctioned off for charity. There were even recent photos of me hiking in the hills with Charlie and Snickers. A shiver went up my spine. Was Rudy Pearson some kind of freakish fan?

With Rudy's mysterious roommate still in the shower, I poked around some more. On the night table next to one of the two queen-size beds I found Rudy Pearson's passport. I flipped through it and stopped suddenly. On the last page was a stamp from Canada. Nova Scotia. Rudy had been there just last month.

The best place to buy monkshead poison. I headed straight for the closet, pulled out two travel bags, and unzipped all the compartments. I found nothing but a few toiletries and paperback novels in the first, but as I sifted through the second one, I discovered a small vial in one of the tiny pockets. It was unlabeled except for a tiny black skull and crossbones emblem on a sticker in the back. I didn't need a label. I knew exactly what it was and where Rudy had got it.

My mind was racing. Rudy must have killed Austin. But why? Should I go directly to the police at this point or try and gather more evidence? Charlie would know what to do. Maybe this person in the shower could shed more light on what was going on. I crept toward the bathroom door with the intent of opening it a crack and getting a peek, but that's when the water stopped running, and I heard someone slide open the glass door and step out of the tub. Probably toweling off. I had run out of time, and didn't want to risk getting caught, so I quickly and quietly left the room. I would have to wait to find out who was shacking up with Rudy Pearson.

When I got back to my own floor, I was halfway down the hall to my room when the door to Juan Carlos's room flew open and Viveca marched out in a huff. Laurette flew out behind her.

"I don't want to see your face anywhere near this room again, do you hear me?" Laurette screamed, her eyes wet with tears.

Viveca kept her face tight, and it wasn't all from plastic surgery. She was stressed out.

Laurette didn't see me in her state. She withdrew back into the room and slammed the door shut. As Viveca passed me in the hall, I gently touched her shoulder. "Are you all right?"

"Of course I'm all right. I knew Juan Carlos was married all along," she said. She was lying. She was fighting back enough tears to fill Niagara Falls, but she wasn't about to cry in front of me.

"Juan Carlos is a boy," she said. "You can never invest much in a boy. I had a bit of fun, and now it's over." This was one steely broad. I had to give her credit. "I'll see you on the set tomorrow, Jarrod."

She kept walking toward the elevators, her heels grinding into the carpet as she went. I pulled out my key and entered my room.

Charlie sat on the bed, his arms crossed, his eyes narrowed and suspicious. "Where the hell have you been?"

Chapter 25

"I was with Bowie Lassiter," I said. No point in prolonging the inevitable.

Charlie nodded, a knowing look in his eye, as if he already knew the answer to his question before he asked it.

"Why couldn't you have just told me you were going to meet him?" he said.

"I couldn't find you," I said, flushed with guilt. "Nothing happened, if that's what you want to know."

Charlie didn't take his eyes off me. He was reading my face. He knew me better than anyone, and he would know if I was going to try and perform a little song and dance. Full disclosure was my best and only course of action.

"I didn't tell you I was going to meet him because I didn't want you to get the wrong idea."

"And why would I get the wrong idea?" Damn. He just wasn't going to let it go.

"I don't know," I said. "He's a good-looking guy, and we weren't exactly on the best of terms when I left to come down here, and . . ."

"And?"

"And maybe a part of me was a little bit attracted to him, but that doesn't mean I would ever act upon it . . ."

There was an unsettling silence. Had I just ruined the best thing that had ever happened to me in my entire life? Was Charlie going to throw his hands up and finally call it quits? My heart stopped, waiting for him to speak.

"Okay."

"What?"

"Okay, fine," he said.

"That's it?"

"Yeah. I get it. Bowie's hot. I'm not blind. Look, I can't expect you not to be attracted to other people. Hell, I am all the time."

"You are?"

"Sure. Look at all the buff guys in uniform I deal with day in and day out. I wouldn't be human if I wasn't attracted to some of that," he said.

"Which ones are you attracted to?"

"Does it matter?" he shrugged.

"Of course it does. I've been wracked with guilt over this, and now you tell me you ogle half the LAPD!"

He gave me a wink. "It's not like I'd ever act upon it." Point taken.

"You were right about one thing," I said. "Bowie's hot."

Charlie grimaced. He may have declared the obvious, but he hated me agreeing with him.

"But you are so much hotter," I said, crossing over to the bed and kissing him lightly on the lips. And the fuse on this potentially explosive situation was temporarily snuffed out.

Still seated on the bed, Charlie wrapped his arms around my waist and pulled me close to him. "Just remember, though, in order for us to stay healthy, we have to be honest . . . about everything." He wasn't scolding me. It was more matter-of-fact. Years of failed relationships talking.

I was really glad he was there.

* * *

Larry Levant shuffled around the shooting schedule and moved up some night scenes in an effort to salvage some of the day after Juan Carlos went AWOL. We were all called back to Coral Gables that evening to film a sequence early in the film where the campers converge after the first sighting of the masked Elmer Fudd madman. Charlie and Laurette accompanied me to the location, where I was rushed through makeup and immediately called to the set to join little Hitler Simon, Viveca, Dominique, and a rather contrite Juan Carlos, who took great pains to explain that he had misread the call sheet. Fat chance. Like anybody would be stupid enough to misread the call sheet. The other inconvenienced cast members had plenty of room to gripe, but I didn't have a leg to stand on.

When Juan Carlos returned to the Ritz Plaza, he never even saw Laurette. Amy Jo was on call to whisk him back to the set the second she laid eyes on him. So everyone was present for the uneasy reunion. Laurette tried her best to put on a brave face, but after a perfunctory hug and kiss, Juan Carlos withdrew from her, clearly uncomfortable by her sudden arrival. He mumbled some feeble excuse about spending the day sightseeing on his own. To her credit, Laurette didn't launch into a litany of accusations about Viveca when she first saw her husband. She was the utmost professional, playing her role of talent manager to the hilt, working overtime to patch up the rift between the production and its star. But Laurette was my best friend, and I knew she would let loose once she got him alone back at the hotel.

Larry was just happy his movie was back on track, and that there was still time to get a few feet of film in the can after a disastrous, wasted day. So he spent little time chastising his leading man. Instead, he barreled forward as if nothing had happened. He offered a quick speech explaining our motivation for the scene, which could basically be summed up in one word: fear.

And then, he bounded back behind the camera with his director of photography, and yelled, "Action!"

I was a glorified extra in this scene, holding my son's hand and listening as Juan Carlos explained the importance of watching out for one another, sticking together, and not allowing this maniac to pick us off one by one. It was the third scene in the picture that said the exact same thing. I was losing any hope that this sinking ship could be anything but a direct-to-video bust. But Juan Carlos was giving it his all again, and doing a bang-up job for once. I had to credit David Martinez. His talents in the bedroom undoubtedly gave our star an extra dose of confidence and charisma on this particular day.

"Cut!" Larry screamed. "Not bad. Let's reload and go again in five." The cast dispersed for makeup checks. Simon howled at his mother, Caitlin, to bring him some apple juice. Viveca grabbed the nearest mirror to check out her face. Dominique kept her eyes pinned on Juan Carlos, who sauntered over to Laurette with a boyish pout, his tail firmly between his legs. Laurette was on the phone to LA and ignored his arm, which had snaked around her back in an obvious ploy for attention.

I turned and looked for Charlie. He was nowhere to be seen. I snagged Amy Jo as she rushed by with her walkie-talkie. "Have you seen my boyfriend?"

"I think I saw him heading into the woods over there. He's probably taking a leak. It's too damn far to hike back to the port-a-johns from here if you really have to go." She kept moving, and with five minutes to play with, I decided to walk down the trail to find him.

It was dark now, and the trees took on a life of their own, blowing in the breeze, sweeping down over me as if I were a lost cherub in a spooky illustrated children's book. I saw some movement ahead, and as I drew closer, I saw the figure of a man, his back to me. I assumed it was Charlie zipping up his jeans. But as the wind blew through a thicket of trees to the right, enough light from the moon seeped through to illuminate the man in front of me. It wasn't Charlie. This man had a much wider frame and was about a foot and a half shorter. When he turned around, I saw the sad-sack face of Rudy Pearson.

"Well, funny how fate keeps bringing us together," I said, surprising him.

"What do you mean by that?" he said, fingering the camera looped around his neck.

"First I see you boating around Star Island taking all sorts of interesting pictures and now I run into you skulking about in the woods," I said.

"I'm not skulking! I'm just getting a story."

"I know. Juan Carlos. You're going to ruin him. Big yawn. The real story is Austin Teboe."

"Who?"

"I think you know who I'm talking about. The poor man who choked down some pretty awful poison at your buddy Juan Carlos's wedding?"

"Oh, right," he said, his eyes darting around to see who else was around.

"How was your trip to Nova Scotia?"

His eyes stopped darting and stared straight at me. "How did you know I went to Nova Scotia?"

I wasn't about to admit searching his room so I decided to play it vague. "I've got spies everywhere."

"I was there covering a soap convention. They're held all over the world, you know."

"No kidding," I said. "So what do you do at one of those things? Take pictures of the stars with their fans? Raffle off *As the World Turns* memorabilia? Buy a couple hits of monkshead poison?"

His eyes went dead and his voice was monotone as he spoke. "What are you trying to say?"

"It's just interesting to me that Nova Scotia is one of the few places you can find that particular poison, and that's exactly what Austin Teboe died from."

"I didn't kill him. I didn't even know him!" He was clutching his camera so tight, I thought he was going to crush it.

"Okay, then what aren't you telling me, Rudy?"

He opened his mouth to speak. Despite the night chill, he was sweating. And then another man, much bigger than Rudy, stepped out from behind the tree a few feet from where Rudy stood.

"Charlie?" I said.

It wasn't Charlie. It was Elmer Fudd. Or Eddie, the big lug playing the killer in the movie in costume.

I smiled. "You gave us quite a start, Eddie. You too lazy to walk to the port-a-johns too?"

Elmer Fudd nodded, and then pulled a long sharp knife out of the sheath attached to his wide, thick brown leather belt.

Rudy froze, unable to move as Elmer Fudd stepped slowly toward him.

"Eddie?" I said.

Rudy shivered as Elmer hovered over him. And as I watched in horrifying slow motion, Elmer grabbed Rudy from behind, hooking one arm around his neck and raising the knife up over his head with the other. And then, in one fast, sweeping motion, he brought it down, plunging the blade into Rudy's chest.

Blood spurted everywhere.

Rudy's eyes bulged, his body convulsed, and as Elmer released his grip, Rudy's body sank to the ground in a crumpled heap.

"Omigod!" I screamed. "Omigod!"

The man removed his Elmer Fudd mask. It wasn't Eddie. It was Wendell Butterworth.

Chapter 26

As Wendell stepped over the dead body of Rudy Pearson toward me, I whipped around and ran as fast as I could through the woods, yelling for help at the top of my lungs. My voice echoed through the night breeze as I kept my arms in front of my face while barreling through an endless barrage of swaying tree branches. I became disoriented from the darkness, unsure if I was even heading back in the direction of the movie set. I ran until my legs ached and I was out of breath, and then I crouched down behind a bush and looked back. There was an uneasy stillness. No sign of Wendell. After a moment's rest, I stood back up and turned around to keep running when I collided with a big man who grabbed me by the arms.

"No!" I screamed. I pummeled his chest and face with my fists, momentarily stunning him. But then, he pushed me away, and raised his hands up to deflect my vicious assault.

"Whoa! Jarrod, stop! It's me!"

Charlie. Thank God. It was Charlie.

"Wendell . . ." I managed to get out between heavy breaths. "Back there . . . he killed a man . . . with a knife!"

Charlie just stood there for a moment, making sure he heard

right, and then with a fierce resolve, he turned to head back, looking deep into the woods in the direction where I pointed. I lunged forward and grabbed him by the shirtsleeve.

"No way are you going near that maniac unarmed! We have to call the police!"

"He could get away!"

"I don't care," I said. "I'm not going to risk him getting you too. He's big and strong and crazy!"

Adrenaline pumping, Charlie was ready to take on this madman all by himself, but I gripped his arm tightly enough to press my point even further, and finally he stopped resisting me, and nodded. "Okay, let's go get some help."

Charlie knew which direction to go, and within two minutes we pounded onto the set, interrupting a take with Viveca. Before Larry could erupt in a tantrum, Charlie had commandeered Amy Jo's cell phone and was dialing 911. I quickly explained what had happened, and a small band of bulky teamsters grabbed some hammers and drills and a couple of lights, and we charged into the woods in pursuit of my childhood nightmare. I led the determined little army to the spot where I had witnessed Wendell stab Rudy Pearson. As we came upon the clearing, there was no sign of Wendell. Or Rudy Pearson's body. There was nothing. One of the grips on the crew shined a portable klieg light from the set on the entire area, and we scanned the leaves on the ground for any traces of blood. But there were none.

By the time the police arrived forty minutes later, the interest of the film crew in my story was waning, and a few started whispering to one another, speculating on whether or not I was drunk and making the whole thing up. You know those attention-seeking actors. Charlie stood firmly by my side. He knew my history with Wendell Butterworth, and his recent creepy appearances in the diner up in San Simeon, at Costco, and on the set of this movie. When investigators finished combing the area, the lead investigator, a handsome African-American man in his mid-forties with a close-cropped beard and a barrel chest, walked over to Charlie and me.

"Your killer must have moved the body in the time it took for you to come back with the cavalry," he said with a shrug.

"Well, can we put out an APB on Butterworth?" Charlie asked.

The investigator shook his head. "No, I'm sorry. We're having a tough enough time establishing that there's even been a crime."

"But I saw him kill a man!" I yelled. Charlie placed a gentle hand on my back, silently suggesting I rein it in a bit.

"Without a body, there isn't a whole lot we can do," the investigator said, trying hard to be sympathetic but anxious to move on to a real crime scene.

"Butterworth has a history of stalking Jarrod," Charlie said calmly. "He followed him down here and weaseled his way onto the set. He's a menace, a danger to society, and I think it's in everybody's best interest that we find him."

"If he's such a danger, why did the parole board up in Vacaville release him?" the investigator asked. He had a point. Without any proof, it was a waste of time trying to enlist the police to help us. Sooner or later, Rudy Pearson's body would have to turn up. Some hiker or a couple of hunters would stumble across his corpse, or a piece of it, or something. And then we'd be in business. But until then, I felt completely exposed. It was as if Wendell Butterworth was anticipating my every move, taunting me, and it scared the hell out of me.

As we walked back to the set, I caught a few looks from the crew. They weren't accusing looks, but they betrayed a sense of skepticism. They had all witnessed my world-class freak-out when Wendell turned up on the set in the Elmer Fudd mask, and they were contemplating my current mental state. Maybe I was so discombobulated from all the stress, I was starting to see things. After all, it was dark in the woods, and swaying branches from a tree can create the illusion of a person, and wouldn't there have been just a tiny spec of blood if Butterworth had indeed stabbed Rudy Pearson repeatedly and then dragged the body away? How could I blame the crew for eyeing me suspiciously? A small part of me was beginning to question what I'd seen out there myself.

Larry wrapped for the day, having completed only half a scene. We were now two whole days behind schedule thanks to Juan Carlos going AWOL and my fantastic murder-in-the-woods adventure. For a young guy, Larry looked as if he was on the verge of a stroke. He was pale, gaunt, and grim. I was about to wish him a good night, but decided the last voice he wanted to hear was mine.

Laurette and Juan Carlos had left for the hotel long before all the drama blew up, and most of the actors had cleared out the minute the police were contacted. Nobody, not Viveca, Dominique, or even the little brat Simon, wanted to be associated with a possible tabloid scandal that could adversely affect their career. There was only a handful of crew members left to clean up and close down the set for the night as Charlie and I made our way to the trailer I shared with several of my costars.

"My bag's inside. Let me just get it, and then we can go," I said to Charlie. Charlie sauntered over to an ice cooler, bent over, and perused the soda selections as I opened the door to the trailer and entered.

"You gave me quite a fright," a deep voice said. I nearly jumped out of my skin before I spun around to find Bowie sitting in a folding chair, his hands clasped behind his neck.

"Jesus, Bowie, what are you doing here?" I said.

"Got a friend in the Coral Gables Police Department. He gave me a ring after your 911 call came in. Came out here as soon as I could," he said.

"Well, I don't think they'll be giving me a Good Citizen Award anytime soon. I'm not sure they believe my story."

"They don't. They think you're making it up to get Butterworth off the street and out of your hair."

I nodded. Big shocker. "Do you believe me?"

"Of course."

"Good. Because I want to hire you."

Bowie raised an eyebrow curiously. "To do what?"

"I want you to prove Wendell Butterworth killed Rudy Pearson. I want you to find the body, tie that freak to the murder, and send his ass to prison. And this time I don't want him ever getting out."

I was shaking. I had kept it together for so long. But now, in front of a man I had known for only a few days, I was coming apart. Ever since the parole hearing in Vacaville, I had been haunted by all those disturbing images from my childhood. Over and over I would see the contorted, wild face of Wendell Butterworth trying to snatch me from my home while I was eating breakfast or attempting to shoot me while I sat in a car with my mother. I had never truly gotten over those traumatic events, and now they were coming up again as Wendell continued to insert himself into my life. I couldn't take it anymore. I just wanted it all to go away. I was tired of worrying, tired of running, tired of waiting for my past to finally catch up to me.

Bowie stood, quietly walked over to me, and put his arms around me. He squeezed me tight and whispered in my ear, "Don't worry, Jarrod. I'll do whatever it takes to make him go away."

"Thank you," I said, feeling weak and helpless, and hating myself for it.

I felt a cool rush of air from outside. Someone had opened the door to the trailer. I looked up to see Charlie's crestfallen face staring inside at me as his old friend embraced me.

Chapter 27

Bowie immediately sensed me tensing up, and let go, turning to see Charlie hovering in the doorway.

"Charlie, man, how long has it been?" he said as he walked over and gripped his hand.

Charlie shook it, but his face remained hard and unresponsive. "Been a while, Bowie. Been a while."

The two friends just stared at each other awkwardly, neither knowing how to break the stifling tension.

"We should get together while you're in town," Bowie offered. "Kick back a few, talk about old times at the academy."

"I'm not sure how long I'm going to be down here," Charlie said. The chill in the air was enough to frost over the smudged, grimy windows on the trailer.

There was a long, agonizing silence. Finally, Bowie said, "Well, you've got my number. Give me a call." And then Bowie turned to me. "I'll get to work right away on that matter we discussed." He wasn't willing to talk about the details of a case in front of anyone but his client. Bowie was the utmost professional. He nodded to Charlie, who had to move to the side to let him pass.

When we were alone, I sighed, and said, "Charlie, he was here when I came in, and I was a little shaken up over the whole Butterworth mess, and he just agreed to—"

"I really don't want to hear it, okay, Jarrod?" Charlie fought hard not to explode. In a way, I wished he would. Get it all out. I could reassure him that nothing had happened, and we would be done with the whole matter. But that wasn't going to happen. He clearly didn't want to deal with me at this moment, and he turned to leave.

"Make sure one of the crew walks you to your car in case Butterworth's around," he said, and then he was gone.

I started to chase after him, but stopped when I saw him climb aboard the last transportation van back to the hotel. He never even turned to see if I was watching as they drove away from the set. I was on my own, not about to stick around for any length of time on the off chance that Butterworth was lurking about. The psycho had already proven he could mysteriously appear anywhere at will, like some ghostly apparition fiercely determined to haunt me. I ran down the wooded path to the parking lot, jumped into the Taurus, locked all the doors, and drove back to the Ritz Plaza in South Beach.

When I got back to my room, the red message light was blinking on the telephone next to the double bed with the tacky red floral print spread. God, I hated this room. I scooped up the receiver and punched the voice mail button, praying it was Charlie wanting to meet me and talk everything out and resolve all this drama over my budding friendship with Bowie.

"Jarrod, it's me. I'm at the Delano in the bar. I need to speak with you right away. Get over here as soon as you get this," Laurette said, her voice frantic. There was a click. The message had been left twenty minutes ago.

The much fancier, hipper Delano Hotel was right next to the Ritz Plaza and it took all of four minutes to get there. When I entered the restored Deco lobby, bathed in milky white draperies hanging from soaring white columns, I quickly crossed to the bar, where I found Laurette hanging off the arm of George Clooney. Damn. She was right. He was staying at the hotel. Laurette had pinned him against the bar and was working on what was probably her fourth or fifth Cosmopolitan. The bartender, dressed from head to toe in white, the signature color of the Delano, watched her with amusement as she prattled on to Clooney about their shared Kentucky heritage, which she'd read about in *People* magazine.

"I understand people from Kentucky, George, being from Lexington myself," she said, her words slow and slurred. "I could really help jump-start your career, get you moving in the right direction."

George flashed his megawatt smile. He was enjoying this. "Yeah, things have been pretty bleak lately on the work front."

"Are you sure you're from Kentucky?" Laurette said, trying to focus on his face.

"Yeah, why?" George said.

"Because when you smile, you've got all your teeth." Laurette guffawed and slapped her knee. Thrilled she'd made a funny.

It was time to intervene. I touched Laurette gently on the arm. "Excuse me. Sorry to interrupt."

Laurette was not happy someone was screwing up her quality time with George. She swiveled around on her bar stool with a scowl, and for a moment, I thought she was too drunk to recognize me.

"I came as soon as I got your message," I said. "What's the emergency?"

Laurette sat up straight, and made an attempt to be lucid and professional. "George, this is one of my top clients as well as my best friend, Jarrod Jarvis." She then leaned into George and whispered loud enough for the whole room to hear. "He's really not one of my biggest, but he is my friend, so I have to say that."

George shook my hand and smiled. "Nice to meet you, Jarrod."

"You probably don't remember, but I played an Amish burn victim in the first season of ER. But I had a lot of makeup on . . ."

"Of course I remember," George said. "Noah Wyle was so stoked to have you on the show. He was a big fan of *Go to Your Room!* He wouldn't shut up about it."

"Really?" I said.

"Oh yeah, he didn't want to embarrass you by making a big deal about it, but every day, he'd pop into my trailer and go—"

George and I did it together. "Baby, don't even go there!"

Wow. I was bonding with George Clooney. Maybe he'd put me in his next movie and I could bid adieu to these cheap horror films. Now I was dreaming.

"Well, I'm meeting some friends so I better go," George said.

Laurette slapped a business card in the palm of his hand and winked at him. "Call me. We'll talk."

He held the card up and, ever the consummate actor, pretended it was like a winning lottery ticket. "Thank you, Laurette." And George Clooney waltzed out of our lives. We both let out an audible sigh.

"He's just one of those people who gets better looking with age," Laurette said, before grabbing the bar rail to keep from falling off the stool.

"People say that about me," I said, hoping she would agree. She didn't. So I took a seat next to her at the bar and ordered a vodka tonic from the bartender.

Laurette grabbed the neck of her Cosmopolitan glass and lifted it unsteadily to her lips, splashing the drink over the sides and onto the floor. She took a small sip, and put it down again. "Juan Carlos ditched me."

"What do you mean ditched you? Did he ask for a divorce?"

"No, nothing like that. We were walking along Ocean Avenue, and we were right in the middle of a serious discussion about our marriage, and how trust is important to me, when suddenly he spotted these two men following us. He got really nervous and ducked inside a sidewalk bar to go to the bathroom, but he never came out. I went inside and looked everywhere. He was gone. I was so upset. And so were the two men who had been following us."

"What did they look like?"

Laurette shrugged. "I don't know. Big guys. One white. One Hispanic."

Javier Martinez's goons. No doubt about it. "Did they follow Juan Carlos inside?"

"No, they hung around out by the street, a few feet away from me. I guess they thought he wouldn't just leave me standing there like a fool. Their mistake."

"Laurette, I can't stress enough the kind of danger Juan Carlos is in. Those men work for Javier Martinez, and he could do some serious damage to both him and you."

"Please, I've dealt with bigger sharks in Hollywood," she said, staring straight ahead toward the entrance to the hotel bar.

"I'm afraid he may already have gotten to Juan Carlos," I said.

"Omigod."

"What?"

"Over there," Laurette said. "The two guys who were following us. They're here."

I whooshed around and saw the two giants, wearing a couple of print silk shirts, white slacks, and sandals, amble in and survey the room. Satisfied, they turned and signaled behind them. Javier Martinez, in a light beige linen suit, swept in with a gorgeous woman in her forties on his arm. She was poured into a tight yellow dress, and boasted a fortune of sparkling Harry Winston jewelry on her neck and wrists. I immediately recognized her as Juan Carlos's paramour and costar, Viveca.

A host, also covered in white, scurried up to them and said in the most pleasant voice he could muster, "Good evening, Mr.

and Mrs. Martinez, I have a private table waiting for you in the back."

I was floored. Viveca was Javier's wife. No wonder Juan Carlos was in such big trouble. He was sleeping with almost the entire Martinez family. Viveca. Dominique. David. Forget Bob Dole. Juan Carlos was the perfect spokesman for Viagra.

"What a slut. She's already married and she's fooling around with my husband. I'll scratch her eyes out," Laurette said, making a halfhearted move to stand up, but one little tug on her sleeve from me, and she was firmly planted back on the bar stool, swaying a bit, but settled.

"As much as I'm a fan of *Dynasty*-style catfights, I'm not sure confronting a mobster's wife is such a good idea."

Laurette's eyes began to well up with tears. "I've been so stupid, Jarrod. So stupid." She laid her head on my shoulder, and I wrapped my arms tightly around her.

"You can't help who you fall in love with," I said. I thought about Charlie. And where he could be.

Laurette opened her purse and pulled out some Kleenex. She blew hard and then wiped some tears away. Out of the corner of her eye, she saw Javier and Viveca disappear around a corner to a private space in the back of the bar.

"That bitch shouldn't have even been in the movie. But her husband was financing the picture, and he only agreed to cough up the money if they gave his wife a big part," she said.

It hit me that Viveca and Dominique were using different last names to conceal both their mother-daughter relationship and their connection to Javier Martinez.

"Javier financed the movie starring a man who was sleeping with his wife and daughter and son? Oh boy. No wonder Martinez hates him so much."

"That dirty cheating louse!" Laurette sobbed. "How could he do this to me? I gave him the best weeks of my life!"

Laurette's cell phone chirped from inside her purse. She pulled it out and snapped it open. Sniffling, she said, "Hello?" After a moment, her face darkened and she turned to me. "Bad news," she said. "He's still alive."

"Where is he?" I said.

Laurette listened and nodded and then hung up the phone. She downed the last of her Cosmopolitan, and slid off the stool. "Come on. We're going to meet him."

"You want me to come with you?"

"Yes. I want you there to make sure I don't kill the bastard."

Juan Carlos had told Laurette to meet him at his former place of employment, the Nexxt Café, a trendy hotspot for the locals located squarely in the middle of upscale Lincoln Road. It was a short ten-minute walk from the Delano, and when we arrived, the outdoor tables were nearly filled to capacity.

"He said he was at a table off to the side," she said as we both scanned the crowd of diners. I spotted him first. He sat alone at a marble table wearing a blond wig, dark glasses, and a heavy brown overcoat. Given the sweltering eighty-degree weather, the sloppy disguise made him stand out like a Hassidic rabbi in an Easter parade.

"There he is," I said, guiding Laurette's gaze with my finger. "I recognize the wig and coat from the movie's wardrobe department."

Laurette gripped my hand as we maneuvered through the myriad of tables to get to Juan Carlos. I whispered into her ear, "Now just stay calm. Let's hear what he has to say. Don't freak him out by laying into him too quick."

"You're right," she said. "We'll just let him talk."

As we circled in front of Juan Carlos and sat down in the pair of empty seats at the table, Juan Carlos didn't move. He just stared straight ahead, his eyes hidden behind the dark glasses.

"You imbecilic asshole!" Laurette screamed. "How dare you

drag me into this mess! What kind of stupid moron are you, seducing the whole family of a sadistic mafia killer? Do you have some kind of death wish?"

So much for letting him talk.

"Don't just sit there, you lying piece of shit! Answer me! Do you hear me? Answer me!" she said, grabbing a fistful of his overcoat and shaking him. He teetered a bit, and then dropped face first into his plastic black bowl of Chinese chicken salad. Juan Carlos Barranco was dead.

Chapter 28

Laurette screamed, panicking the other diners and alerting the wait staff that something was seriously wrong. The wide-eyed hostess picked up the phone and dialed 911 when she spied us hovering around a slumped-over body in a bulky over-coat and a blond wig askew, revealing wavy jet-black hair underneath.

I grabbed Laurette and hugged her tightly as curious patrons craned their necks, most probably wondering if it was the food he was eating that did him in. With one arm draped around Laurette's back comforting her, I reached down with my other and casually lifted Juan Carlos's wrist and felt for a pulse. Nothing. He was definitely history. I wished I could muster up some kind of emotion, maybe a passing sadness, but what I wound up doing was suppressing elation. Every instinct was telling me Laurette was much better off without him.

"I can't believe he's gone," she cried, the words barely audible between sobs. I was not about to point out that three minutes ago she was ready to poison him herself for his multiple infidelities.

Even with a restaurant full of witnesses, I was not about to leave Juan Carlos's corpse alone for even a second. I had learned my lesson after witnessing the brutal slaying of Rudy Pearson, and with his body still missing, it allowed Wendell Butterworth to roam around free to stalk and murder me at his convenience.

The police arrived within minutes, followed by paramedics in an ambulance. The hostess with the big wide eyes pointed at Laurette and me accusingly, as if she had seen us do away with him ourselves, and the cops descended upon us to ask a barrage of questions. Charlie always told me to tell the cops everything during an interrogation. Don't leave anything out. You don't want something coming back to haunt you later. So Laurette and I spilled it all. The murder in San Simeon. Juan Carlos's extramarital activities. And most importantly, his making an enemy of Javier Martinez. The cops froze. They didn't like hearing that name. The last thing they seemed to want to do was rattle Martinez's cage. No telling what kind of trouble a man with his connections could stir up. Did Martinez own these guys? After I mentioned the Martinez name, the cop asking the questions briskly changed the subject.

"Any other enemies he had you can think of?" the cop asked Laurette.

"He was an actor with the lead in a feature film," she sniffed. "Half of SAG would like to see him dead."

The CSI investigator arrived to examine Juan Carlos's body. He was a hefty bald man in a blue windbreaker with a distracting mole on his left cheek. He wore plastic gloves and ate walnuts from a zip-lock bag as he scanned the corpse for any clues. He'd touch the head looking for bruises and then pop another nut in his mouth. Then he'd check the cold, dead arm, and follow it with another nut. I was completely grossed out. He caught me watching him and snickered.

"Doing the Atkins Diet. These walnuts are very low in carbs."

"That's a terrible diet," Laurette managed to get out between sobs. "In fact, the doctor who came up with it died of a heart attack."

"No, he didn't," I corrected her. "He fell on the ice and went into a coma."

"Please," she said. "That's what they wanted you to believe. Weight Watchers is the way to go." Even a grieving widow can be allowed a quick evaluation of the best weight loss programs.

The CSI investigator crumpled up his empty zip-lock bag and stuffed it into his coat pocket. "No outward signs of foul play. Could be a heart attack, or stroke, something like that."

"He wasn't even thirty!" Laurette said.

"I'm just speculating here. I need to conduct an autopsy for any definitive answers. Then we'll see if there are any traces of poison in the bloodstream."

Poison? Monkshead? That raised an interesting question. What if Juan Carlos had been taken out with a hit of monkshead? There were certainly enough people who wanted to see him dead. Javier Martinez. Viveca. Dominique. Maybe even David. Not to mention half the cast and crew of *Creeps*. The only one I could safely rule out at this point was Rudy Pearson. I saw him murdered with my own eyes. Unless his ghost did it. But Rudy could have been in cahoots with any one of the other suspects. He at least knew one person here in Miami. I heard him or her taking a shower when I cased Pearson's room. And he could have easily shared the poison with his accomplice before Wendell fatally stabbed him. I had to find out who that person was.

With the cops ignoring my bombshell about Javier Martinez's hatred of the deceased, I didn't trust them anymore so I decided to modify Charlie's helpful advice when interrogated. I neglected to mention the Rudy Pearson murder and the whacked-out psychosis of Wendell Butterworth. It would only incriminate me. If any one of them had a pipeline to the Coral Gables Police Department, they would find out my habit of showing up at a crime scene and start to suspect me of being some kind of serial killer who calls the cops for kicks after committing a murder.

Although Laurette did admit she wanted to hang her husband up by the balls after discovering his multiple infidelities, the cops had no concrete proof tying either of us to Juan Carlos's death. The CSI guy wasn't even prepared to list the death as a homicide at this point. So after a two-hour marathon of questioning, we were told we could leave, but that it would be wise of us not to leave the Miami area.

As we hiked back to the Ritz Plaza, Laurette stared straight ahead, as if in a trance. The shock of all the revelations she had encountered since arriving in Florida were starting to have an effect on her, and I felt she was close to a complete breakdown. I lured her up to my shabby room with the promise of a couple of stiff drinks from room service. When we walked into the room, we found Charlie on the bed, reading the paper.

"I'm glad you're back," I said. "You're not going to believe what we've just been through."

He lowered the paper, and glared at me. The vision of me hugging Bowie was apparently still fresh in his mind. There was a palpable tension lingering in the air. Laurette wasn't about to indulge us because she was having the worst day of all. She recounted everything to Charlie, whose anger subsided as she related all the dramatic details. He was mesmerized. And when she'd finished, he stood up, crossed over to her, and grabbed her in a warm hug.

"Honey, I'm sorry you've had to go through this," he said as she laid her head on his big shoulder.

"Somebody up there doesn't want me to be happy," she said, sniffling.

Charlie lifted her chin up with his thumb and forefinger until she was looking directly into his eyes. "Juan Carlos never would have made you happy. I'm sorry he died, but in time you'll see you deserve so much better."

He had her attention. And mine.

"He lied to you. He cheated on you. And he would've drained you financially and emotionally. Laurette, you're a beautiful, vibrant woman, and I know there's a man out there who is looking for you, and will appreciate you, and love you for who you are, not what you can do for him."

He squeezed her tighter, resting his chin on the top of her head, and said, "You and Juan Carlos, it never felt right. There wasn't a lot of trust there. And trust is the foundation of every relationship. Trust and communication."

He was looking at me when he said this. His piercing eyes were like a sword through the heart. But now was not the time to worry about us. Laurette was hurting too much.

"You're too good to me," Laurette cried as she pulled away from Charlie and held out a hand to me. "Both of you. I'd be lost without you."

I smiled, took her hand, and we hugged. The phone rang. Charlie slowly backed away to give us our best friend moment, and answered the call.

"Hello?" he said. I saw his face get hot and red, but his voice remained steady. "He's a little busy right now." Bowie. It had to be Bowie. God, this was getting more out of hand by the minute.

Charlie sighed and scribbled something on the pad of paper on the nightstand.

"All right, I'll tell him," he said and then slammed down the phone.

"Who was it?" Laurette asked.

"It was for Jarrod," he said as he tore the piece of paper off the pad and handed it to me. "Bowie wants you to meet him at this address."

"Did he say what it was about?" I asked meekly.

"No," Charlie said.

"I'm one of his clients now. Maybe he has some information about Wendell Butterworth's whereabouts or maybe he found Rudy Pearson's body . . ." I said.

"Look," Charlie said, walking back over to Laurette and putting a strong, muscled arm around her shoulders. "I don't feel right about you running all over Miami while Butterworth is on the loose, but I certainly can't stop you from doing what you're going to do. So go."

"You can come with me if you want," I said meekly.

"I think one of us should stay here and be with Laurette, don't you?" he said.

He was right. I wanted more than anything to stay and patch things up with my boyfriend and be a supportive shoulder for my best friend to cry on. But if I didn't find Butterworth and prove he was a homicidal maniac, then I would never be able to sleep at night ever again.

"I'm sorry," I said, and then I quietly turned and slipped out the door.

Chapter 29

When I arrived at the *QE3* houseboat, it was already dark. The moon illuminated a shimmering carpet across the bay, and for a city the size of South Beach, it was unsettlingly quiet.

I tapped on the door of the boat and waited. I wished Charlie had come with me. That would have been one way to allay his fears that I was having some kind of secret affair with Bowie. On the other hand, he was right. Laurette was upset and fragile, and it was best that one of us stay with her tonight.

Bowie opened the door, and motioned for me to come in. He was sweating, his face was tight, and his eyes betrayed a distinct uneasiness.

"What's going on? Did you find Wendell?" I said as I followed him inside. I jumped with a start when I saw my stalker, Wendell Butterworth, tied to a chair in the middle of the room, a piece of duct tape over his mouth.

"Omigod!" I said, spinning around to Bowie, who quickly shut the door to shield the scene from any passersby. "What happened? How did he get here?"

"I've been quietly tailing you since you asked me to help," he said as he circled around me and headed straight for the wet bar. "Since he kept popping up to scare you, I figured he'd turn up again eventually. And he did. I caught him loitering outside your hotel."

Wendell was slumped over in the chair, his eyes shut tight. I cautiously moved toward him to see if he was breathing.

"He's alive. Don't worry. He's just pretending to be asleep so I don't harass him with any more questions," Bowie said as he poured himself a generous glass of scotch and downed it one gulp.

Now I was sweating. "I don't understand. Why are you holding him prisoner? I didn't ask you to—"

"Look, I approached him outside the Ritz Plaza. When I got too close, he pulled a knife on me. Luckily during my military training they taught me how to kill a guy with a quarter, so he wasn't too hard to take down," Bowie said.

"But this isn't exactly legal, is it? I mean, he may belong behind bars, but that doesn't give us the right to—"

"I don't care," Bowie said as he lifted his fatigue green tank top up to reveal a deep cut sliced across his torso. "The son of a bitch got me. Hurt like hell. But not nearly as bad as the hydrogen peroxide I used to clean it out with. Damn."

"Why didn't you call the police?"

Bowie marched over to Wendell, grabbed a fist full of his hair, and yanked his head back. Wendell's eyes popped open, full of fear.

"Because then we'd never find out what he did to that soap reporter's body. By keeping him here, we can work on him until he tells us what we want to know. Isn't that right, Wendell?"

Wendell struggled in the chair, but it was halfhearted. He knew it was useless. Bowie knew how to tie a knot. After all, he was a Navy Seal. And probably a Boy Scout to boot.

Bowie ripped the duct tape off Wendell's mouth, knelt down, and spoke quietly into his ear. "Where is he, Wendell? Tell me and I'll let you go."

Wendell turned his head away defiantly. Bowie grabbed his chin and jerked his head back toward him. "Talk to me, Wendell. I'm not a patient man."

"Maybe we should turn him over to the police . . ." I said, my stomach flip-flopping. This wasn't what I'd had in mind at all.

"I'm not going to ask you again," Bowie said, slapping Wendell hard across the face. Wendell groaned, but remained steadfast in his silence. Bowie slapped him even harder.

"Bowie, stop!" I yelled, rushing over and grabbing his wrist to stop him from going another round. "I don't want this."

"This loony tune has been stalking you since you were a kid. How many nights' sleep did you lose thinking he was right outside your window? And now you want to show him some mercy?" Bowie said, his eyes blazing, his muscles taut. He stared me down.

Wendell gazed at me with pleading eyes, his mouth open in a state of shock. And then it hit me. I had him. Right in my corner. Bowie had provided the perfect setup. I leaned down to Wendell and gently stroked his face and smiled at him. He had never received such an affectionate gesture from me, the object of his obsession. He didn't know quite how to react.

Bowie clamped a big paw on my shoulder to pull me away from him, but I shook him off. "I'm sorry he hurt you," I said, staring straight into Wendell's eyes.

Wendell went limp. He looked at me and smiled. A tear slowly streaked the side of his face. He couldn't believe what he was hearing.

"I guess I always knew, but there were so many people in my life who couldn't accept it. They filled my head with all sorts of horrible thoughts to keep us apart. But I can't deny your love for me anymore. You do love me like any true soul mate would. And I love you too."

I threw my arms around him and squeezed tight. At first he tensed up, but as the reality of what was happening sank in, he burrowed his head in my chest and sobbed. In his mind, I had finally come around.

I glanced back at Bowie, who had quickly caught on to what I was doing. He gave me an encouraging wink.

I carefully lifted Wendell's head off my chest and tenderly raised it up so we were face to face. I offered him a warm smile. He sniffed and cleared his throat and squinted his eyes to rid them of the onslaught of tears.

"The truth shall finally set us free, Jarrod," he said, beaming.

"I know, Wendell, but this guy here, this evil man, will never let you go until you tell him what he wants to know."

"I don't know . . . He wants me to go back to prison. I don't want to ever go back, do you hear me? I wouldn't make it, " he said, his voice shaking.

"We'll tell him what he wants to know, and then we'll go away. We'll leave the country. Make a new life somewhere else," I said, ready to shoot my hand out to accept that elusive Emmy Award that I had been chasing after for so many years.

Wendell scanned my face, not a hundred percent ready to believe I was sincere. I had to seal it with a kiss. I softly brushed my lips across his cheek and whispered in his ear, "I just want to be with you, away from all this like we're meant to be."

Wendell took a deep breath, and released it, allowing years of frustration to escape his body. After all this time, his soul mate had finally come home. He then turned to Bowie and said, "A tool shed."

"Where?" Bowie barked.

"I didn't have to drag him far. It's right near—"

A burning smell wafted up, and I stood up and looked around. "What is that?"

Bowie took a whiff and then, with a start, flung his body forward. "Jarrod, watch out!"

I caught sight of the lighter pressed into the palm of Wendell's hand too late. It must have been in his pocket, and he managed to get ahold of it and burn right through the ropes binding him. He freed himself, and shoved me aside as Bowie pounced on him like a cougar. Wendell head-butted Bowie with such force, he flew back, smashing against the wet bar, jostling it enough so that bottles of scotch, tequila, and vodka tipped over and fell, smashing Bowie over the head. Glass shattered everywhere, and Bowie, half-conscious, drooped down to the floor.

Wendell was out of the chair like a shot, and took advantage of the opportunity to flip Bowie facedown on the floor, and quickly bind his hands together with the singed rope.

"I'm tired of listening to you," he said as he picked up the roll of duct tape off the coffee table, tore off a nice long piece, and pressed it over Bowie's mouth. Wendell stared at Bowie for a moment, debating on what to do next, and then he marched over to the kitchen area, scrambled around in a drawer, and studied the blade of a sharpened steak knife. He walked back over to Bowie's prone body and hissed, "Don't you worry, Jarrod. He won't be bothering us anymore."

Straddling Bowie, he raised the knife in the air. I sprang across the room and grabbed ahold of his arm. "No!" I yelled, trying to pull him off Bowie. He swatted me aside like an annoying housefly.

"Boy," he said sternly. "Stay out of my way."

He raised the knife again. This time I hurled myself between Bowie and the blade, hoping to dear God he would stop short of stabbing his "soul mate." Luckily he did.

I had to give the performance of a lifetime. "Wendell, listen to me, please," I said. "We don't need more police chasing us. If you keep killing, we'll never have any peace. And isn't that what we both want? To be left alone in peace?"

Wendell's stone face relaxed into an admiring smile. "You're right, Jarrod. You're a good boy. Smart boy. I'm so proud of you."

"The people on the other boats may have heard all the commotion. Someone might have called the police. We should leave," I said, motioning him to join me. I just wanted him to step away from Bowie before he changed his mind and plunged the knife deep into his back.

We walked outside, and Wendell veered toward my rented Taurus. He had been following me for so long he knew exactly what kind of car I was driving in Miami. Wendell opened up the driver's side door to get in, but noticed me hanging back.

"Come on, boy, what are you waiting for? Let's go."

I hesitated. Every childhood fear was rising up inside of me. I was about to get in the car with the man who had stalked me for over two thirds of my life and had tried to kill me twice.

Wendell could smell my fear, and he melted. "Being scared is nothing to be ashamed of, Jarrod. We've all got things we're afraid of," he said with an understanding smile. "And I know you're worried about all the people who are going to chase us and try to separate us again."

I nodded, playing along for lack of a better plan.

"Chances are we will get caught eventually and they will take you away from me. But there's one surefire way to make sure that never happens."

"What's that?" I asked, not sure I wanted to hear the answer.

"The only way we'll be safe and together is if we leave this world. Right now."

I shuddered. This was the Wendell Butterworth I knew and loathed.

"I'll kill you first. Nice and quick. You won't feel a thing," he said as he reached into his pocket and pulled out the steak knife. "And you wait for me at the light. I'll be right behind you."

Chapter 30

Wendell took a step forward, raising the knife over his head. I slowly began backing away.

"Don't be scared. You won't feel a thing. I promise," he said. And that's when I turned and hightailed it out of there. I bolted down the sidewalk running along the marina, yelling at the top of my lungs for anyone who could hear me. I wrenched my head around and caught sight of Wendell, huffing and puffing, as he chased after me.

"Jarrod, come back!" he bellowed before he had to stop and catch his breath. It was my dumb luck that Wendell hadn't spent his long years behind bars working out at the prison gym. I was in much better shape from my many hikes in the Hollywood Hills with Snickers. I stayed well ahead of him.

I spotted a pair of headlights in the distance and debated whether or not I should run out into the road, but the car was coming too fast and shot by before I had a chance to get the driver's attention. I heard Wendell wheezing a few hundred feet behind me as he closed the distance between us. Instinctively, I sprinted to my right, but quickly discovered I was running down a dock slip housing a line of expensive yachts. When I reached the end, there was nothing but Biscayne Bay ahead of me. I could hide on one of the boats. Wendell would be hard pressed to find me. Screaming for help at this point might not be the smartest move. Most of the owners were out dining at the finest restaurants South Beach had to offer, and it would only lead Wendell to me. I spotted a darkened white cruiser with the name CHARLIE'S ANGEL stenciled in blue across the bow. It was enormous and easily worth a couple of million. It probably had a lot of compartments and closets for me to hide. I made a dash for it, but stopped suddenly when the moon illuminated the big, bulky form of a man gripping a steak knife. Wendell stood motionless at the other end of the dock, trapping me.

"Why are you running from me, boy?"

I whipped my head from side to side, searching for some way, any way, to escape. Wendell cautiously started to walk toward me. The only sound I could hear was the rocking of the wooden dock against the gentle waves lapping into shore and the steady approach of my stalker's footsteps.

There was nowhere to go. I knew it. Wendell knew it. I turned and sprinted straight off the dock in a swan dive, silently praying Wendell had never learned how to swim. I hit the bone-chilling water and swam for my life, as far out as I could. Other than fishing Dominique out of the surf, I hadn't swum since I played the son of a Midwestern tourist who accidentally steals a cache of diamonds from the Hawaiian mafia in a *Magnum, P.I.*, episode in 1984. One of the native gangsters tries to drown me off Waikiki Beach as a warning to my father, but I manage to swim away from him. It took nine takes to get right. I nailed it every time. The guy playing my attacker had had too many mai tais at lunch and had trouble hitting his mark.

My arms and legs ached after a few minutes, and I stopped and treaded water while I tried to rest up. I looked back at the dock, maybe a hundred feet away. Wendell stood forlornly at the edge, staring out at the moonlit bay.

"Jarrod? Jarrod?" he wailed.

I bobbed up and down in the waves, trying to keep my breathing steady. Don't panic. Just stay here, and pretty soon he may give up and leave and I can swim back to shore. I worried my legs wouldn't be able to tread much longer. I was spent. What a choice. Stabbed by a stalker or death by drowning.

A light hit my eyes, blinding me. I squinted and tried to focus. Had I already drowned and this was the light where I was supposed to meet Wendell? I heard the rumble of an engine and smelled gasoline as a motorboat pulled up in front of me. A hand reached out, hauling me up over the side and into the boat. I had been rescued.

Coughing and sputtering from the salty seawater, I said, "Thank you so much for picking me up. There's a guy on the dock who—"

For the first time I was able to see my rescuers. Two giants. One Caucasian and one Hispanic. Martinez's henchmen. I spun around to jump over the side, but the Hispanic grabbed a fistful of my shirt and yanked me back, shoving me down on a hard wooden seat in the back of the boat.

"Relax, will you?" he barked. "Enjoy the ride."

I sat silent, staring at them, wondering how far out we would go before they tied a cement block around my ankle and sent me hurtling to the ocean floor. But after a brief ten-minute ride, we drove up alongside an impressive cruiser, nearly twice the size of all the other boats docked in the marina. On the bow, I saw the name VIVECA II in big bold lettering. He'd named a boat after her, and she still felt the need to go sleep with a sleaze like Juan Carlos. But who was I to judge? The two henchmen wore loud flower print shirts and khaki shorts. Not exactly the butchest bad guys you would ever run across. But what they lacked in fashion style, they made up for in pure bulk. They hustled me up the ladder, and I braced myself for my first face-to-face meeting with Javier Martinez.

I was led into the private quarters and through to a back office deep inside the boat. I didn't see any other people aboard except for us. Viveca and the kids were probably in town wondering what had happened to their beloved paramour. The Caucasian rapped on a shellacked wooden door with a gold plate that said PRIVATE, and a gruff voice said, "Bring him in."

The door opened to reveal a brightly lit space with a glass-top table and high-back chair, four televisions, computer, phone, fax, everything. Rupert Murdoch could run his corporation out of this place. Javier Martinez in an open floral print shirt and white slacks, a look only an intimidating mafia don could ever get away with, stood up and offered me a warm smile.

"Well, Mr. Jarvis, at last we meet," he said. "Can I offer you a cocktail? I make an excellent margarita. My entire family swears by it."

"I'm fine, thank you," I said, a little confused by his hospitality. "First of all, Mr. Martinez, I want you to know I appreciate your . . . associates . . . picking me up when they did. They saved my life." I went on to explain my history with Wendell Butterworth and his endless pursuit of me leading up to the last few hours. Martinez listened to my story, wide-eyed and fascinated. When I'd finished, he took a big gulp of his tequila sunrise and set the glass down.

"Sounds like a very nasty business," he said dryly.

"Oh, I'm sure it doesn't even compare to what you're used to," I said, instantly regretting it. Here I was on his turf, surrounded by his thugs, and I was being flippant like Bruce Willis in his umpteenth *Die Hard* sequel.

"You'd be surprised," Martinez said with a smile, his eyes downcast. "I'm not as brutal and ruthless as most people think. Nobody's going to do a show on HBO about me anytime soon."

"Why did you bring me here?"

Martinez looked up at his goons and waved them away. They turned and walked out, closing the door behind them. "You've been following me. You and that private eye, what's his name, Bowie something . . ."

"Lassiter," I said.

"Right. And I want to know why."

"Okay, um, well, I'm not sure really where to begin, but a dear friend of mine recently married someone you might know . . . Juan Carlos Barranco."

Martinez picked up his glass and squeezed it so hard, I waited for it to crush in his hands. But he caught himself, and finished off the drink with one swig. "Yes, I know him. Too well, I'm afraid," he said.

"Well, another man connected to you, Austin Teboe, died of poisoning at Juan Carlos's wedding, and the trail has led me here . . . and to you."

"You think I'm behind Teboe's murder?"

I awkwardly shifted position. "Well, um," I said, "he did work for you. And he did betray you by leaving. And you do have a reputation for . . ." I stopped myself. This wasn't exactly my smartest hour accusing a mobster of murder. But I had to know the truth.

"I had no reason to get rid of Austin. Yes, he left me high and dry to go work in some restaurant. But he came crawling back, wanting his old job. I said no. It was a question of loyalty. He had disappointed me once. I was not going to let him do it again. But I never held a grudge. Now the other one, the actor, now that's another story."

"He's dead too."

Javier raised a brow, genuinely surprised. "Really? How?"

"Poisoning. My guess is it was the same kind used to kill Austin Teboe."

A sly smile crept across his face. "Well, I may be guilty of a lot of things, but lately my biggest crime has been just trying to make my family happy."

"What do you mean?"

"My daughter Dominique was dating that Barranco character. I never liked him, or the effect he had on her. He got her all
excited about the movie business to the point where she had
stars in her eyes. She wanted to be an actress. She heard some
low-rent horror movie was in town looking for funding, and she
came and begged me to invest. She figured it would ensure she
get a part in the picture. It's hard to say no to your only daughter. In fact, I've never said it to her, so I agreed. Then, before I
knew it, my wife came to me and told me not to write the check
until the director promised to cast her in a role too. It was turning into a damn Martinez family production."

"Did you know Juan Carlos was playing the lead?"

"Of course not. I hated the bastard. I would've shut the whole
damn movie down if I had known. Viveca and Dominique went
to great lengths to hide that key piece of information from me."

"So when did you find out?"

"That self-promoting son of a bitch couldn't resist announcing in one of the local papers that he was back in town starring in
a new film. A member of my household staff saw it and brought
it to my attention. He had already broken Dominique's heart
once, and I was afraid he would try again. I told him if he ever
came near my daughter again, I would cut off his head, so I had
my boys follow him around to make sure he didn't try to contact
her . . ." His voice trailed off. He stared out a portal at the vast
ocean.

"They saw him up north," I said. "At the Sand Drift Motel,
with—"

"David," Martinez choked out. "My son."

We stood silent. Martinez poured some more tequila, stirred
it around with his forefinger, and raised the glass to his lips. "I
was ready to kill him right then and there. But things only got
worse . . ."

"Viveca?"

Martinez nodded. "She left clues all over the place. And there was a lot of tension between her and Dominique, so it was only a matter of time before I put two and two together. At that point, the sick mother fucker had signed his death warrant."

"So you had him killed?"

Martinez shook his head. "No."

"Mr. Martinez," I said. "You have a history of offing men who cross your family."

He stared at me blankly. "I don't know what you're talking about."

"Your daughter Dominique's ex-boyfriend Calvin. He mysteriously disappeared after breaking it off with your daughter. Are you telling me . . . ?"

Martinez laughed. "I didn't kill him. I just threatened him. Told him if I ever saw his face again, I would slaughter him and his entire family. He ran off scared. Last I heard he was working as a bartender in Havana."

"But why hasn't he tried contacting his family? They're worried sick."

"He will eventually. When he thinks it's safe. I can have a certain effect on people," he said proudly.

"So you had nothing to do with Juan Carlos's murder?"

"I'll be honest with you. I had every intention of doing it. And I wanted to do it all by myself. I wanted him to see *my* face as I squeezed the last bit of breath out of his skinny, weak body." He snapped out of his fantasy and looked at me. "But I guess someone else got to him first."

I believed him. There was no reason for him to lie. He could've confessed and then just fed me to the sharks.

"Jarrod, I respect your need to find out what happened to Austin and the actor. I have no problem with that."

"Okay," I said warily.

"But let's set the record straight. Feel free to poke around all you like, and solve your little murder mystery. But when you dig for your information, just be sure you don't come across anything that could prove hazardous to your health."

"Like what?"

"Like anything related to me. I'm telling you right now, I had nothing to do with either of those deaths. But I am embroiled in certain activities that need to be kept under wraps. If you unwrap them, then we have a problem."

"I get the message. Loud and clear."

"I suspected you would."

"Am I free to go now?"

"No," Martinez said, standing up and coming around the desk. "My wife and children should be arriving at any moment. I believe you know them all. I'd like you stay for dinner."

"Oh, I don't know if they really want to see me . . ." I said.

"If they've heard about Juan Carlos, I'm sure they all must be in mourning. I'll need your help in cheering them up," he said as he gripped my arm, signaling to me that I didn't have a choice.

I would've preferred being fed to the sharks.

Chapter 31

Martinez was kind enough to allow me to freshen up in one of the guest staterooms. I used the opportunity to pick up a shore-to-land phone and immediately call the *QE3*. I was afraid Wendell Butterworth might have doubled back and finished off Bowie, whom we'd left tied up and gagged on his houseboat. The phone rang and rang and I finally got his machine. I hung up and dialed the Ritz Plaza. When the operator put me through to my room, Charlie picked up the phone on the first ring.

"Hello?" he said. I could tell he was worried.

"Charlie, it's me," I said. "Look, I don't have time to explain, but I need you to go over to Bowie's houseboat and make sure he's all right."

"Why?"

I quickly explained everything, and when I'd finished, he said, "Where are you now?"

"On Javier Martinez's boat. Somewhere out in the marina."

"What?" Charlie said, more than a bit concerned.

One of the crew rapped on the stateroom door. "Mr. Martinez is requesting your presence in the dining room, Mr. Jarvis."

"In a minute," I called out.

"Mr. Martinez isn't used to being kept waiting," the crew member said.

"Okay, be right there," I said, then spoke fast into the phone. "Charlie, I have to go. I really don't want to piss this guy off. Please, just go make sure Bowie is all right."

The crew member outside the door inserted the key and turned the knob. I didn't want him catching me on the phone, so I hung up, and smiled at him as he stepped inside. He was short and squat, a balding Latino in a crisp white uniform, his pressed shorts showing off some hairy, knobby knees. He stared at me sternly.

"I love the little duck soaps in the bathroom. Can I take some home with me?" I said, hoping I would be able to actually go home at some point.

He wasn't amused. He just held the door open for me, and I passed him with a shrug. He escorted me to the dining room, and made sure I went inside before quietly retreating. I had entered the lion's den.

Javier sat at the head of the table, Viveca to his immediate right, Dominique and David on his left. Javier watched with glee as his wife and children finally noticed me. Viveca nearly spit out her peach schnapps. Dominique stared daggers. And David strained trying to place me, probably having a vague recollection of seeing me at the Sand Drift Motel.

It was obvious Javier hadn't mentioned I would be tonight's special guest. He had a sick sense of humor, and enjoyed catching them off guard like this.

Dominique spoke first. "What's he doing here?"

"He's my friend and I've asked him to join us for dinner," Javier said, barely able to contain himself he was having such a good time.

"I didn't know you and Dad were friends," Dominique said,

barely even looking at me. "Is that how you got cast in the movie?"

"No," I said. "We've only recently met."

"We've discovered we have something in common," Javier said as the same crew member that brought me to the dining room rushed in to refill his boss's glass of bourbon.

"And what's that?" Viveca asked.

"A mutual loathing of your dearly departed Juan Carlos," Javier said. There was a deafening silence, finally broken by Javier's almost merry voice. "Jarrod, can I offer you a drink?"

"Just some water, thank you, Mr. Martinez."

"We're friends, Jarrod, call me Javier," he said with a wink.

So this is how Miami crime bosses got their kicks. Stirring the pot at home. I never saw someone have such a good time.

David finally spoke up. "Have we met?" He looked me up and down.

"No," Javier answered for me. "At least I don't think so. But Jesus and Abe first saw him up in that little town north of Vero Beach. Sebastian. Where you were last week. With Juan Carlos."

Another long, painful silence. David looked down at his clean, shiny, empty plate guiltily. I knew Viveca and Dominique both knew that the other was sleeping with Juan Carlos, so I tried reading their faces to ascertain if they knew about David's involvement with him as well. Both remained still, and stone-faced, and silent. They definitely knew. Talk about a family affair.

The wait staff arrived with a sumptuous feast of pan-fried scallops as an appetizer, shrimp salad, a delectable pecan-crusted catfish, and a very expensive French white wine with a name I couldn't pronounce. Javier was clearly a lover of seafood given the rather one-sided menu, and mother, son, and daughter dove in with relish, obviously relieved that the food could serve as a distraction from the excruciatingly uncomfortable circumstances.

None of them had any idea how much I knew about their individual escapades, though Viveca flaunted it on the set every chance she got. Of course, how could she ever imagine that I would at some point be joining the family for dinner on their yacht? Javier stuffed huge bites of catfish in his mouth, and chewed with his mouth open. Smack. Smack. Smack. I could easily understand why Javier had such deplorable table manners. Who in their right mind would want to mention it to him? Viveca and Dominique exchanged furtive glances. David sat sullenly, poking at the shrimp on his salad plate with a tiny stainless steel fork.

He then took a small bite of scallop, and hurled it back onto his plate. "It's overcooked . . . again," he huffed. "I wish we could get Austin back."

"Well, we can't because Austin's dead," Javier said, shooting an annoyed glance at his son. "And dead people are useless in the kitchen."

"Maybe if you had let him come back, he wouldn't be dead," said Viveca.

Javier's face reddened. "Austin left us high and dry for greener pastures. Loyalty means everything to me, Viveca. You know that," he said, and then glared at the entire family. "You should *all* know that."

"I miss him," Dominique said quietly. "He was a good man."

"Good man. Good man. Austin Teboe was a traitor." Javier spit out his catfish. I jerked my head to the right to avoid a bull's-eye. "None of you ever took the time to really know him. You just liked the way he prepared your food. The three of you have proven time and time again that you're not particularly good judges of character."

Nobody dared to respond. They all looked down at their food and continued eating. Nothing made much sense anymore. Austin Teboe had quit working for the Martinez family. But did that necessarily provide the motive for a family member to poison him? And Dominique had been the only Martinez present at the time Austin Teboe was murdered. So everybody not there was pretty much cleared. So who did kill him? And why? And what about Juan Carlos? Javier said he didn't do it, and I was predisposed to believe him. If he had done it, he probably would have bragged about it after all the humiliation Juan Carlos put the poor guy through, sleeping with his entire immediate family. No. I was pretty sure Martinez was innocent, at least of the Austin Teboe and Juan Carlos Barranco murders. But what about the rest of the family? Juan Carlos had broken Dominique's heart, toyed with Viveca's affections, and slept with David while also banging his mother and sister at the same time. Probably recycled his sweet nothings too. No, there were plenty of motives to choose from. But as I looked around the table, I didn't see a smidgeon of guilt or remorse, just pure unadulterated grief. These people were in mourning. They should have been rejoicing. Juan Carlos wouldn't be around anymore to lie, steal, cheat, and play a sad little ditty on their heartstrings. But none of them were willing to look at that side of him. They chose to focus on his positive attributes, whatever they might be. Just as Laurette had. All I could imagine was just how good he must have been in bed.

I decided that although this family was wildly dysfunctional, there wasn't a murderer among them outside of their mobster father. So if no one in the Martinez family killed Juan Carlos, then who did? I was no closer to solving this puzzle than I was when my plane touched down in Miami a few weeks ago.

The knobby-kneed crewmember burst into the dining room, his face tense. "Excuse me, sir," he said to Javier.

"Yes, what is it?"

"We're under attack."

Javier stood up, and threw his napkin down. "What?"

"Two men are on board. Our security cameras caught them climbing over the deck railing. And they're armed."

"Stay here," Javier said to all of us, and hastily followed the crew member out. We all sat frozen for a moment, and then jumped up at the same time and dashed out of the room and up the narrow steel stairs to get a good view of the action. By the time we'd reached topside, a swarm of Martinez's men were searching the boat. The intruders had yet to be found. Javier barked orders and nervously paced the deck. He caught sight of us peeking out from the door leading to below deck.

"I told you all to stay put! I want you to go to your staterooms now!" The family knew better than to defy orders from the master of the house twice, so they all solemnly retreated. Since I didn't have a stateroom, I figured he didn't mean me. So I took the opportunity to poke around. Who were these men? A rival mob family? The feds on a raid? And how on earth did I get caught in the middle? As I passed a midsize rubber dingy, a pair of hands grabbed me from behind and hauled me over behind it. The attacker wrenched my arms behind my back, and before I could call out to my good friend Javier, someone else in front of me cupped a hand over my mouth.

"Quiet, Jarrod, it's me," Charlie said, looking very sexy in a black skintight wet suit unzipped far enough to show off his broad, furry chest.

"What are you doing here?" I whispered urgently.

The man holding me from behind let me go, and said, "We came to rescue you." It was Bowie.

"Rescue me? I don't need to be rescued," I said in a hushed voice.

"When you called me to tell me you were on Martinez's boat, you sounded nervous," Charlie said.

"I was late for dinner," I said. I turned to Bowie. "Are you okay?" I could feel Charlie tense up the minute the words came rolling out of my mouth.

"Yeah, Wendell never came back. I was hogtied in my living

room until Charlie thankfully showed up," Bowie said, also looking sexy in the same black wetsuit.

"You guys better get out of here before Martinez finds you. They saw you on the security cameras, and it's only a matter of time before—"

A flood of lights blinded all three of us as Martinez and his men, armed with flashlights and pistols, swooped down on us. We all threw our hands up in the air to surrender. We were too outnumbered to try anything.

"Who are you?" Javier asked Charlie and Bowie brusquely. "What are you doing on my boat?"

"They're friends of mine," I said, with an upbeat smile. "I was hoping there might be room for them at dinner."

Chapter 32

Unfortunately Javier wasn't in the mood to resume dinner after the dramatic invasion. And it was lucky for us he decided not to kill any of us for ruining his meal and nearly causing him a heart attack. He knew three bodies washing ashore was a headache he didn't need at the moment. Instead, he had his crew escort Charlie and Bowie topside and to the small speedboat they had tied to a post just a few hundred yards from the yacht.

As I was heading back up to the deck of the boat to join them, a stateroom door creaked open, and a voice said softly, "Jarrod, come in here. I need to tell you something." It was David Martinez. We hadn't exchanged two words ever, and now he had a burning need to confide in me. I looked around to make sure Daddy wasn't spying on us, and then slipped inside his stateroom.

"What is it?" I said.

David shut the door and locked it. "I know Juan Carlos was a shit. Deep down I've always known it. But I couldn't help myself. He had a power over me."

"And a lot of other people," I added.

David nodded. "I know. But I want to know who killed him. It's tearing me up inside now that he's gone, and I have to know."

"I'll do my best."

"Do you really think there might be a connection between Juan Carlos's death and Austin Teboe's?"

"Yes."

"Then maybe this will help you somehow. After my dad refused to rehire him, Austin fell into serious debt and really needed some cash. He showed up at the house one day when he knew Dad was away to ask me if I could help him somehow, maybe talk to Dad for him, and he walked in on me and Juan Carlos fooling around in the sack."

"Did he already know about Dominique and your mother?"

"Everybody knew about Juan Carlos dumping Dominique. It was very messy and very public. It's what drove Juan Carlos out of town. I'm not sure if Austin knew about Juan Carlos and my mother though. But the fact that Juan Carlos was bisexual and sleeping with me and my sister, well, he figured he had enough."

"Enough to do what?"

"Austin was hiding out from loan sharks by the time word leaked out that Juan Carlos was marrying some TV agent out in California. He was penniless and desperate. So he went out there to blackmail him. If Juan Carlos helped him out financially, he'd keep quiet and my father would never have to know that his gay son was sleeping with the same man who destroyed his daughter's heart. Dad would never have to know any of what was going on behind his back."

"How do you know that was what Austin was planning?"

"Because Dominique saw him at the wedding. She figured out what he was going to do, and confronted him about it. He certainly didn't deny it."

"So did your sister poison him to protect Juan Carlos?"

"No. She says she didn't and I believe her."

"Then what about Juan Carlos? He could've retaliated and

poisoned Teboe at the wedding. You were as close to him as any-body. Surely you might have some idea if it was him."

"Juan Carlos was a lot of things, but he was not a murderer. I think if you find out who killed Austin, you'll find out who killed Juan Carlos."

"What about you, David? You certainly had a lot to lose if your father found out. Maybe you sent someone out there to do the job for you."

"Would I be telling you all this if I had? I'm hoping this gives you the information you need to find out who murdered Juan Carlos."

He had a point. Why implicate yourself to such a degree if you were guilty? My initial hunch was right. No one in the fam-ily was responsible. But this key piece of dirt opened up a host of new possibilities. A blackmail scheme. But Juan Carlos must have refused to play ball. Teboe threatened to put in a call to Martinez. And an hour later Austin Teboe was dead. It sure sounded like a textbook case of murder. Juan Carlos knocked him off before he could talk. But Juan Carlos was never away from Laurette's side at the wedding. There was no way he could have poured the poison in Austin's champagne. No, it was im-possible for Juan Carlos to have pulled it off. Besides, no one else but Rudy Pearson had possession of the lethal monkshead poison. But why would Rudy Pearson have reason to murder Austin Teboe? It was clear on the bus ride up to the Hearst Castle that the two didn't even know each other. Unless Rudy meant to poison someone else. Yes! Austin could have swallowed the poison by mistake. Rudy despised Juan Carlos for some rea-son, and wanted him dead. When Austin keeled over instead, Rudy decided to follow Juan Carlos to Florida and finish the job once and for all. It made perfect sense. But since Rudy was al-ready dead by the time Juan Carlos died in his Chinese chicken salad, someone else must be behind that murder.

I left David in his grief and went topside where the knobby-kneed crew member waited to show me the plank, or ladder rather, that led me down to the speedboat where Charlie and Bowie waited for me. As Bowie revved the engine, and we began the short trip back to shore, Charlie put a hand on my knee.

"By the way," he said. "I had the guys back in LA call in a few favors with the Miami Police Department. They let me take a look at the toxicology reports that just came back from the lab."

"And?" I said.

"It's official. Juan Carlos died from a hit of monkshead poison."

Bowie stole a glance at Charlie's hand resting on my knee. He grimaced. It was clear he had developed some feelings for me. And I felt wholly responsible. But I couldn't iron out those problems now. This new surprise just raised more unanswered questions. Who other than Rudy had access to the stash of monkshead? There was that mysterious roommate taking a shower in Rudy's room while I was searching it, but I had no idea who that might be. Maybe he or she took over for Rudy after Wendell killed him?

When we reached the dock, I told Bowie what I had learned from Javier about his cousin Calvin. Bowie was taken by surprise by my news. It was the first solid lead he had heard in months. It was clear he was anxious to get on it. He mumbled his good-byes and quickly disappeared inside the *QE3*. Charlie and I got into the Taurus and headed back to the Ritz Plaza.

I turned to Charlie. "Thank you for rescuing me," I said.

"No problem," Charlie said.

"I love you," I said, and meant it.

Long, long pause. He really wanted me to suffer a little bit before finally relenting. "I love you too."

When we got back to the room at the Ritz Plaza, Charlie sat me down on the bed. "I meant what I said in the car," he said.

"I know. So did I."

He stared at me sharply, trying to read my face for any signs of insincerity.

"From the moment we met, until now, and forever," I said.

"So you're not leaving me for some muscle-bound ex–Navy Seal with his own boat?"

"Never was, never will," I said.

Charlie slowly nodded, considering, and then he said, "Well, I'm leaving you. Your director, Larry Levant, came out to me on the set, and we really hit it off, and one thing led to another and well—"

I whacked him with the pillow. We both laughed. I started to unzip his black wetsuit all the way down to the lower regions when the phone suddenly rang, disrupting the mood. Sighing, I scooped it up and said impatiently, "Yes, what is it?"

I heard a bright, cheery, familiar voice. "Hi, Jarrod, it's me, Amy Jo."

"Hi, Amy Jo. What's up?"

"Well, given the recent tragedy, the producers have decided to shut down production indefinitely." I had forgotten that some people might consider Juan Carlos's death a tragedy.

"I see. Well, I'm sure it's for the best."

"So we need all of the cast to clean out their trailers ASAP," she said. "Like right now."

"It's kind of late, isn't it?" I said.

"Most of the cast did it this afternoon. You were nowhere to be found. I kept calling and calling. You really should tell us when you're going to take off like that." Mean, vicious Amy Jo was suddenly reemerging.

"I'll get my stuff first thing in the morning."

"We really need you to do it now, Jarrod. The crew wants to pack up all their equipment and caravan it back to California in the morning. And we promised the city of Coral Gables we would leave the park cleaner than when we found it, and that won't happen if your belongings are littered all over the place."

"Fine. I'll go out there now."

"Good. I sure do appreciate your cooperation," she said, her mind already onto her next job. I was about to hang up when Amy Jo said, "Oh, Jarrod, by the way, some guy left a message for you at the production office about an hour ago."

"Who was it?"

"He didn't say. But he said he left you something in the tool shed on the set, and you really need to go pick it up."

"What tool shed?"

"You know, the one out in the woods a few feet from the set. Stella from makeup keeps some hairbrushes and hand mirrors, stuff like that in there for safekeeping. But she couldn't find the key this morning, and that thing's a bitch to open. So bring a crowbar."

"Did the person say what it was he left me?"

"No. Just that it's someone you've been looking for." She paused and then giggled. "The receptionist must have written this down wrong. It has to be 'something,' not 'someone.' She makes it sound like there's a person in there."

"Thanks, Amy Jo," I said robotically as I hung up the phone and looked at Charlie, my face drawn and pale.

"What is it?" Charlie said. "What's wrong?"

"I think I know where Wendell Butterworth stashed Rudy Pearson's body."

Chapter 33

After I told Charlie what Wendell had said about the tool shed and not having to drag Rudy's body far, he unzipped his suitcase, rummaged through it, and drew out his gun. He stuffed it into his shoulder holster. "I'm going with you this time," he said.

"Believe me," I said, "I'm not about to go out there without you."

We headed out the door and down the hall.

"Do you know where the shed is?" Charlie said.

"I'm not sure I remember ever seeing it. But it has to be in the vicinity of the set."

We reached the bank of elevators, and I pressed the "down" arrow button. After a few moments, the bell rang and the elevator doors slid open. Laurette and Larry Levant stepped off. Larry had his arm around Laurette's waist. She was bleary-eyed and giggly.

Larry smiled weakly. "I found her in the bar. She was drowning her sorrows. She's had a rough time of it."

"He's so sweet," Laurette slurred. "Isn't he sweet?" She turned to Charlie and me. "Well, don't you think so?"

"I'm sorry," I said. "I thought it was a rhetorical question. Yes, he's very sweet."

"And probably gay too," Laurette said. "Just my luck. Or bi. Like my husband. I mean, my dead husband. The jerk." Laurette teetered, but Larry's hand on the small of her back steadied her. Laurette fought to focus, and squinted to get a good look at the two of us, or from her blood alcohol level, all six of us.

"I've told her four times I'm not gay, but she won't believe me," Larry shrugged. "What do I have to do to prove it?"

Laurette stroked a finger down his cheek. "I've got a few ideas." Then, she burst into tears. "What am I doing? I've been a widow for less than two days."

"It's okay, sweetheart," I said. "Juan Carlos wasn't exactly a role model for fidelity, and I know a woman should take her time after the end of a relationship, but after what that bastard put you through, I say go for it."

"Thanks, Jarrod," Larry said. "She's a cutie, isn't she?"

I smiled. Laurette glared at me through her blurry vision.

"Yes," I said quickly. "She is. I'm sorry, Laurette, I thought it was another rhetorical question."

"You're my best friend, Jarrod," she mumbled as she started sliding down the wall. Larry had trouble holding her up. Charlie and I swooped in to give him a hand. Once Larry had her in his grasp again, Charlie and I stepped back as the bell rang again, and another elevator arrived. Charlie reached out and held the door open.

"Jarrod, we better go," he said.

"Where are you two off to?" Laurette called out as Larry attempted to maneuver her down the hall.

"Back out to the set," I said. "I think we may have found Rudy Pearson."

Laurette stopped cold, grabbed the wall for support, and sobered up a bit. "Excuse me?"

"We'll explain later. After you've had some coffee," I said and got on the elevator. Laurette wrested herself free from Larry, and charged back up the hall and to the elevator. She stuck her hand in to stop the doors from closing.

"I don't want you two going out there tonight. It could be dangerous. Call the police, and have them come with you," she said.

"I called the police the last time, and when they showed up, I couldn't prove anything had happened. They think I'm some screwy actor making up stories. If we find anything, then we'll call the police."

Charlie opened up his jacket far enough for Laurette to see his holstered gun. "We'll be fine, Laurette," he said.

I gently pried Laurette's fingers off the elevator door. "I'll call you as soon as we get back. I promise."

"Be careful," she said as the doors closed on her worried face.

When we reached the set in the wooded park just outside Coral Gables, most of the props and equipment had been packed up and the area cleared. There were a few trucks and trailers locked up tight in the parking lot, but no one from the crew was around. It was completely dark now, and Charlie and I stuck close together as we surveyed the area for any sign of the mysterious tool shed.

The temperature had dropped to the low fifties. It was cold for Southern Florida and there was a biting breeze that made me shiver. It also could have been the macabre circumstances of searching for a butchered body that gave me chills. I led the way, Charlie right on my heels, as we walked down a path leading away from the set. It was the spot where I had witnessed Wendell Butterworth stab the life out of Rudy Pearson. When we reached the clearing, the trees swayed ominously around us, blocking the moonlight, making it that much darker.

"You see anything?" Charlie said.

261

"No," I said. The truth was I was seeing a lot of things. When I was a little boy, I watched the John Carpenter horror classic *Halloween* on late-night TV. Jamie Lee Curtis played a nubile young babysitter stalked by a vengeful escaped mental patient named Michael Myers. He wore an eerie, white mask over his face, and stalked unsuspecting teenagers in the neighborhood accompanied by a disturbing, bone-chilling film score. It had an undeniable impact on me, and for several weeks after that, I saw the masked face of Michael Myers everywhere. On the street, outside my bedroom window, in my closet. Everywhere I turned there he was. And on this night, after all I had experienced at the hands of Wendell Butterworth, I saw his face. Everywhere. Peeking out from behind the trees, waiting for us down the path, hovering above us in a tree branch. I couldn't shake his image, and it began working the knots in my stomach.

"Jarrod, down here!" Charlie said as he pounded off down a hidden trail I had missed. I ran after him, not wanting to lose him from my sight. When I caught up to Charlie, he was standing still in the middle of the path, his gaze fixed on a small wooden shed, about six feet in height, not more than four feet wide. There was a steel padlock around the rusted door handle.

I looked at Charlie, my eyes wide with anticipation, and the knots in my stomach twisting tighter. "You think this is it?"

Charlie shrugged. "I guess there's one way to find out." He picked up a rock and banged it against the padlock. Nothing. Not even a scratch. He tried again. No luck.

"Amy Jo was right," I said. "This is going to be a bitch to open."

"Stand back," Charlie said, drawing his gun out of his holster. I did what I was told and Charlie aimed the barrel right up against the lock and pulled the trigger. There was a loud pop, and it made me flinch. The padlock snapped off. Charlie put his gun away and lifted the broken lock off the door handle.

"You ready?" he said.

I nodded, and watched as he gripped the handle with his right hand and slowly opened the door. The first thing I saw were Stella's beauty supplies lined up on a small shelf that ran across the top of the shed, and then I saw him. Rudy Pearson sat almost in a lotus position on the floor, covered in dried blood, his eyes wide open in terror. Wendell had told the truth. His body had been right under our noses the whole time.

I stepped back to get a good look. "Oh, shit."

"Come on, Jarrod, let's call the police. This is all we need to get Wendell off the streets for good."

Charlie started back up the path. I took a moment to stare at the dead body. Who else would have to die before the authorities realized what a menace Wendell Butterworth was to society? I took a deep breath, and turned. Charlie stood still, halfway up the path. Why had he stopped? And then, just beyond him, I saw the face of Wendell Butterworth. Was this my mind playing tricks on me again like it did when I was a kid with Michael Myers? A part of me prayed it was just my imagination, but I knew better when Charlie went for his gun. Before he could snatch it out of the holster, Wendell rushed forward with a shovel raised over his head and cracked it down on Charlie's skull. Charlie crumpled to the ground.

"Charlie!" I yelled, and ran to him. Not even concerned with Wendell at the moment, I knelt down and saw a trickle of blood stream down Charlie's forehead. He moaned softly. Thank God he was alive.

"Why did you betray me, boy? We had a chance to escape to a place where no one would ever bother us again, and you ran away! Why?" Wendell stepped forward, still gripping the shovel.

"Because you've been bad. Very bad. You've hurt my friends. First Bowie. Now Charlie. Who else have you hurt, Wendell?"

Wendell glanced down at the still body of Charlie and pointed an accusing finger at him. "He was the one who wanted to hurt *me*. I was just protecting myself. Same with the other one. And Juan Carlos."

"What about Juan Carlos?"

Wendell didn't answer. His fingers tightened around the wooden handle of the shovel.

"Did you poison Juan Carlos?"

Wendell's eyes were blank, as if I were talking to a robot. He didn't respond. He just stared off into the distance.

"Did you somehow get your hands on some of Rudy's poison and use it to kill Juan Carlos?"

Wendell looked at the ground and shrugged, like a schoolboy brought to task for shooting a spitball.

"I don't understand, Wendell. Why? Why would you go after Juan Carlos? The facts just don't add up."

"Because Wendell didn't kill him," a voice said from behind me. I spun around and gasped at the smiling corpse of Rudy Pearson. He was on his feet, and very much alive. "I did."

Chapter 34

Rudy Pearson lifted his heavy body up out of the shed using the wooden door for balance. He pulled a white handkerchief out of a pocket in his trousers and began scrubbing off the dried blood on his face.

"Pretty nifty, huh?" he said. "Blood looks so real."

I stood a few feet away from him, my mouth agape, still somewhat in a state of shock. "I don't understand, Rudy. Why did you go to all that trouble to make it look like Wendell killed you?"

"Too many people knew I hated Juan Carlos, especially you. I would've been the first person the cops came looking for."

Wendell stepped over Charlie's inert body, and lumbered up behind me. I felt his presence, his hot breath on my neck, but stayed calm. The last thing I was going to do was make a sudden move and spook him.

"You knew I was hot on your trail after I found the monkshead poison in your room," I said. "So you manipulated Wendell into helping you set all this up."

Rudy grinned and nodded. He was rather proud of himself. I didn't dare to turn and see what Wendell was doing.

It was clear now that Wendell was Rudy's mysterious roommate at the hotel. He was the one taking a shower when I found the monkshead poison. All the facts kept spinning around in my head. It was an incredible rush of information, and I felt I was reaching up and grabbing pieces one at a time to fit into the puzzle.

"Why? Why would Wendell help you?" I said.

"Because I promised to help reunite him with his soul mate if he did as he was told. And look, I did," Rudy said as Wendell pressed his giant hand around my bicep in a steel-like vise grip. "See how happy he is, Jarrod? Just don't disappoint him by running away again. He suffers from separation anxiety, not to mention a white-hot temper."

I glanced up at Wendell, who squeezed my arm so tight, the pain shot through my entire body. I winced.

"Look at the big lug," Rudy said. "He was like a kid in the candy store when we were setting this whole thing up. He loved all the fake blood and makeup we stole from the set to make my murder look real. And the crew never even missed one of the retractable prop knives we lifted while you were shooting your death scene. Once we had you convinced Wendell had stabbed and killed me in the woods, I was free to poison that bastard Juan Carlos."

"Now you can just disappear and start over, and Juan Carlos can never hurt you again," I said.

"That's right," Rudy said, a euphoric grin slinking across his face.

"Why, Rudy? Why did you hate him so much?" I said.

Rudy clenched his fist, and stared at the ground. Just the thought of Juan Carlos sent him spiraling into an internal rage.

"Did he sleep with you too?" I said.

"No!" Rudy snapped. The thought of it disgusted him. "I'm not some love-starved, pathetic, needy, blithering idiot like that Dominique girl. I would *never* allow myself to manipulated by that piece of shit."

"You two obviously have some kind of history," I said.

"Yes, we did. When we were struggling actors, we both went up for the same parts time and time again," Rudy said, eyeing me for my reaction.

This was indeed a surprise. I had no idea Rudy Pearson had ever acted before. And given his rather slovenly appearance, I was hard pressed to believe he and Juan Carlos had ever competed for the same roles.

Rudy gauged my reaction and sighed. "I used to look a lot different."

I didn't want to set him off so I remained silent, still very much aware of the giant hand squeezing my left arm and the formidable presence of a much taller Wendell Butterworth standing behind me.

"It was the late nineties," Rudy said. "I gotta tell you, I was a real hunk. Worked out every day. Surfed on the weekends. My acting teacher kept telling me I was leading man material in my scene study class. But I just couldn't catch a break. My manager wasn't sending me out on any auditions. My prospects looked pretty bleak. I was about to quit the business and start looking around for something else to do, when a friend of mine came to me and said he heard they were looking for a good-looking, sexy guy around my age to play a professional rugby player from England to romance Tori Spelling for a story arc on *Beverly Hills 90210*. Man, I was perfect. I had just finished a short run doing a Noël Coward play at one of those small equity waiver theaters on Santa Monica Boulevard. I had perfected an English accent, and I knew how to play rugby. But my manager was useless. She said she couldn't even get me in to see the casting director. So I took matters into my own hands. I bluffed my way in. And I blew her away. I remember her saying, 'Where the hell have you been?' She took me straight to the producers and they loved me. I even tested with Tori. We flirted. I could tell she thought I was cute. It was pretty much a done deal."

Rudy let the stained handkerchief slip from his fingers and drop to the ground. He kept staring at the ground, remembering. "I had it in the bag. My manager, who actually took me out to dinner after she got the call, was busy negotiating the contract. I was going to appear in seven out of the first thirteen episodes of the new season, with an option for more. I had such a good feeling about it. I kept having dreams that I'd make such a great impression, they would reshoot the opening credits so they could put me in with the other cast members. You know, shots of me on the beach messing around with Luke Perry and Jason Priestly, pinching Jennie Garth's ass. That kind of stuff."

Rudy's eyes welled up at the memory, the lost opportunities, another Hollywood dream shattered.

I knew the rest. The rumors about Juan Carlos sleeping with the married executive producer to land the role of the sexy rugby player.

"Juan Carlos was runner-up for the same part," I said. "If they couldn't close your deal, they were going to go with him. He found out they were going to cast you, so he decided he had to do something about it. One of the executive producers had the hots for him, and he knew it. He used that to his advantage. Started up a big romance. That poor woman probably never knew what hit her."

Rudy nodded. "She should've known better. Actors will do anything for a part. She was a fucking executive producer! How could she not know that?"

"People, no matter how cynical, can often be blinded by love, or lust," I said, wondering at what point it was that I had suddenly turned into Dr. Phil.

"They gave it to him," Rudy said, almost spitting out the words. "He gave her multiple orgasms so she made sure they gave it to him. That fucking lowlife user. I was supposed to be the big cheese! Not him!"

"That's Hollywood," I said, instantly regretting it. Rudy

stared at me with contempt. I shrugged. "We've all got a story like that."

"My one big shot, and he stole it away from me. I spiraled after that. My manager used the botched deal as an excuse to drop me. I couldn't even get hired to be a cowhand extra on a fucking *Dr. Quinn, Medicine Woman*. I started eating too much, gained about a hundred pounds. I started drinking too much, smashed up my car, and got arrested for DUI. It was downright tragic. I was three months behind on my rent. I didn't know what I was going to do. I just sat at home watching soap operas all day and downing bottles of gin. I was becoming a fucking cautionary tale!"

Wendell loosened his grip, and for a moment, I had a chance to run. I could have made it out of the clearing, and into the woods, but I just couldn't leave Charlie. There was no telling what they might do to him. I had to make sure he was safe, even if it meant giving myself over to Wendell.

"Finally, the girl who lived next door to me was going out of town to visit her folks in Iowa or somewhere. Her mom had some kind of a stroke and she had to get home fast. She wrote freelance articles for *Soap Opera Digest*, and offered to pay me a hundred bucks if I finished up a couple for her while she was away. Hell, I figured it would be a cinch. I knew everybody on all the shows. I'd been watching them every day for the last six months. So I wrote them for her and they loved what I did. Then she recommended me to the magazine, and they started giving me my own work. An article here, an article there. And before long they offered me a staff position. Can you imagine the humiliation of writing fluffy profiles on those people? I was supposed to be one of them! They should have been writing profiles about me!"

"But things got better for you," I said. "You moved on and forgot all about Juan Carlos."

"That's right. Until they cast him as that rapist/preacher on

The Hands of Time and the magazine asked me to do a fucking cover piece on him. I did it, but then he started to get bigger and bigger. He was popping up everywhere. Commercials. TV movies. I couldn't get away from him. It was driving me mad!"

"So you decided to get rid of him once and for all. You got your hands on some obscure poison while you were covering that soap convention in Nova Scotia, crashed the wedding at the Hearst Castle, and spiked some champagne intended for Juan Carlos. Trouble was, he had you booted off the premises before you could make sure he drank it. Poor Austin Teboe gulped it down instead. The wrong man died. So you had to try again. You couldn't stop until you killed the man who cost you your ticket back into the big time."

Rudy's eyes grew wide. He stared numbly at me. "*Back* into the big time? What are you talking about?"

"Oh, come on, Rudy," I said. "I knew the minute you recited your trademark line. 'I was supposed to be the big cheese!' I'm figuring Rudy is your real name, and you no longer go by your stage name . . . Cappy Whitaker."

I sized up his portly frame, the receding hairline of orange hair, a few freckles spread out over his fleshy cheeks. He had changed so much. But the eyes were a dead giveaway. They still had that same twinkle from those long ago Kraft Macaroni and Cheese commercials. I was face to face with Cappy Whitaker. The one who made a lasting impression in a Disney adaptation of *The Prince and the Pauper*, the one who played Debbie Reynolds's grandson on a short-lived situation comedy, and the one who landed on the cover of *People* magazine after Wendell Butterworth tried abducting him from a Santa Monica beach. He was also the Cappy Whitaker who wrote to the parole board in Vacaville, California, to request Wendell's immediate release from prison.

"So, Rudy, did your grandmother make you change your name in order to stand out at auditions?" I said.

270

He nodded. "You know, it's funny, Jarrod, when we were kids, we basked in so much attention. Everybody loved us. They did anything for us. Gave us everything. And then, when a lot of us hit puberty, they took it all away. And what were we left with? Pretty much nothing. My grandmother didn't have much use for me after the parts dried up once I turned thirteen. I was all alone. Not you, of course. You got *Go to Your Room!* That kept you going another few years. And I've seen you on TV now and then. You've managed somewhat of a comeback. Congratulations."

Charlie moaned softly a few feet away from us. I wanted to run to him, get him some medical attention, but it would do neither of us any good if Rudy or Wendell snapped.

"But nobody wanted me anymore," Rudy said. "Nobody but Wendell Butterworth. Without fail, he wrote me a letter from prison every damn week. Never missed one. And not only that, he sent me cards for Christmas and every year on my birthday. He was the only one, Jarrod. After years of fame, he was the only one. I was so lonely, one day in a weak moment, I wrote him back. I knew he was whacked out and crazy, but hell, I didn't even care at that point. I just wanted somebody to talk to."

We both glanced at Wendell, who stood silently, his eyes blank, as if in a trance.

I looked at Rudy. "So you became pen pals?"

Rudy laughed. "We sent each other all kinds of puzzles and games. Can you imagine that? I befriended the man who tried to kidnap me. My childhood stalker. My grandmother blew every cent I had ever made as a child actor. Wendell was the last tie to that whole life of fame and fortune. I found him to be a fucking comfort, if you can believe that."

"So when the authorities up in Vacaville were going to release him, you wrote a letter of support."

"Damn straight. Why wouldn't I want my only friend to be free? It worked too. Look at him. He's a free man. Free to do anything he wants."

271

"The only problem is," I said, swallowing hard, and trying not to panic. "What he wants to do is to kill me and then kill himself so we can be free together on the other side."

Rudy considered this for a long moment before looking at both of us and smiling. "Well, Wendell was there for me, so in all fairness, I need to be there for him. And if that's what he wants, then I don't want to stop him."

Rudy called out to Wendell. "It's time, Wendell."

Wendell snapped out of his trance. He bent down, roughly turned Charlie over on his back, reached into the holster strapped across his chest, and pulled out his gun. He stood back up and pointed it at me, a loving smile on his face.

Chapter 35

"We've hung around here long enough, Jarrod," Wendell said warmly. "It's time for us to go." He released the safety on the gun and pressed back on the trigger.

"No!" a voice hollered. It was Charlie. He was conscious. He seized Wendell's right leg, and jerked it back with all of his remaining strength. Wendell tumbled just as the bullet fired. It nicked my left ear, drawing blood. As he went down, Wendell shot at me again, but this time his aim was way off. I heard an agonizing scream from behind me, and whirled around to see Rudy clutching his right arm, real blood seeping through the sleeve of his coat over the dried fake blood.

"He shot me! The fucker shot me!"

It was only a flesh wound. I heard a scuffle and turned back around to see Charlie on his feet, his arm wrapped around Wendell's neck, trying hard to subdue him. But Charlie was dizzy and weak from the blow to the head, and was no match for the much stronger, much bigger man. He flung Charlie off him like a piece of lint. Charlie hit the ground hard, and rolled down a hill of leaves until he smacked into the trunk of a tree. Wendell pounded down toward him. I couldn't let him get near Charlie. I couldn't allow Wendell to hurt him anymore.

"Wendell, come back. We can leave. Right now. You and me."

Wendell stopped in his tracks, and slowly turned to look at me. His face was full of hope but mixed with mistrust. I had betrayed him before, and he wasn't sure if I was being straight with him. But at least it took his mind off killing Charlie.

"Don't you worry, Wendell, I'll make sure your boy here doesn't play any more games with you," Rudy said as he came up quick behind me, twisting my arm up behind my back and pressing the cold, sharp blade of a knife against my throat.

Wendell stared at the two of us, in a state of utter confusion.

Rudy hissed in my ear, "Just so you know, this isn't one of those retractable prop knives, Jarrod. This is the real thing." He pressed the blade harder against my skin to prove his point.

"He's hurting me, Wendell," I gasped, trying desperately to appeal to Wendell's paternal side.

Wendell threw out his hands at us and cried, "Let him go, Cappy. He belongs to me. Not you."

Rudy didn't move.

"I said let him go!" Wendell bellowed so loud it echoed in the night breeze.

"You always preferred Jarrod to me," Rudy said, scowling. "I did so much for you. I sent care packages to you every week in prison, I wrote letters to the governor pleading for your release, and I was a better soul mate to you than *he* ever could be! So why, Wendell, why did you always prefer him to me?"

Wendell opened his mouth to speak, but no words came out.

"Tell me, Wendell," Rudy said, grabbing my shirt collar and pressing the blade so hard a small drop of blood slid down over my Adam's apple. "Tell me now or I cut his throat!"

Wendell, with downcast eyes, said softly, "Because Jarrod had a hit series and, well, you never did."

That was it. Rudy just couldn't face any more rejection. He

was going to kill me. I had to take action now to save myself or at least die from trying. Cappy and I had long ago gone up for the same guest-starring role on *The A Team*, and I had won the part. I played a general's son kidnapped by a ruthless band of mercenaries that the much-decorated officer had abandoned in the jungles of Vietnam. They were out for revenge and I was the target. At one point, Mr. T tries to rescue me, and I mistake him for one of the bad guys, so I elbow him in the solar plexus, knocking the wind out of him. Had Cappy been cast instead, I never would have learned that move. And it wouldn't have saved my life at this moment. I slammed Rudy as fast and hard as I could. I felt the rush of air escape from his mouth, the shock of the blow forcing him to loosen his grip on my arm. The knife sliced across my neck as he stumbled back, but not deep enough to puncture my wind pipe. Rudy was only momentarily stunned. As I sprung forward to get away from him, he tackled me around the waist and we landed facedown in the dirt. He snatched a handful of my hair and started pounding my face into the dirt. I scrounged around with my hand for the knife he'd dropped, and finally my fingers felt the sharp blade. I circled my fingers around the handle, and raised it up to defend myself, but Rudy must have seen me out of the corner of his eye. He stopped driving my skull into the mud long enough to grab at my arm holding the knife. We wrestled and rolled for possession of it, clubbing one another with our free hands and kicking each other with our legs. Rudy tried prying my fingers off the knife handle one by one, but I had a tight hold on that sucker and I wasn't about to let go. That's when he kneed me in the groin, and I felt the strength rapidly drain from my body. I roared in pain, instinctively dropping the knife to protect myself from another blow, and it gave Rudy enough time to snatch up the weapon, shove me down on my back, and straddle my waist. He raised the knife high over his head, cackled with relish, and sneered, "And . . . action!"

As he brought the knife down, I shot my arms out to stop him from plunging it through my heart. Everything seemed in slow motion. Our eyes locked together, our bodies entwined, both our hands struggling to gain possession of the knife in a desperate last-minute murderous standoff.

Suddenly a burst of light blinded both of us. The whole woods lit up as if daylight had sprung upon us. Wendell looked skyward, probably expecting a UFO to land in the clearing. Rudy squinted, covering his eyes from the oppressive light. I recognized what it was right away—a powerful, megawattage klieg light used to illuminate a set. Whoever had turned it on had just rescued me from certain death.

I used the distraction to shove Rudy off me, and scramble to my feet.

"Who is it? Who's there?" Rudy screamed.

Larry Levant stepped into the light. He had a handheld Panavision film camera strapped to his shoulder and was aiming it at Rudy. "Drop the knife, Rudy. You don't want us filming you committing a murder, do you?"

Rudy stared into the camera lens, almost wistfully. Probably somewhere in the back of his mind, he was saying, "I'm ready for my close-up, Mr. Levant." He let the knife slip from his fingers and drop into the leaves. Larry kept approaching him slowly, cautiously, until he was right up in his face with the camera.

"You've got a very expressive face, Rudy," Larry said. "You really should be in features."

"Really?" There was a slight smile on Rudy's face. He loved being back in the spotlight.

Wendell, mystified by the goings-on, made a sudden break for it. The person holding the klieg light flashed it in his face, and he stopped suddenly, blinded and disoriented. Five police officers swooped in and wrestled him to the ground, cuffing his hands behind his back. The light shut off, and I saw the smiling face of Laurette as she set the bulky light down on the ground and ran over to hug me.

"Do you honestly believe I would let you two come out here all alone at night without backup? Are you all right, honey?" she said in her usual motherly tone.

I nodded as I watched more cops swarm into the clearing and surround and arrest Rudy Pearson. He didn't put up a fight. He just kept staring at Larry's camera, smiling, as the police carted him away.

"Did you hear Larry Levant?" Rudy said to one of the officers. "He thinks I should be in features."

I swiveled my head around frantically. "Charlie!"

He was sitting upright, against a tree, as a paramedic stitched up his head wound. Laurette and I ran over to him.

"Charlie, are you okay? I was so worried!" I said.

He reached out and squeezed my hand. "Paramedic says I need something like fifteen stitches. You know what that means?"

"What?"

"Lots of recovery time at home. With you tending to me. You've played a lot of parts in your career, Jarrod. It's time you played a nursemaid. And I mean twenty-four/seven. For as long as it takes for me to feel better. Making sure the patient gets everything he wants." He patted my butt with his free hand. "And I do mean *everything*."

"Absolutely," I said. I was just so damn happy he was alive and well, and still willing to put up with me, that I would have agreed to anything. He deserved it.

Laurette clasped her hands over ours and beamed. "Who would have thought that both of us would be lucky enough to find the love of our lives, Jarrod?"

Charlie and I exchanged baffled looks and then turned to Laurette. "I'm not sure I get what you mean, Laurette," I said gently. "Juan Carlos didn't exactly turn out to be your fantasy man."

"Oh, I know, I'm sorry he's dead and all, but good riddance to that good-for-nothing asshole," she said, crinkling up her nose in utter distaste before returning to her excited smile and motioning with her head. "I'm talking about Larry."

"You just met him," Charlie said.

"I know, I know, but sometimes you just know. I think he's the one."

"Laurette . . ."

"Look, I know I've said that before . . ."

"At least four times."

"Well, if you're going to keep a record of my romantic life, then okay, sure, but Larry's different. And I know I've said that before too. And I know you've questioned my judgment in the past, but I think this time I'm really turning a corner! No more bad choices in men. From here on in, it's all about Larry."

"He's an egotistical film director, Laurette," I said.

"And you know how I'm a sucker for creative types. Now I'm not going to rush things this time. I'm going to take things slow, let things unfold naturally."

Charlie and I knew Laurette was past the point of no return, and our best course of action was to just smile and nod to appease her.

"But there's a three-year wait to book the Hearst Castle for a wedding. I can't count on a last-minute cancellation like last time. So it probably won't hurt to book it now." Laurette fished out her cell phone from her coat pocket. "Excuse me, I won't be able to focus on anything until I at least know my name is on their calendar." And she headed off to make her call, winking and cooing at a poor unsuspecting Larry as she passed by him.

The paramedic stitched up what he could, but suggested Charlie drop by the hospital to consult with a doctor and make sure there wasn't a concussion.

Charlie drew our clasped hands to his mouth and kissed my

fingers with his soft, gentle lips. "Can we go home now, babe?" he said.

"Yes," I said as I helped him to his feet. "Just as soon as the doctors give their okay."

"I want to sleep in my own bed. I want to play ball with Snickers," he moaned. "I'm done with Florida."

I slid my arm around his waist, and with my support, he hobbled back toward the Taurus. He was still woozy from the head injury, so I held on to him tight to make sure he didn't lose his balance. I don't remember ever holding him that tight. And at that moment, I knew I was never, ever going to let go of him again.